⊙∂∂∂∂∂–○ ○–₵₵₵₵₵₵⊙

THERE WAS A roar from the students around him as they were plunged into darkness. Behind them, the exit signs of the school shot red light across the campus, and from tinny speakers on poles above their heads, a siren began to blare. The school's intercom system ripped across the grounds, Dr. Richardson's voice.

"Students, please return to your dorms. The maintenance sweep is beginning."

Evan sprinted toward the cross, faster. He threw his elbows into passing plebes, ducking under their arms. The crowd thinned as he got to the back, sprinting over the chapel steps, along the side of the church, through the red-tinted darkness. He landed on the platform and sank to his knees before the cross.

He was alone. Emma wasn't there.

⊙∂∂∂∂∂–○ ○–₵₵₵₵₵₵⊙

ALSO BY SAMUEL MILLER

A Lite Too Bright

REDEMPTION PREP

SAMUEL MILLER

KATHERINE TEGEN BOOKS
An Imprint of HarperCollins Publishers

Katherine Tegen Books is an imprint of HarperCollins Publishers.

Redemption Prep
Copyright © 2020 by Samuel Miller

Library of Congress Cataloging-in-Publication Data

Names: Miller, Samuel, author.
Title: Redemption Prep / Samuel Miller.
Description: First edition. | New York : Katherine Tegen Books, an imprint of
    HarperCollinsPublishers, [2020] | Audience: Ages 13 up. | Audience: Grades
    10-12. | Summary: Told in multiple voices, teens at a preparatory school for
    the exceptional in the forests of Utah uncover a larger mystery after a student
    disappears.
Identifiers: LCCN 2019026848 | 978-0-06-266204-0
Subjects: CYAC: Missing persons—Fiction. | Preparatory schools—Fiction.
    | Schools—Fiction. | Secrets—Fiction. | Mystery and detective stories.
Classification: LCC PZ7.1.M588 Red 2020 | DDC [Fic]—dc23
LC record available at https://lccn.loc.gov/2019026848

Typography by David Curtis
21 22 23 24 25   PC/LSCH   10 9 8 7 6 5 4 3 2 1
❖
First paperback edition, 2021

for leah, leb, seth & joe—

(another mission completed on the never-ending quest to
convince my siblings i'm cool)

men wiser & more learned than i have discerned
in history a plot,
a rhythm, a pre-determined pattern . . .
these harmonies are concealed from me.

i can see only one emergency following upon another as
wave follows wave.

—H.A.L. Fisher

i view my fellow man not as a fallen angel,
but as a risen ape.

—Desmond Morris

REDEMPTION PREPARATORY ACADEMY

fifty miles east of Black Rock, Utah

October 19, 1995

Day 40

Testimonial: Emmalynn Donahue.

Year 1995–1996. Day 24.

When I came here, I thought I was blessed.

I remember my parents were so excited. We didn't apply for it or anything, we'd never even heard of it, so the first few times that my father answered the kitchen phone and heard a man introduce himself as a member of a "recruitment department," he thought it was a telephone salesperson, and he hung up.

They invited us to a Recruit Day in Des Moines, and my dad drove us there, four hours in the truck. We thought it would be full but there were only six of us, two potential students and our two parents each, in the conference room at the Days Inn. The other girl's name was Melissa.

They told us that recruitment was incredibly selective, that we'd been chosen because of our accomplishments. They read long lists of names—famous inventors, politicians, and presidents of million-dollar companies—then added ours to the end. They showed us photographs of the campus on a projector screen and told us the school was funded by private donors, so we wouldn't have to pay a dime for tuition. My mom cried.

I was fourteen when that happened. I thought it was the best day of my life.

My dad drove me to Utah in the truck, eighteen hours, for the start of my freshman year. When we got there, he put my suitcase on the bus and got right back in the truck. He said stuff like this didn't happen to people in our family, so I should be sure to take advantage of it. He told me to take lots of pictures for my mom, because she would want to know what it was like to be given an opportunity like this. He said he would come get me in May, and that he would pray for me every day, and that I should pray too, to have the strength to not screw this up. Then he drove off and left me there, feeling blessed and alone.

The first person I met was Leia. She was from Beirut, and when she was eleven, she won a science competition that had ten thousand people in it. There aren't even ten thousand people in our town. She needed to take an airplane to come to school here, but she could, because the country of Lebanon was giving her free flights so she could be at this school. The next person I met won a math competition in Germany. The next person I met spoke twelve languages. All I did was write a poetry book in English.

My dad couldn't come get me in May. He lost his job when the furniture factory moved to Mexico, then the truck in a drunk-driving accident, so I stayed at the school over summer break, reading books and walking around the forests. There was only one phone on campus and you had to pay $1 per minute to use it, so my mom would write me letters instead, telling me about how Kansas looked in the summer, and how my old friends from middle school were starting to look like adults and work at the Dairy Queen, and how my dad loved me, even if he couldn't come get me again this summer. At the end of every letter, she would write, *There are more than a million people in Kansas, but no one is our Emma. You are our most special girl.*

She still writes me letters, but they're not as long anymore, and they don't come as often. She hardly ever mentions my dad. She's given up trying to understand my life here, so she doesn't ask. In the last one, two months ago, she told me she didn't think about me first thing in the morning anymore, and that she thought it was "nice to be moving forward." But still, at the end of the letter, no one is their Emma. I am still their *most special girl.*

I used to love when she said that, but I don't think I want to be special anymore. The most beautiful flowers are the ones that get picked, but what good is a dead flower?

I don't remember what it was like to be fourteen and in love with the possibility of this place. I don't feel worthy or important. I don't write poetry anymore.

I've been here four years, and I don't think I'm blessed. In fact, I'm afraid I might be cursed.

PART I.

evening mass.

EVAN.

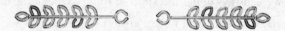

THE OVERHEAD LIGHT flickered as he waited for her to enter the dormitory hallway.

His door was wide open and he stood just inside the lip of it, angled toward the hall. It was Day 40, which meant he'd lived across the hall from her for forty days, and this was the first day he'd left his door all the way open. He'd covered his walls with basketball posters and lit a candle that smelled like pine trees. His hair was long enough now that it was starting to turn upward at the bottom, like the boy she said she liked from *3rd Rock from the Sun*—Joseph Garden Whoever He Was. He'd even found one of his signature button-ups in the Lost and Found.

It was delicate, being in the right spot at the right time. It usually involved several minutes of standing in the right spot, waiting for the right time, and sometimes being placed in the right dorm and waiting forty days. Today, he held a Goosebumps book to his face, pretending to read and staring over the top at the hinge across the hall where at any moment, her door would open, and Emma would come gliding out.

He checked his watch: twenty minutes to mass. A few students passed but none of them noticed him standing at attention behind the book. It was easy to blend in at Redemption; the fact that everyone came from different parts of the world meant students were always doing unexpected things. One of the lessons you learned in week one was to always look the other way, and before too long, you didn't have to try. It was better that way. Forty days on this floor, and only two or three other students knew his name.

Across the hallway, the hinge creaked open, and Emma rushed out the door with her head down. She turned left.

Evan leapt forward, brushing past her in the opposite direction. His right hand dropped, and the book slipped from between his fingers, but he kept moving down the hall away from her.

He counted off ten seconds before chancing a look back. The Goosebumps book hung in her doorframe, blocking the latch.

Emma walked alone to church every Thursday night. Twenty minutes early, down the Human Sciences dorm hallway to the stairwell in the lounge. A stop at the water fountain on the way. The third pew in chapel. Hands crossed the whole time. A solo prayer at the outdoor cross afterward. A walk back with Neesha. A painted smile every time some plebe tried to say hi to her. A half hug for every pretend friend. Emma lived in a loop.

It wasn't just Emma. The whole world was like that. In a loop. You could find a pattern in anything, if you stood far enough away from it. Day becomes night, success becomes failure becomes success becomes failure, green becomes yellow becomes red. All of it could be predicted.

And beaten.

That's how you win at chess. You can't solve the game; the game is objective. There's an absolute mechanical parity to the pieces on both sides of the board. You solve the other person. You study their pattern. Every time they sacrifice a pawn to protect their bishop, they tell you about their carelessness. Every time they bring a castle back to protect their queen, they reveal an insecurity. Most people broadcast their mistakes before they even know they're going to make them. So you load up not where they're weak but where they're going to be weak, and when they inevitably play the part they've been telling you they're going to play, you take them.

Evan rushed down into the Human Sciences Lounge and out into the fog. It was thin today, the kind you could see through. The chapel was a quarter of a mile across the lawn, and the yellow light atop the wooden cross was the only one on the school's back complex to guide the students. They were told to walk carefully through the fog, with their eyes on the ground, following the network of dirt paths, avoiding the rock formations and wild grass in between. He ran, his eyes up, around a slow-curving path that banked along the forest, until the gold in her hair broke through the fog, twenty feet ahead.

Emma stopped at the mouth of the path and stared into the mass of students. People came from all directions toward the stairs of the chapel, but where she stood, slightly elevated, it gave the illusion that they were all converging on her. She hid her eyes as a group of instructors passed. Someone tried to wave but she wasn't paying attention. Evan followed her gaze and noticed a dark-purple-and-yellow jacket, hovering near the woods. By the time his eyes found Emma again, Aiden Mallet had descended on her.

Evan kept moving in a wide path around them, settling on one of the benches in front of the chapel. Aiden was trying to hug her, and she wasn't hugging back. Her eyes were fixed on the ground. Her arms were around her chest like a protective vest. Her fingers were twitching against the sleeves of her sweater.

Evan held his breath. This was it.

Aiden was a terrible boyfriend. He could barely read and write; he sucked at math, history, science, and philosophy. He could shoot a basketball, but that was a useless skill. He was attractive by American standards, with thick blond hair and broad shoulders, but to Evan he looked like a floppy-haired Hulk. He had one real value, but it was universal and easy to understand: Aiden was rich. His parents owned a chain of grocery stores on the East Coast, and he was their only child, and the heir apparent to their fortune.

None of that would have mattered if not for Emma. If not for Emma, Aiden would have been just another zero-value life filling the void of everywhere else. But he wasn't. Something about being popular and rich and average at basketball gave him the right to Emma, and everybody went along with it, because it's high school and that's how the pattern is supposed to go. And Aiden went along with it, because that's how the pattern of his life had always been. But Aiden didn't deserve her, and Emma knew it, and Aiden knew it, and he'd made her life miserable for it.

But Emma had been altering her routine to avoid him. No more Wednesday morning breakfasts. No more walks home from mass. No more looks at him during church. No more invitations to her dorm after curfew. Aiden's days were numbered, and today, they'd run out.

Evan sat on the edge of the bench, watching the conversation in his reactions, between groups of passing students. First, Aiden was nervous. He knew what was coming. A group of Year Ones stood in the way, so Evan craned his neck around them. Aiden was holding Emma's shoulders to stop her from speaking. Evan sat up even further on the bench. A seven-foot-tall boy ran in front of them, so he slid left, just in time to see Aiden's face morph into a smile.

"Hey."

Evan's face fell. Aiden was still smiling, bigger, and nodding along.

"Hey!"

Standing over her like a hungry lion, he mouthed one word; a question and an answer, a confirmation and a lifeline; the worst possible word that could come out of his mouth—*"Tonight?"*

"Hey!"

A large gloved hand grabbed Evan by the shoulder, and he fell backward.

"Can I sit here?"

Peter Novak was six foot three and razor thin, draped in a puffy orange coat, blocking the light from the top of the cross.

He nodded to the bench next to Evan and sat without waiting for a response.

"So," he said, burying his hands in his pockets. "You're the kid who beat the chess computer?"

Evan nodded.

"Yeah, when my girl told me that, I thought, 'No, that's Bobby Fischer.' You're not Bobby Fischer, buddy." Peter was from Eastern Europe, so his vowels were thick with an accent, but he was also on the debate team, so he spoke at two times the normal human speed, spitting as he went. "I guess you could do it too, but . . . that's gotta suck, right? Being the second guy to invent the wheel? I mean, we kinda only need the one wheel."

Peter hadn't looked away from Evan; Evan hadn't looked back. Silently, he absorbed all the *S2—Subtext* possible. Condescension was a means for establishing social control.

"What're you looking at over there? Not much view from this bench, buddy. And I gotta say," Peter said, inching closer, "I feel like I'm seeing you everywhere. Weird, right? Why do you think that is? Evan? Why d'you think that is?"

He felt his hair rise. Take the *S4—Emotion* out of it, and *S5—Rationale*. There was no reason for Peter Novak to know his name, unless Peter was paying attention to him.

"It's a small—"

"Gotta talk louder than that."

"It's a small school."

Peter tilted his angular nose down, like he was trying to

pry a silent answer from beneath Evan's skin. Aiden and Emma were gone, swept into the chapel with the wave of students around them. "I'm gonna go," he mumbled, but as he tried to stand, Peter's left arm slammed him back into the bench.

"I know what you're doing, you little plebe," Peter said. "*She* knows what you're doing."

"I—I'm not . . ." Evan tried to squirm around him but failed. His body went limp.

"I don't know who you think you're helping here, or why you're following her, but knock it the fuck off, okay?" Peter let go of him and stood up. "My suggestion? Get a new hobby. Find your own thing."

And he was gone, leaving Evan alone and out of breath on the bench. A few students nearby rolled their eyes in pity and continued into the chapel. One plebe girl tried to offer him a hand to stand but he ignored it. He didn't need the help.

He didn't care, either. It didn't matter what Peter thought of him. Peter's life wouldn't matter anyway. Peter was a plebe. He'd graduate from Redemption and find a lifeless job. He'd make a few women miserable. He'd mow his lawn a million times and get back problems. He'd die. Peter would come and go from Earth without anyone ever acknowledging that he was actually there. Peter would never exist for a larger purpose, and he would never know true salvation.

But not Evan. He had a purpose. After stepping inside to confirm Emma was secured in the third row, Evan disappeared out the back door of the chapel.

NEESHA.

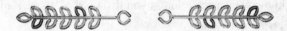

TEN MINUTES BEFORE evening mass, at the stone well two hundred yards north of the wooden cross, wearing a dark-purple-and-yellow Adidas windbreaker. Those were the instructions.

Neesha waited with her hands balled into fists, leaning against the inner break of a tree. On the top of the Wah Wah Mountains, and every mountain in the southern Rockies, water condenses faster, so when the sun disappears and the wet heat of the day is left to night, it becomes a thick white fog, clinging to the top of the mountain. Redemption was built on the edge of the fog line, which meant most nights, it came rolling in slowly and suffocated the school until dawn. She liked being outside to watch as it was settling, slowly obscuring everything in the distance until you could only see twenty feet in any direction. It was like watching the world shrink in minutes. *Souffle de dieu*, the instructors called it. *The breath of God.*

Twelve minutes to mass. Her feet were soaking wet. She'd been in such a hurry to get out, she forgot her all-terrain shoes, and now her Skechers were sinking into the mud. She could feel the cold sneaking up the arms of her jacket and in the holes of her jeans, squeezing her skin and setting off ripples of vibrations. She stood stiff, soaking the drawstring of the jacket with saliva as she chewed it.

Nine minutes to mass. Something started to feel off; she could always tell when something was wrong. Her mother told the story of a night in Chandigarh, when she was eight. They'd been walking home from temple, and as soon as the sun had fully set, she stopped and started crying. Her father tried to carry her forward, but she collapsed to the ground, refusing to cross the Ghaggar River. She insisted they walk around it, an extra kilometer to get home. The next day, her mother ran to tapri to get a newspaper, expecting to see reports of a drowning, or a car driving into the Ghaggar, but there were no tragedies in Chandigarh. Or if there were, she didn't get far enough past the front-page headline to find it: JAHAR DEVASTATED BY FLOODING. Rains in the nearby Patna region had destroyed entire villages. It was like an attack; the rainfall was so sudden and violent that survivors felt certain it had been sent as a punishment, starting with the first drop right at sunset.

It wasn't scientific, but it was proof: she had a good sense for these things, even if she wasn't always exact on the details.

Seven, six, five minutes to mass. Something was definitely off. Maybe she'd been given the wrong instructions, or maybe whoever she was supposed to meet had seen that it wasn't

Emma waiting and turned around. Either way, she wasn't going to wait and miss mass to find out. She shoved both of her arms against the sides of the tree, pulling hard against the mud to lift herself up, but the branch wasn't strong enough. It split with a loud crack.

"Neesha?"

Her hands shot in opposite directions and her balance swung forward. She hit the mud hard, her whole body sinking into it, and rolled onto her back, cracking open like an egg.

Above her, a dark-purple-and-yellow Adidas windbreaker was floating in the breath of God, glaring down.

"*I fucking knew it!*"

She could see a dark brown face below the hood. "I knew it," he said again, high and tentative. "Oh, this is so messed up!"

He pulled his hood back. Ahmad Galbia—Zaza, as he had been called since he was seven years old—had a thin layer of black hair that stopped too high on his forehead, and a wide face, but maybe that was because his narrow glasses threw off the proportions. For as many times as she'd seen him, and it was many times—in the lab almost every day, weekends included, for three years—he'd never been this animated.

"As soon as I heard about this, I was like, 'That's Neesha's project,' I just had to see it for myself and I was fucking right! Do you have any idea how much shit you're in right now?"

She groaned as she pulled herself up from the ground, bringing her face-to-face with him. He was short, only a few inches taller than her.

"They'll end you. They'll confiscate your work, they'll take away the project, and they'll ban you from winning the trophy—"

"Money, please."

He shut up.

Neesha smiled, watching his hand hover over his pocket. "What?" she asked. "Are you going to *not* buy it?"

He sighed and dropped a clean white envelope on the stump between them.

"What are you even doing here?" she asked as she began to count. "It was supposed to be someone from the basketball team."

"I am on the basketball team—I do the stats."

"And the dirty work."

"I guess."

He didn't say anything else. It said an embarrassing amount about his self-esteem that he was willing to run an errand like this for guys who cared so little about him that they asked him to run an errand like this.

"Where's Emma?"

"Not here."

"Why?"

"She had to make a phone call."

"That's strange."

"No it's not," she said reflexively, but it was a little strange. Part of the agreement she'd made with Emma a week ago was that Neesha would never be the one to take anyone's money. But tonight, for their biggest sale yet, Emma had begged her to step in.

"How many people know you're doing this?" Zaza asked.

"Where is this money coming from?" Neesha ignored his question, asking her own as she tucked the first thousand back into the envelope.

"Um." He rubbed his head. "I don't know. I guess everybody pitched in. I think somebody's parents—"

"God, Aiden is so fucking rich."

"Yep. It's crazy. He's completely divorced from any kind of real-life proportionality. His mom will ask him, like, 'Do you want to order a waterbed for your room?' And he'll be like, 'Yeah, but let's get two or three, just in case.' Which sounds like it would be great but it actually creates real problems, like, what is he even gonna do with the extra waterbeds—"

"This is only half of it."

Zaza's eyes flipped back and forth in the dark. "Yeah." He rubbed the top of his head again. "That's what Emma said. Half for her, half for you."

"You pay in full. What we do with the money after has nothing to do with you."

"Are you sure? Emma said to split it up—"

"No, we don't split it up!"

"Okay, okay," he said, throwing his hands up. "Feels like we could just go to Emma—"

"Put it on the stump."

He frowned at her, then reached into the same pocket and removed an identical envelope, staring at it a moment before handing it over. Neesha's breath steadied as she counted in silence.

"Just for the record," he said. "You have the same motivation I do to lie, and if I go back to Emma—"

"I'm not lying."

"—she'd be more likely to believe *you*, which makes *me* more susceptible to getting screwed than you. So if you compare the odds that one of us is lying—"

"Shut up."

He did.

It was an exhaustingly typical attitude. It was always the innocent ones who expected the most, like because they were a television version of nice, they believed they were entitled to everyone's best behavior, even though usually their manners were being weaponized to some end, like sex, or stealing large sums of money.

"Okay, we're good," she said, dropping a small baggie of clear pills on the stump in place of the envelopes and turning to carve her way down the mountain.

"You're making a mistake." Zaza hadn't moved behind her. "All this, for a couple grand? It's not worth it."

"Yeah, it is," Neesha muttered to herself without looking back.

She took a wide route back to the chapel, wiping the forest off as she ran. Zaza was right, but not in the way he thought he was. He was right that it wasn't worth it for the money. The extra cash was nice, to buy cigarettes off the maintenance workers or send money home to her mom for her sister's birthday. But that wasn't what made "all this" worth it—it was the trophy.

The Discovery Trophy was a four-foot, diamond-studded beaker that sat at the front of Dr. Yangborne's classroom all year round. At the end of the year, it was awarded to the most innovative breakthrough in the C-School. More than just the physical award, it came with a full-ride scholarship to California-Berkeley, a full legal team to register and patent the product, and a commitment to find manufacturing. The students who won it were immediately elevated from senior high students to practicing chemists. Previous winners had gone on to be the heads of labs and CEOs of pharma companies. In her Year Two, she'd come in fourth, with a hormone booster she created from scratch; she refined it in her Year Three and finished in second. This year, she'd gone a completely different direction, synthesizing something new, effective, and useful.

And she was going to be able to prove it.

She slid into the first open seat she could find, five rows from the back and off the center aisle of the chapel. As soon as she sat, the organ ripped through the sanctuary, starting the music. Everything shook as the pipes screamed—the windows, the pews, the Bibles tucked into the seat backs. The overhead lights bowed into darkness for a moment, then popped back on. The whole complex was on an old grid, relying on two hundred miles of cable to get power from Salt Lake, so sometimes, when the draw got to be too much, electricity would dip in and out. Instructors had jokes for it; others had learned to ignore it entirely. Father Farke, for his part, used every blackout as an opportunity to shout, "Alas, his light has arrived!" Neesha wanted to remind him that, because the light was supposed to be constant and blackouts were a temporary interruption, it was actually the opposite—his light had disappeared.

The prelude ended, leaving everything in the church still once more. The whispering stopped and Father Farke made his way to the front to select a holy candle-lighting person. Emma had volunteered.

Emma loved this shit. She was one of the people at the school who was actually a Christian. Neesha had never been to church before Redemption and found the whole thing to be creepy. The chapel was far too big for the number of students, and every window had a still-frame Bible story stained into it—the American version of the stories, where the characters were white and the Middle East looked like Texarkana. The biggest mural, in the very front, was a forty-foot rendering of Noah's ark, in which twelve super tall and *super* naked passengers flew a boat away from a raging flood. Craziest of all, clouds of smoke billowed from a source just out of the frame.

She assumed the choice to put it at the front of the church was some kind of warning to students. Come to mass or die in a fire.

Emma moved quickly, candle to candle, checking over her shoulder behind her. Neesha sat up, watching. Usually Emma was graceful, but tonight she looked uneasy. Behind her, a student let out a light moan, and Emma checked over her shoulder. The bells on top of the church rang out, and Emma leapt, nearly knocking over one of the candelabras.

As Father Farke moved into the announcements, Emma carried a single candle back up the aisle toward Neesha, slowly, to protect the fragile flame in her hands. She kept her eyes focused forward, past all the students who watched her, until she got to Neesha. She glanced to the right, ever so slightly, and she held up one finger in front of the candle. A question.

Neesha raised her hand to her face and scratched her nose, with one finger. Her answer.

It was the code they'd developed; the simplest binary form of communication: 1 meant good, 2 meant bad; 1 meant success, 2 meant failure; 1 meant yes, 2 meant no.

Emma smiled. Neesha smiled back. The lights of the chapel flickered on and off.

AIDEN.

AIDEN STARED AFTER where she'd just disappeared into the back of the church; she didn't bother to look in his direction.

". . . faster around picks, that's the only way we beat these fucking giants, you know? Shoot them out the gym."

He'd made himself impossible to ignore, combed his hair back just the way she always did it up for him and smiled with a poster-quality apology face. Still, she looked the other way.

"Plus, I'm trying to show off this jump shot for the scouts, okay? Make it fucking rain a little, you know? Splash splash? Aiden? Hello? What do you think?"

Dirk was talking down at him from a two-inch height advantage. All the guys were listening.

He cleared his throat. "I think you guys talk about basketball too much."

"*Please.*" Dirk's breath smelled terrible. "Just this week, care a little bit, please? I'd like to play in the professionals."

Aiden rolled his eyes. "Yeah, alright, I'll get off faster, just as long as you can get your giraffe-ass body out far enough to set them."

Everybody but Dirk laughed.

"Besides." Aiden stared forward. "The scout's coming to watch me."

Because the school was so remote, the basketball team played three games a year, and only one in their home gym. Next Tuesday would be their first exhibition, against the previous years' McDonald's All Americans, and Coach Bryant had confirmed it for them in practice today—the Dallas Mavericks were sending a scout. Aiden hadn't told the guys, but it was his dad who called the scouting department, to set up the trip. He was the one they were coming to watch.

"Just don't be mopey forever, okay?" Dirk asked. "You look like Eeyore for last two weeks. Your game looks like it, too."

No one on the team disagreed.

"Really?" he asked. "Alright, well, keep talking this shit and see how much you even get the ball next week."

Dirk's shoulders fell. "You're right, bro. My bad." The rest of them nodded apologies.

"By the way," he said, leaning forward, patting Zaza's shoulder, speaking loud enough for everyone to hear. "Hold on to that five hundred for me till later, okay?"

Zaza nodded, and the group was silent. Aiden tried one more glance at the back of the church, but Emma wasn't there.

The flickering lights in the chapel were getting much worse, bowing in and out every few seconds, graduating to a strobe.

Aiden's parents had sent him to Redemption with that one goal in mind—make the league. There were other schools, other teams, but his dad decided Redemption was the clearest shot. They'd sent coaches to his AAU games with crazy facts and figures about their success. When Coach Bryant visited, he brought two NBA players, Redemption alums, who used words like "revolutionary" to describe the system. They sold him on that dream that he'd come here, train with the best, showcase for the scouts, and go straight to the draft. For four years, he'd followed that path, starting since his Year One, and leading the team in scoring since Year Two. In four years, he'd never missed a practice, or shorted a workout, or sat out a scrimmage.

Now, here he was, a week away, and all he could think about was the fact that his girlfriend was ignoring him. Whether she knew it or not—and how could she not?—Emma was jeopardizing the most important week of his life.

"Emma told me to meet her tonight—" he started to whisper to no one, but as the lights dimmed again, he was interrupted by a moaning noise, like the drone of an alarm.

"Oh . . . oh . . ." It echoed through the church like a warning siren, but all the guys in his section groaned.

"Fucking Eddy," Dirk muttered.

Aiden leaned forward to find where Eddy was sitting. Faces were flashing left and right, snapping around in search of the noise. It looked like some of the students were blinking incessantly, others clenching their jaws. He couldn't tell if it was actually happening, or inside his own eyes, but students everywhere seemed possessed with tiny, almost unnoticeable shakes.

The entire congregation had a vibration.

Eddy got louder and louder. "Oh . . ." His voice was wailing, quivering in every corner.

"Oh, oh—" Dirk yelled. "Just get to it already!"

The whole sanctuary laughed.

"What is that?" a Year One asked.

"This kid Eddy," Dirk explained. "He's a weird boy. Very messed up."

"I think he's possessed," someone else whispered.

"Oh . . . oh!"

The lights of the chapel began to flicker violently, much faster than before, waves of power drops coming in and out like a storm cell was descending on the mountain. Up and down the congregation, students shuffled restlessly around the old pews creaking and cracking below them. Aiden could hear their panic in the grinding of their teeth, coming from all around him. Why was it so loud?

"Well . . ." Father Farke spoke over Eddy's moaning, his microphone still working. "We'll have to wait for the Lord to allow us to continue." He stepped back from the pulpit and made his way to the window, watching the sky like he was waiting for something to happen.

And something did happen, but it didn't come from above. It came from the fifth row. The moaning turned into screaming, and the screaming turned into a recognizable word—

"*No!*"

Students in the front started to crash into the center aisle, screaming and knocking over the candles. With no light, Aiden couldn't see where they were running, or what they were running from, but the screaming just got louder.

"Go, go, go!" Next to him, Dirk started shouting and shoving. Aiden backed up, standing on the pew to let them pass. Two huge candles at the front of the chapel roared to life, and Aiden got his first clear look at the chaos.

Eddy was standing above the herd, swinging his arms wildly, screaming like he was in pain. He had a Bible in one hand and his other balled into a fist, lashing at the bodies around him. Those bodies had fallen over each other trying to get away. A bigger kid tried to subdue him and Eddy squared up the Bible against his head. The kid fell backward, holding his eye.

At the front, Father Farke and the other clergy members were huddled, scared. The rest of the instructors were still assessing the situation from the balcony. No one was moving toward the center aisle. Someone needed to stop this. Aiden saw his moment, and he charged.

The backs of the pews were about five feet apart, only a few inches of wood but enough for him to catch and propel himself to the next. He leapt around students, row to row, straight for where Eddy had picked up another Bible and was throwing it into the crowd.

He landed on the pew next to Eddy, catching him by the arm before he could swing forward again. Eddy tried to bring his other hand in to help, but Aiden curled over to receive the blow with his back. Eddy was a small kid, but his fists were surprisingly fast and strong, burying themselves below Aiden's ribs before pulling back and hitting him again, two, three, four times. Aiden snaked his left arm around Eddy's chest, and with a half-nelson grip, he lifted, driving Eddy off the ground, off the pew, sending them both crashing into the center aisle.

Eddy's body writhed in pain, and Aiden used the moment to look up for a staff member. He could hear them shouting, but a wall of students surrounded them, standing on pews to create a grandstand. Eddy cowered below him, his gray Metallica T-shirt stained with blood. "No," he was still shrieking. "No! No! No!"

"Can somebody help him, please?" Aiden shouted. The crowd just roared in response.

Aiden turned back. "Relax!" he shouted down at him. "Eddy, you have to relax!"

Eddy snapped back and Aiden took no chances, capturing both of his hands and driving them backward into the carpet until Eddy stopped trying to fight.

His body went limp, and for a moment, Aiden felt his advantage. Maybe he'd lost his shit for a second, but at this moment, Eddy was a defenseless student, half his size, collapsed and bleeding underneath him, squashed like a bug against the chapel floor. The worst part was his eyes, now bruised and lost in a mess of hair, were staring straight up into Aiden's, terrified.

Aiden stood again and spun to face the crowd. "Come on! Let somebody through!" A few staff members had fought their way to the front of the crowd, Dr. Richardson and three men in maintenance uniforms. "Does anyone know what's wrong with—"

He heard it before he felt it, the crowd screaming, a second before Eddy's shoulder snapped into his spine, pile-driving him forward into the holy water basin in the center aisle. He felt his forehead smack against stone, and his world went cold.

The last thing he heard were the bells of the church, ringing out forever across the empty, warm, black space into which he was falling.

NEESHA.

SHE FELT A pair of hands pull her from the ground and she swayed in small circles, blinking to find her vision. She must have rolled several feet, because she was behind the pews now. It had been such a violent moment, with no light and a hundred students trying to push past the bottleneck of the center aisle. She was pretty sure she'd been thrown to the ground but it was hard to know who was doing what on purpose; people were falling over each other.

"Are you okay?" It was Leia, one of her Chem School classmates, dragging Neesha to her feet. "We're over here, come on."

Cold air hit her face; someone had opened the back doors of the chapel and students were streaming out. She followed Leia to a pillar in the back of the chapel. A few of the other C-School kids were milling in the corner, trying to get a look at the front of the church.

"What the *fuck*?" someone asked. "Did Aiden just kill Eddy?"

"I think Eddy almost killed Aiden," Leia said.

"Why was he freaking out?"

"Something about lights."

"The lights?"

Neesha could barely hear them. There was a muffled ringing in her ears; her face was flushed with blood. Flashlights at the front of the sanctuary started flickering on, swirling light through the abstract shapes and colors of the room.

"Students, return to your dorms immediately," Father Farke announced from the pulpit. "There will be no open campus this evening. Return to your dorms, *immediately.*"

Neesha looked to the front of the church, expecting to see Emma rushing in with concern. It was her boyfriend, after all. But Emma wasn't there.

"Are you okay?" Leia had been watching her sway back and forth.

"I think I got kicked in the face."

"Let's have a cigarette, it'll balance you out," she said, and started leading them toward the door.

Neesha felt for them in her pocket, removed them, and then felt the pocket again. It was empty. She froze. The crowd continued to push them forward as she slapped at her pockets.

"What are you doing?" Leia asked. Several arms against her back prodded her forward, but instead she dropped to the floor.

"Get up!" Someone nudged her with their knee.

"What happened?" Leia crouched next to her.

"My envelope," Neesha choked.

"Envelope?"

Neesha crawled out of the path of the students and felt blindly. "It's gone."

"What was in it?"

She didn't respond.

"Neesha, what was in the envelope?" Leia grabbed her by the wrist and squeezed.

Systems crashed in her brain. Neesha went crawling back toward the center aisle, toward where she'd first hit the ground, but there were still students plowing toward the rear exit. "What the fuck are you doing?" disembodied voices shouted down at her; "Holy shit, get off the floor!" and "Are you okay?" from faces that she didn't have time to notice. She went row by row, but the light from the candles didn't reach the aisles so the floor beneath the pews was pitch-black shadow. The center aisle cleared out, and Neesha slumped against one of the pews.

"Would someone . . . take it?" Leia asked from the ground behind her.

Neesha swallowed. Yes, someone would take it, but only two people knew about it. Emma, but it was her money anyway. Which left—

She stood up abruptly. As the last few students left the church, she thought she might have seen a dark-purple-and-yellow hood go up as it disappeared into the fog.

EVAN.

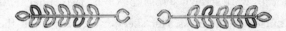

OF ALL EMMA'S patterns, the most important was the ten minutes she spent at the base of the school's wooden cross, alone after mass.

The cross was forty-five feet tall. Its arms were so high that the constant wind and rain of the mountain had battered them into drooping downward in the middle. When you sat on the metal platform below, the cross appeared to stretch upward into the clouds, the light at its peak shining straight into heaven. Emma sat there alone every Thursday night, collapsed to her knees in front of it, transforming from the Emma of this world to the Emma of the next. When he pictured Emma in his head, this was how he saw her. This was where his mission had to begin.

He set his watch. He had thirty minutes to get back before the end of mass.

Inside the dorm, everything was quiet. The Goosebumps book was still hanging where he'd left it. He didn't hesitate, standing tall for the cameras and sliding inside.

Emma's room was heavy with the smell of her, a thick, fruity department store perfume, and dimly lit by bedside lamps. There was a split down the center, between Neesha's perfectly organized bed and desk, and Emma's side. Half of her clothes were strewn across the floor. Two of her textbooks were buried in the mess. Her sheets were tangled at the base of the bed.

There were photos taped all along the wall, but a few obvious gaps suggested some had been torn down. Most of the photos weren't taken at Redemption, but what Evan assumed was her family home in Kansas. Young Emma was undeveloped but perfectly recognizable. The same thin blonde hair, but cut just below her ears. The same hundred-watt smile, but missing a few teeth. She had photos smiling with her mom, smiling with her dad, smiling at her church confirmation, smiling at what looked like a birthday pool party.

Then came the Polaroids from Redemption. A picnic with some instructors, a photo on a bench with Neesha, a Bible study with Father Farke. All of them were sterile and detached.

Emma didn't smile in photos anymore; she hardly ever took them. She'd stopped going for walks to take her journal into the forest. Her conversations with friends were less than a minute long. She'd stopped doing her homework. Two days ago, she slept all day, instead of going to class. Emma was broken. She was crying out, but no one was listening.

Except him. He was listening.

By the foot of the bed, there was a photo with Aiden, his

arms wrapped around her, suffocating her. Evan ripped it down.

There was one surface on Emma's side of the room that wasn't in disarray. The only item on her desk, a small, leather-bound notebook, sat perfectly centered, waiting for him to discover it.

Emmalynn Donahue / Testimonial Journal / Year Four.

Below the title was Redemption's crest, a half oval with crescent moons and a book, shining upward into the school's credo: *You are the light of the world.*

Evan sat in her chair for a few moments without moving, his heartbeat rising as he stared into the cover, its jacket cracked from use, unsure where to start. With two fingers, he pulled back a single page.

Day 1. Sigh. Another new year, another opportunity to get this right. I see myself in the face of every new student, their eyes wide enough to reflect my own, smooth skin where my creases have formed—

He retreated, pulling his hands off the surface quickly like it was hot to the touch, his temples pounding. The front cover fell on top of the journal again.

This was it. Ever since May fourteenth, he knew the pattern of Emma was fragmented. Everyone else was so directional and readable, but Emma curved, cut, and folded into herself. Everyone else could be predicted by patterns of desire and familiar endgames, stepping on others to get the things that they wanted. But Emma submitted herself to them, swam with their currents, felt their pain. Emma's mysteries grew out of her subconscious. Poetry was her translation and her salvation. The testimonial journal was full of her poetry. This was the key to the pattern, the key to the mission, the answer to every riddle.

He flipped through the journal, scanning each page, trying to find the poem she'd read for him five months earlier. On Day 9, he found it, decorated with the same doodles that brought the rest of Emma's writing to life. His heart beat faster, twice its normal speed.

I'll hold your place next to me, eternally, endlessly.
This world was never big enough, but you still tried to make a place for me—

There was a knock on the door behind him.

He almost fell backward out of the chair, grabbing for the desk to stabilize himself. He held his breath and squeezed to prevent his muscles from vibrating. No one knew he was here; no one had any reason to think that the room wasn't empty.

There was another knock. "Open, open." It was a man's voice, not one he recognized, with what sounded like a Russian accent. "We know you're in this room."

Evan's pulse accelerated as he searched for options. He could try the window, but it was a three-story drop to the rocks below.

There were places to hide, but the man's *S2—Subtext* told him he wasn't going anywhere, and if the *S3—Intention* was to punish him, the best he could do was lie. Often, a half-truth could reduce the *S8—Consequence*.

"We can hear you stomping around," the voice said, knocking louder. "Not very subtle."

His throat closed. He tried to breathe through his nose like Mom had taught him, but it wasn't working. He couldn't think about his safe place. All he could focus on was the punishment that was coming for him. Missing mass was inexcusable. Being in her dorm would make Emma mad. The mission would be over before it could even start. The handle shook like someone outside was using a key. He reached quickly for it and slammed it open.

There were three maintenance workers in the doorway, wearing dark gray plastic suits and black vests full of supplies. The man at the center was massive; at least six foot five, because his head nearly touched the fluorescent ceiling light above him.

"Ah." The one in the center, the owner of the accent, cocked his head. "You are not Emmalynn Donahue."

Evan stared blankly back, giving him no *S2—Subtext*. "No."

He checked a clipboard in front of him. "And . . . you are also not Neesha Shah?"

"No."

"So then . . . who are you?"

"I'm Evan."

"Huh. Okay." He didn't look upset. But he did look serious. "Where is Emmalynn?"

"It's just Emma. She doesn't like Emmalynn."

"Okay then, where's Emma?"

Through the walls of the building, the church bells began to ring. The notes they played were discordant, too close in pitch to be pleasing to the ear. Instead, they hung in the air, unresolved and tense. "She's at mass. Like everybody else."

The maintenance man stared for a moment, then walked around him into the room. His arms were almost as wide as Evan's chest. Evan noticed he was breathing heavy, unfamiliar lungs reacting to thin mountain air.

"So what are you, then?" the man asked. "Her boyfriend or something?"

"No," Evan answered quickly. "Not her boyfriend."

"Then why are you here?"

"She asked me to grab her homework for her before mass. I'm just running a little late."

The two men outside the room stood at attention. Their reason for being there wasn't clear, but the *S2—Subtext* was obvious: intimidation.

"Did you get it?" the man asked, starting to thumb through her books.

"Get what?"

The man looked up. "Her homework?"

"Uh, yeah." He patted his backpack. "Got it in here."

"Good. Such good friends. Everybody here, such good

friends." He tapped the center of her desk. "Where's her . . . the progress journal?"

"Testimonial journal," one of the men outside said.

"Yes, that."

Evan shook his head. His hand clutched the top of his bag. "I don't know."

The man stared at Evan now. He could feel his body reacting to the pressure, his testicles migrating north at accelerating speeds.

"Well," he said. "Were you going to mass, or . . . ?"

Without a word, Evan backed out of the room, avoiding the men outside the door, and started away from them.

"Hey." The man inside the room leaned out. "If you see Emma, let her know Yanis is looking for her."

Evan walked quickly down the hallway and stairs, trying to get far enough away to make sense out of the interaction. He was certain his life at Redemption was over. Everything he'd done demanded a punishment hearing or at least a write-up. But none of that had happened. Yanis didn't care.

The seizing in his chest and throat returned, ten steps out the back door. *S5—Rationale.* He'd broken major rules, and Yanis didn't care. Which meant whatever Emma had done, it was much, much worse than that.

Why was a maintenance worker trying to find her during mass? She was sitting in the third row of the chapel twenty minutes ago; why were they looking for her now? What had happened to Emma?

He heard noise from the chapel as he approached, not one voice but dozens, moving toward him through the fog. It was too early for mass to be over; someone was outside the chapel. Before he knew it, the entire student population was moving against him, plugging the walkways to the chapel. He jumped to a rock in the wild grass to avoid being run over.

"What happened?" he tried to ask the mob of students.

"They let us out early!" someone responded. "Eddy had a panic attack!"

His eyes fled to the back of the chapel, where the light at the top of the wooden cross was flickering. He leapt forward from the rock, launching himself into the crowd and starting to fight his way through. In between waves of passing students, he could catch only half glimpses of the metal platform at the base. He thought he saw a shadow pass over it, standing at the bottom of the cross, kneeling, but by the time he fought his way out of the crowd, it was gone. The yellow light on the top of the cross went out.

There was a roar from the students around him as they were plunged into darkness. Behind them, the exit signs of the school shot red light across the campus, and from tinny speakers on poles above their heads, a siren began to blare. The school's intercom system ripped across the grounds, Dr. Richardson's voice.

"Students, please return to your dorms. The maintenance sweep is beginning."

Evan sprinted toward the cross, faster. He threw his elbows

into passing plebes, ducking under their arms. The crowd thinned as he got to the back, sprinting over the chapel steps, along the side of the church, through the red-tinted darkness. He landed on the platform and sank to his knees before the cross.

He was alone. Emma wasn't there.

PART II.
maintenance sweep.

Testimonial: Evan Andrews.

Year 1994–1995. Day 1.

First and foremost, I do not fully understand the purpose of the testimonial journal. Dr. Richardson says it's to *"keep a constantly updating record of how our minds and bodies are responding to the challenges of Redemption Preparatory"* so that we can *"create emotional awareness and have an open relationship with our progress."* But it seems as though the entire school is designed as a metric to test progress; self-assessment hardly feels necessary. Also, I feel my self-assessment may be subjectively unbalanced in my favor. I guess that's the point. *S6—Honesty.*

Dr. Richardson said the best way to establish a natural rhythm with the journal was to treat it as a person, as though a trusted confidant asked at the end of every day what I've been doing and how I've been feeling. This is silly. I see no need to recall past events, as I have already experienced them, making the practice of emotional deconstruction both irrelevant and unnecessary (*S6—Honesty*), particularly to an unconscious conversational partner. However, I'd like to be successful at Redemption—

So hello, inanimate journal.

I woke up at 4:00 a.m. to take two flights, from Burlington to Newark, and from Newark to Salt Lake City, with my mother and my father, and then they rented a Ford Escort and drove me to the Redemption pickup station. The bus ride took four hours, straight into the mountains. After an hour, most of the buildings and houses from Salt Lake City were gone. By two hours, we stopped seeing even small towns and fuel stations. By three hours, we had to drive slowly because there was too much fog to see far in front of the bus. By four hours, we arrived at Redemption.

It doesn't look like the photographs. Not in a way that's misleading, but the photographs failed to capture the full context. The GRC, the central school building, is state of the art, but you don't see the age of its stone walls or feel the impenetrable strength of its physical structure. You can see that there's a network of hallways connecting the academic buildings and dormitories, but until you're walking through them, you can't appreciate just how complicated their construction must have been. In the overhead map, it looks perfectly geometrical, like a chessboard, but in person, it feels like a maze.

My father helped me onto the bus, loading my three boxes one by one, then turned the car around immediately. He said goodbye quickly and reoffered his parenting creed: "It all makes sense if you take the time to understand it." My mother sat in the passenger side with a blanket over her legs. She had to stay in the car, instead of getting out to hug me. She told me that she understood why I was going to school, and if I ever wanted to come home, I should.

It occurs to me as I write this that seeing her seated there is the last full sensory experience that I will have of her for nearly nine months. Only sitting at my desk now am I noticing how irregular this is. For a machine pattern, it would be categorically dysfunctional. I notice the breaks. I can hear silence that is usually her reaction to the television. I can smell the unaffected air of her not being seated in a reclining chair next to me.

But my pattern will adjust. I've already begun preparation for my first day of classes. I've organized and cataloged my clothing. I've charted my walking route on days of class. I've made a list of foods available in the lunchroom.

I should say, I met another person, earlier. A girl. Her name was Cara. She was also a Year One, and she lived two floors down from me. She was sitting on the grass outside as I measured the distance to my first class. "What are you doing?" she asked. Seeing no benefit to the conversation, I *S5—Rationalized* that I should lie and tell her "nothing." She asked where I came from, and despite the fact that I had little interest, I asked as well. Cara is from Illinois. She was recruited to Redemption because she led an effort in Chicago to beautify the city through botany. I find pursuits of beauty to be as unnecessary as conversations filled with cursory personal information, but I chose not to tell her that. The *S8—Consequence* of the statement would not be worth the *S6—Honesty*. Instead, I continued measuring my walking distance between classes.

I should introduce you to this thought pattern. *S1–S8* are shorthand code for the eight steps of socialization, the key components of a program developed by my parents to assist me in conducting short-term conversations, for the purpose of building long-term, meaningful relationships. *S1—Input, S2—Subtext, S3—Intention, S4—Emotion, S5—Rationale, S6—Honesty, S7—Response, S8—Consequence.*

I am not, nor have I ever been, a strong communicator. When I was in elementary school, other students found my behavior so abrasive they assigned me a special teacher, Mrs. Duckworth. When I continued to punch and hit my classmates, Mom was forced to create a more intentional solution to the problem of my inability to interact with other human beings.

After intensive training and application, I have fully adopted the eight steps of socialization as a permanent pattern of thought. While many find this exhausting, I find it liberating. Every conversation follows this pattern, meaning the eight steps of socialization provide the backend code to all human communication; every miscommunication can be traced to a break in the code.

The whole world is really a pattern, if you stand far enough away from it. It all makes sense, if you take the time to understand it.

Here is an example. When Dr. Richardson says to me on the new student tour, "Evan, we really think you're going to excel here," *S2—Subtext* forces me to acknowledge that she is paid by the school to ensure that I have a good experience, so her *S3—Intention* is less sincere interest in my good ability, and more interest in doing her job, which involves making me feel comfortable and desired. This is an understandable behavior; everyone must first look out for their own self-interest. However, *S5—Rationale* tells me that there is no *S4—Emotional* investment to be made. Instead, I'll simply respond, "Thank you." I have developed no feelings of emotion or affection toward Dr. Richardson.

I would be remiss to not mention that I have identified in myself a feeling of excitement that is approaching the level of irrationality. Finally, I can sense that I belong to a structure that deserves my intellect. The possibility for growth is apparent; the only question that remains to be answered is, how much will I grow? What will I accomplish? For what will I strive the hardest? To what will I devote myself?

EVAN.

EVAN PUSHED HIS way through the Human Lounge and into the academic building.

The number of routes that could be taken inward toward the GRC approached infinity. The five schools at Redemption were interconnected by a grid system of perfectly laid circuits, forming an outward-branching cell around the nucleus: the GRC. Tonight, the Human Lounge to the Human School to the P-School to the GRC was the most discreet.

Redemption Prep opened in 1975, built on the bones of the Griou Research Center. The GRC was the creation of five science professors from Princeton University who shared a vision for their work: total seclusion, full immersion, rooted in the worship of Jesus Christ. With nearly unlimited resources from Princeton, each of them built their dream facility, in pursuit of their respective fields of study: Dr. Carl Yangborne, chemical science; Dr. Gerard Roux, brain science; Dr. Luc Simon, physical science; Dr. Lisle Bouchard, robotic science; and Dr. Cynthia Richardson, psychology and human science.

But their research required help, and no qualified scientists wanted to live on a mountain in Utah, a hundred miles from civilization. So instead of hiring professionals, they recruited young, hungry minds with exceptional skills—fifteen- to twenty-year-olds—and trained them. When they realized the armies of young scientists they were training were much more valuable than the research, the five labs became the five schools: Chem (C-School), Brain (B-School), Physical (P-School), Robotics, and Human Sciences. Each school built its own facility, with classrooms, a lounge, a library, and a dormitory. On the back lawn, they built housing for the staff, housing for the maintenance workers, and a chapel, to ensure that the school's mission stayed rooted firmly in Christianity.

Other than the geography and the layout, Redemption was just like Spring Hill High School in Montpelier, where Evan had gone for two semesters. There were 940 students. There was a basketball team and a theater. There were bathrooms that always smelled terrible, and required classes nobody wanted to take. There was a lunchroom, surrounded by student lockers, right in the center of the GRC.

Only one light was on in the Human School as Evan passed through, in the lobby of the school's head instructor, Dr. Richardson. She had an office just off the lounge, with her own waiting room and phone booth. Eddy sat alone in the waiting area outside.

Evan kept his head down and continued through the P-School gym, and waited at the entrance to the GRC, a ten-foot, vacuum-sealed door with an iron bar across the front, locking it in place. The GRC's locking system was interconnected and exact. All five doors would open on staff-member request at one of the terminals, for five minutes exactly, before they relocked. They weren't separate locks either. The same metal piping ran through the walls of the circular building, locking them simultaneously.

Moments later, Dr. Simon and Aiden emerged on the other side of the lunchroom, and the metal bars over the doors released. Evan slipped inside behind them and set his watch.

Taking the four-digit combination to a locker by watching someone wasn't difficult. Most people's hands block the combination numbers themselves, but that's not really what you're looking for. Instead, you set your eyes on one single, recognizable dial marking, and watch its movement with every turn. Then after they leave, you take the final number, where their combination ended, and you re-create the pattern backward from the final number. Emma's final number was twenty-two, backward fifteen to thirty-seven, forward eight to twenty-nine, backward twenty-nine to fifty-eight.

Fifty-eight, twenty-nine, thirty-seven, twenty-two. The locker clicked open effortlessly.

Emma's locker was still full.

In the center, there was an uneven stack of textbooks, magazines, and lined notebooks. He picked them up, one by one. She drew in pencil in the margins, mostly abstract phrases stylized and dotted with illustration. *You're just a kid*, she'd written on the first page of her *The Art of Feeling* textbook, the *j*'s and *i*'s and apostrophes replaced by stars. There was a single *Holy Life* magazine at the bottom, worn at its creases. The address printed on the back was to Cynthia Richardson—Dr. Richardson—at an address in Black Rock, Utah. He thumbed through it, watching the margins, and stopped on the second to last page. Emma had scribbled a Bible verse: *Put on the full armor of God, so that you will be able to sit firm against the devil. —Matthew 7:20.* Evan ripped it from the magazine and held it briefly to his chest.

He traced the titles of the textbooks again. *Into Feeling*, her compassion training book; *The Art of Understanding*, the paperback they used in her Applications of Empathy class; and *Richard Simmons' Never Give Up: Inspirations, Reflections, Stories of Hope* by Richard Simmons, for her Inspiration in the New Millennium elective.

He stopped. If they'd been set back in order, based on her classes that day, *The Art of Feeling* should have been on the bottom. He pulled it out again.

When he gripped the book by its cover and shook the edges, a small page fell from the center, exactly what he'd been looking for. He recognized it before it even hit the floor. He'd seen Emma writing on this same crumpled piece of paper dozens of times. He'd tried a few times to get close enough to read it, but Emma was always more cautious when this paper was exposed. He picked it up carefully. Without unfolding it, he could read the name at the bottom. It was written hastily in black marker and underlined twice.

Zaza Galbia.

AIDEN.

"KEEP LOOKING FORWARD," Dr. Simon said, his fingers pressed under Aiden's jaw. "Let me know if you experience any pain."

"I swear to God," Aiden said, resisting as the doctor's thumbs worked their way up the back of his neck and scalp. "I'm fine."

"Please, refrain from language." The doctor was wearing the same black suit that most instructors wore every day. "By your own account, you've likely experienced a contusion of some sort, and may very well be concussed. If there is internal bleeding here, we will need to stop it right away."

"It was a bump on the head. That's it."

"Always in such a rush, all of you students."

Aiden pictured Emma, seated alone on the stands of the school's outdoor basketball court, waiting for him in her over-sized yellow raincoat. *Tonight*, she'd promised.

"I have homework," he told the doctor.

"Sure, sure, sure." Like several members of the adminis-tration, Dr. Simon had traces of a French accent buried under

American pronunciations. "And for Mr. Napoléon, it was *just a little* stomach ulcer. And for Mr. Caesar, it was just a little flesh wound, nothing more. What's that behind you in the theater, Mr. Lincoln? Just a little *bump on the head?*"

"What are you even talking about? Lincoln was shot— *fuck!*"

The doctor's thumbs reached a pressure point on the top of his head. Aiden could feel the pain in his toes.

"Profanity," he barked, and lifted a finger to Aiden's face. "Look. Blood. From the top of your head."

"One time I bled from my eyeball in a basketball game."

"Your blood is surprisingly thin." Behind him, it looked like Dr. Simon might have raised his glove to his mouth and smelled it. "Your file doesn't list any condition—"

"Can you just put a Band-Aid on it or something?"

"Yes." The doctor resumed his position over Aiden's scalp. "But we will need to shave your hair—"

"No!"

"Stitches it is, then."

For twenty minutes, the doctor worked, prodding and pulling at the top of his scalp. Aiden could feel the pressure at the edges of the wound as Dr. Simon cleaned it, but he hid the pain, smiling and reminding the doctor he was fine to leave.

The knot in his chest was getting tighter every minute. A maintenance sweep was about to start, probably because of the chapel, and the school would enter lockdown mode. If the staff was moving dorm to dorm, checking on every student, Emma wouldn't wait long for him.

But it wasn't just about tonight. There was more to the knot than that. He had felt it when they talked before mass, too, painfully tight. She was so distracted. She barely looked him in the eye, even when he told her point-blank he didn't feel like she cared about him anymore. She'd been like this for two weeks now, avoiding him, shorting their time together, falling asleep early on nights he was supposed to come over. Tonight, he could feel himself racing to cut her off in the middle of sentences, afraid that if she reached the end, she would get all the way to breaking up with him.

"We'll have to sit about an hour as the stitching settles," the doctor announced.

"I'm not sitting for an hour." Aiden stood, pulling his head out of Dr. Simon's reach.

"Sit down! I'm not finished—it's still bleeding!"

He looked in the mirror. A section of his hair had been pulled away for the wound, and the small scissors were hanging from a string. He took them himself and cut the string at its source. "There." He handed them back to Dr. Simon. "Can I go?"

"At least let me wrap it," the doctor said, exasperated. Aiden nodded, and he went to work, pulling a thick, tan cloth around Aiden's head and knotting it at the top. As soon as the doctor removed his hands, Aiden was headed out the door.

"Mr. Mallet," the doctor called. "You'll need medication."

Quickly, Aiden returned to the room and watched as the doctor opened a cabinet that covered the full width of the wall. Inside, hundreds of tiny, colorful drawers were labeled with words he didn't recognize—hydrocodone, oxycodone, amox-icillin. As Dr. Simon bounced between them, Aiden noticed a file sitting next to his own on the counter.

"Can I ask something?"

"If you must."

Aiden gestured to the folder. "What happened to Eddy?"

"I'm sorry?"

"Eddy."

"Ah, that's right. Hit his head. Same as you. He will be fine."

"No, I mean . . . why did he do . . . that?"

"I'm sorry?"

Aiden balanced himself. "He started screaming in church—"

Dr. Simon's hand landed on the table, covering the file. "There is something wrong with his central nervous system," he said. "Stress-induced. We will figure it out, and we will fix it."

Aiden watched the doctor for another moment, studying the way he moved. Everyone lied differently, but usually avoiding eye contact and offering short sentences was a strong clue.

The doctor handed him a small bottle. "Don't you have homework?"

Aiden nearly sprinted through the hallways on his way back, strong-arming Year One plebes rather than waiting for the post-mass hordes to clear the hallway. Left and right, peo-ple offered him high fives. "Dude, Aiden, that was so sick!" one plebe shouted. One group of Year Twos broke out into applause. He burst through the P-School Lounge and out into the fog, not stopping until the school's outdoor basketball court was in view.

It stood alone, surrounded by a cage of wrecked fence. There was one light on it, in the corner, so it cast hard shadows on the blacktop. This far from the school, the sweep sirens faded into the noise of the forest. Alone, pacing atop the bleachers, he saw her silhouette.

The school had forgotten this court existed when they built the indoor gym and removed the cameras years ago. On the first night that Emma convinced him to sneak out after curfew, they came here, with a quilted blanket and a water bottle of vodka she bought off a maintenance worker. They sat inches apart on the splintered stands, passing the bottle back and forth and talking about everything. She told him all of her favorites—her favorite stars, her favorite sounds, her favorite trees, her favorite people. He told her he didn't have any, and she said it was okay, but he owed it to himself to pay better attention. Since that night, the stands had become their spot, the source of every good night they had. But it had been at least a month since the last time they were here.

"Emma?" he called out.

The pacing stopped. She leaned against the top bleacher.

"Emma?" he asked again, her silhouette disappearing as he reached the entrance. The fence gate fought back as he pushed, grinding against the concrete.

She leaned over the stands, staring blankly down at him, and his heart dropped.

It wasn't her.

Testimonial: Neesha Shah.

Year 1995–1996. Day 21.

Emma just hung a photo of us on her wall.

She left the room thirty minutes ago, but I can't stop staring at it. It's a disgusting picture, really, up my nose on the bench near Human. We were walking there yesterday, on our way to class, when she stopped and sat, then patted the seat next to her like I should sit, too. She took her Polaroid camera out of her bag and before I knew what was happening, she was holding it out with her arm and snapping the photo.

She's smiling. I look like I'm trying to stop the photo from happening. She looks like Julia Roberts. I look like I just saw Julia Roberts getting murdered.

I don't think I've ever seen a photo of myself on someone else's wall. My family didn't do pictures, and the only photos at Kimberley International were taken for the brochures, of the beautiful students reading under trees or testing fake compounds in plastic beakers. One time, my friend Aanya took a photo of everyone at her birthday party, but when I saw it on her dresser, she'd folded it so you couldn't see me. She said there just wasn't room in the frame.

Emma and I aren't photo-on-the-wall friends, or waste-a-Polaroid friends. We're not even walk-to-class-together friends, we were just leaving at the same time yesterday. She has a hundred other friends, better than me, and a boyfriend, Aiden. She gets invited to parties that happen after curfew and sits with the basketball team at lunch.

Still, there I am, one of the ten photos on the wall. You can see everything that's different about us, starkly contrasted in those two square inches—Emma's hair is straight and golden, mine's curly and black; Emma's teeth are perfect, mine have a few noticeable gaps; Emma's smile is practiced, mine is forced—but we're both in there.

I've only known Emma for twenty-one days, and already, she's making me question the way I've lived for seventeen years. She asks simple questions, dumb questions, but questions that I can't answer, like "Why?" and "What if you didn't?"

Last night, she listened to me drone on for hours about how my project had failed to show any results, and how I'd never win the Discovery if I was only allowed to experiment on fucking rats, and then she asked, "Why do you let it have so much power over you?"

"Because it matters more than anything else that I do here!" I said.

"But what if it didn't?"

I know the work I'm going to do will be important, and the

lives I'll change will be immeasurable, and my family will get to live in a house with both a pool and a sauna inside it. I know exactly what the future is supposed to look like, if I just give myself to it completely.

But what if I didn't?

Is there a version of myself who isn't obsessed with her work, a girl I've never met, who laughs with her friends in the lunchroom and hangs a wall full of pictures behind her bed? Is there something further down inside me, a plane of existence where accolades and trophies melt away into perfectly normal, golden days of nothing to do and no one to please? Have I been squinting so hard in a single direction, at a distant future, that I've made myself blind?

I don't know why you guys moved me from the C-School to the Human dorms. Probably to mess with my head. I definitely don't know why Emma put a photo of us on her wall.

It seems like it's all happening for a reason. Maybe one day I'll learn what that reason is.

NEESHA.

TO BE SAFE, Neesha made the walk up and back to the stone well twice, to make sure the envelope hadn't fallen out. The woods were creepy at this time of night, full of foreign sounds, animal noises; the wall of fog created a separation between the world of the school and the world of the unknown around it. At one point, she felt something creeping up on her, and spun just in time to catch a branch, swinging harmlessly back and forth.

She hurried back to the dorms, empty-handed. If she was quick, she might be able to get to Zaza before the sweep and get her money back. She couldn't stand the idea of going to Emma with nothing, spending an entire sweep locked in their room in bitter disappointment. Emma had trusted her with this; she wasn't going to fail so spectacularly on her first try.

As her footsteps crunched along the path, she noticed a shuffling noise, like the swish of plastic against plastic. It got louder as she got closer, but it wasn't coming from the school; it was coming from in front of her, across the lawn. The sound began to morph, hiccuping like human laughter, human voices, and then footsteps.

She froze in the middle of the path, staring at it. A flashlight clicked on; a tiny, solitary beam, shooting toward the school. Another flashlight clicked on. Then another. Then three more. Then an entire army, too many to count, at least fifty beams, moving and circling and scanning in all directions.

In one unified motion, the flashlights began to advance. The siren shifted up a pitch, and the school's intercom system ripped out once more across the grounds.

"All students must presently be in their dorms. The maintenance sweep is beginning."

She stood frozen for a moment, watching them. She'd never seen a sweep from the outside before. Usually they were just drills or extra precautions during storms when there were serious electricity problems. One time, in her Year Two, a boy named Yasmani fell asleep in the forest, and they called a sweep for the two hours it took to find him.

She started to walk back toward her dorm. *It's not worth it.* That's what Zaza had said in the forest. Of course it was worth it—the work was incredible, far more revolutionary than anyone else's at Redemption in her four years. But, she realized, she'd never actually pictured the consequences. Every time she brought it up with Emma, Emma told her not to worry, people got away with breaking the rules all the time. But that wasn't entirely true. *Emma* got away with breaking the rules all the time. And Emma wasn't here anymore.

Neesha walked faster, down a separate, wider path, around the march of the flashlights. *You're all of us now*, that's what her mother had told her, with a kiss on the forehead at the drop-off for the bus. *We're all with you.* She meant it as a promise that the family would support her and watch over her. But as the tape had played back in her head over the years, warped from repetition, it started to sound more like a threat. You're *responsible* for all of us now. We're all *counting on* you.

No one in her family had found their footing in America yet. They'd moved from Chandigarh so she could go to Redemption, but back in Salt Lake City, things kept getting worse. Her father's position had slipped at his company, and he was made to go through Americanization training; her mother, her brother, and her brother's wife couldn't find consistent work. The only one who liked it here was her sister, but all of them sucked it up, for the promise of cashing their golden ticket— Neesha's brain.

What if the school found out about Apex? How would she be punished? And what would her mother say about that?

The Human Lounge had cleared out by the time Neesha was inside. Only the highest frequencies of the sirens were audible through the stone walls, but red lights popped and flashed intermittently down the connected hallways. She took the stairs, two at a time, checking over her shoulder for flashlights. When she reached the third floor, she turned the corner into her hallway and froze—

In the flashing lights, she could make out five staff members, each wearing the school's plastic protective suits, congregated outside her room.

"Neesha." One of them noticed her from down the hall; she couldn't tell who. "We need to talk to you."

She felt the weight pushing down against her shoulders.

"When was the last time you saw Emma?"

AIDEN.

"HEY, BUDDY," THE voice said to him from above, quick and sharp, with an accent. "Who's that?"

He rounded the bleachers, turning into the light. It was a tall guy, skinny but with a puffy orange jacket hanging from his shoulders. "Wait," he said. "I recognize you . . . Peter, right?"

He nodded. "Yeah, Peter Novak, buddy."

"We met Year One, you were in my orientation group. For capture the flag. I'm Aiden."

"Cool."

"What are you doing out here?"

Peter cleared his throat. "Seems like a nice night for a sit. You?"

Aiden ignored the question, instead scanning the court for something he might have missed. There was no other entrance to the cage, and no movement around them. It was just the two of them.

"You're looking for Emma?" Peter asked.

"Yeah, we were supposed to meet after mass, but . . ." Aiden pointed to his head.

"Goofy look, man."

"It's not a look, it's a bandage. I was bleeding from my head after that kid slammed me into the altar."

"Why'd you let a kid slam you into an altar?"

"I didn't let him, he was freaking out and I stopped him from hurting anybody. You don't remember this from mass?"

"Oh, no, I got the fuck outta there. What a mess."

"Huh. She must have gone back before the sweep. . . ."

Aiden's skin was crawling. He was sweaty from the run, but it was more than that. The prickly sense that something was wrong, the feeling that someone was watching him, the palpable weight of the mist in the air—all clung to him like moisture.

"Yeah . . ." Peter looked nervous.

"What?"

"I came straight from mass, buddy," he said. "Emma hasn't been here."

Aiden looked at him. "No offense, but you probably don't know who I'm talking about."

"No, I know who Emma is. I was supposed to meet her, too." He felt the impact in his stomach. "Are you serious?"

Peter nodded.

"For what?"

Peter squirmed a bit. "For important, personal business between me and her."

Aiden couldn't control himself; he leapt up the bleachers, two at a time, his hands flying straight for Peter's jacket.

"Easy, easy," Peter said, moving away from him. "I was buying! It was a transaction!"

Aiden froze, halfway up the bleachers.

Peter peeked up from where he was crouching. "Jesus, be careful with that energy, buddy. I can see your insecurity from here."

Aiden sat, rubbing his face with his hands. She never came. She probably never even planned on coming. She'd lied.

"Sorry, buddy." Peter sat next to him. "Looks like you might've been wrong about some stuff." He felt Peter's hand on his back. "Whoa, you're sweaty. Did you run all the way out here?"

Aiden nodded. They sat in silence for a long couple of minutes, his brain racing through everything she'd said to him tonight, everything he'd done in the last two weeks. He'd been afraid that if he didn't make it out in time, he'd lose her, but the truth was, he never had her at all.

"Let me ask you something," Peter said, still watching him. "You're taking right now, yeah?"

Aiden hadn't noticed, but his hands were active, grabbing uncontrollably at the bottom of the bandage around his head.

"Yeah, you're *up*. Here." Peter held out a water bottle. "Gotta stay hydrated, bro. Apex will fry your shit."

Aiden took it and drank. He nearly emptied the bottle, handing it back to Peter with a small reservoir in the bottom. "I took one on my way here."

"You got more?"

Aiden shook his head. "Not on me, but I just bought five hundred for the team."

"Five *hundred*?"

Aiden shrugged. "It's not really a thing to me."

He could feel Peter surveying him more critically. "Are you the prince of some country or something? Did you invent a hair product?"

"My dad owns some grocery stores."

"Huh." Peter put a dip of tobacco in his cheek. "Now, you're a basketball player, right?"

Aiden nodded.

"You any good?"

"There are NBA scouts coming to watch me next week."

"Jesus, are you serious? Man, some guys have all the luck."

"It's not luck," Aiden spat back. "I work for my shit."

"Sure." Peter spat on the ground in front of them. "Just saying, no one's going to pay me millions of dollars to be in debate. I didn't even get recruited here to debate. They just thought it was cool I could speak twelve languages, then stuck me with an activity."

Peter watched him for another long minute, even though Aiden was making it obvious he wasn't interested in talking. "Are you still here?" Aiden asked finally.

"Yeah, sorry, buddy. Just trying to figure this out."

"Figure what out?"

"You're trying out for the fucking NBA next week, and tonight you're sprinting out here, during a sweep, to meet your girlfriend, who didn't even show up?"

"So?"

Peter shook his head. "Nothing. Just interesting."

The sirens shifted, faintly droning in the background, raised a half step, and they heard the far-off announcement that the sweep was starting. "Alright, that's the edge of my patience," Peter said, moving down the bleachers. "Good luck, buddy."

He stopped once he was on the ground and turned back to Aiden. "I hope she shows up. Kinda looks like you lost yourself up there."

"What the fuck is that supposed to mean?"

"Nothing. Good luck next week, buddy." Peter shrugged and strolled off.

Aiden sat alone for another ten minutes, overreacting anytime a sound echoed from the forest or the school behind him. The last time they were here, just the two of them, Emma confided something in him. What did she say? He could barely remember, but it was serious, about flowers and her parents, how they treated her. She'd said something that didn't make sense, how she didn't want to be special, or how she wished people would pay less attention to her. It was hard to listen to Emma when she was in one of her hopeless moods. She'd talk like the sky was falling, then forget it all the next day. But this one was different.

Whatever it was, he hadn't done anything about it then, and it was too late to do anything about it now. Emma had moved on to whatever was more important than him, and he was left here, in their spot, alone.

EVAN.

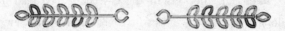

"PEACE BE WITH you," a maintenance worker said, standing in the doorway, blocking most of it.

"And also with you," Zaza said from his desk chair.

"You know the drill, right? I'm gonna look in all your stuff, you've gotta open it for me, you signed up for this, et cetera?"

"Yeah, sure thing."

Evan tucked himself into the doorway. His face was a few inches from the frame of the door, and he flinched every time the red light behind him exposed his position.

"Do you think it's weird they make you all dress like janitors?" Zaza asked. He leaned back comfortably, like he had nothing to hide. If he did know something about Emma, he certainly wasn't going to give it up to a random maintenance worker.

"No way. I had to sweep some of the labs in the chemical science building one time—I don't know what kind of crazy shit they've got going on in there." The maintenance worker had walked across the room and was looking in Zaza's closet. "How'd you get the solo dorm?"

"Two years. Since late in my Year One—"

"That's lucky."

"—when my roommate had a mental breakdown."

"Less lucky."

"It's fine. Half the kids in the C-School have had mental breakdowns. Mostly the ones who don't win their reviews."

"Win their reviews?"

"Yeah, we get judged one-on-one against a classmate, so only half the people pass. It's stressful."

The man knelt to scan his flashlight under the bed.

"What are you guys even looking for?" Zaza asked.

"Just trying to ensure that everyone is accounted for."

"So someone's missing."

"We don't know that yet."

"And you think they might be under my bed?"

"She could be anywhere. Students here are too smart for their own good."

"So it's a she."

The flashlight reached its farthest point under the bed, the light swallowed to a single spot by a blanket, and Evan took three silent steps into the room. His body must have pushed an air current, because as the light came leaking back out, Zaza's head turned to the hallway. Evan breathed through his nose, watching from between the door and the wall.

"When will the lights come back on?" Zaza asked. "I've got three sets due tomorrow morning for O-Chem."

The man hoisted himself back up. "Don't you guys have stuff for candles?"

"Yeah, but I can't really compare three forty-cell spreads by candlelight." On Zaza's desk was the school's basic-issue set: two wax candles, a copper holder, and a small box of matches. They were told in Year One that given the frequency of power outages and maintenance sweeps, they'd need to get used to working by candlelight.

"I'm sure previous generations had it much worse than you."

"They also knew a lot less and died a lot younger."

The maintenance worker didn't respond, so Zaza lit his candle. The man used his flashlight to scan the room once more, down to the carpet, up to the exposed stone in the ceiling. Evan held his breath, praying.

"Sometimes," he said, the beam hovering two feet over Evan's head, "I think the people who built this place had never been inside an actual building before." The light whipped back to Zaza's face at the desk. "Lights will be on when we're done."

The door slid shut with a soft click behind him. Zaza leaned back with a heavy sigh, *S2—Subtext* suggesting a release of tension, his fingers, legs, and neck dropping to assume the curvature of the chair. From his inside jacket pocket, Zaza pulled out a baggie of silver pills and dropped them on his desk. He fell forward, burying his face into them, letting out a guttural moan.

"It's Emma."

Zaza shot up. "What the fuck?"

"That's who they're looking for," Evan said quietly. He'd moved to the bottom of the bed.

"Evan?" Zaza recognized him immediately. They'd met

twice, once during his Year One orientation, and once when they were placed on the same team during a physical activity day. "What are you doing here?"

"I'm looking for her."

"Who?"

"Emma. I just told you."

"Okay," Zaza said. "But what are you doing *here*? Actually— *how* are you here? There's a sweep going on. Did they not see you out there?"

"It's not complicated." Evan talked to his thumbs.

"Jesus." Zaza took a breath. "How'd you know that they're looking for Emma?"

"Because she's missing."

"Pretty sure I saw her in church."

"She disappeared before it was over."

"And you came to see me, because . . ."

Zaza slid the candle toward Evan's face, and he felt the heat curling against his cheek, leaking into his eye. It hurt so he backed away, blocking the direct wave with his hand and wincing, shorter than his shadow. "You saw her," he mumbled.

Zaza was slow to nod. "Yeah, I mean, I saw her before church. I don't know how you know that, but you're right."

"Why?"

The siren outside shifted pitch and grew louder. "Are you gonna get in trouble for being here?" Zaza asked. "Not in your dorm?"

"I have four minutes."

"How could you possibly know that?"

"What did you say to Emma?"

Zaza stood for a moment, then sat back against the top of the desk, blocking Evan's view of the bag of silver pills. "How old are you, anyway?"

"Fourteen."

"*Fourteen.*" He kept looking directly into Evan's eyes, while behind him, his left hand slid the pills behind a photo on his desk. "That's young. So you must be crazy good at something."

Evan rocked back and forward a few times. "Chess," he said.

"That's right," Zaza said, smiling. "Second kid to beat the chess computer. Champion of the robots. I forgot that was you. Chess is pattern recognition, so . . ." He thought for a moment. "You've figured where they're starting and how fast they're moving, built a model—" He pointed to Evan's watch. "And you know that you have four minutes to talk to me."

"Three. Please tell me why Emma came to see you."

"You know," Zaza said, "any analyst would tell you that there's way too many variables for the level of certainty you're demonstrating now."

"I just want to find her."

Zaza sighed. "I bought some books from her—"

"You don't have any classes," Evan cut in. An *S6—Honesty* reflex.

"Fiction books, man." He reached across his desk, holding copies of *Animal Farm* and *Fahrenheit 451*. "I didn't really know her that well."

Evan's eyes started to scan the room.

"I'm sorry, Evan. But can I give you a piece of advice, as a friend? Don't get involved in this. Wherever Emma went—if she actually did go somewhere, like you're saying—it's for a good reason. And it's just not gonna be good for you to get involved. Trust me."

Evan didn't answer. Usually, when people said "trust me," there was another *S3—Intention* involved.

"I'm sure she just went for a phone call or something, and she'll be back as soon as she's done. She used to talk on the phone all the time—"

"Talk to who?" Evan sat up. There was a phone number at the top of Emma's list of names.

Zaza shrugged. "I figured you'd know. Since you guys were so close."

Evan looked straight into Zaza's eyes before his gaze fell to the desk, then to the chair in front of it. Hanging unceremoniously from the back was a dark-purple-and-yellow windbreaker.

Evan stared at it. Zaza had come to mass less than a minute before the service started, with mud on his shoes. One minute after that, someone else came back. "What about Neesha Shah?"

In the wind leaking in through cracks in the walls, the flame of the candle swung, and Evan could feel it passing onto and off his face, but his expression didn't change. He hadn't modulated his emotional performance since he'd entered the room.

Zaza shifted uncomfortably, but before he could answer, Evan's watch started to beep.

Zaza smiled and nodded to the door. "Time's up. Hope there weren't any breaks in the pattern. Variables are a bitch."

emma donahue investigation.

neesha shah—year 4.

transcription by MONKEY voice-to-text software.

YANIS (Administration) _ Hello. Checking. Checking. Checking. Good. There it goes. Please say your name for our voice-to-text software.

NEESHA SHAH (Student) _ Your what.

Y _ Voice to text. Look. It prints what we say. As we say it.

NS _ Okay. Nee Shu Shaw.

Y _ Huh. Bad spelling. How long were you roommates with Emma.

NS _ Just this year.

Y _ Did you know her before this year.

NS _ I met her in year one. But we didn't talk.

Y _ Why not.

NS _ I don't know. She hung out with cool people. I didn't.

Y _ Who did you hang out with.

NS _ C School kids. I guess.

Y _ C School kids aren't cool.

NS _ We had different social groups.

Y _ Emma had a lot of friends around school.

NS _ I guess.

Y _ It's kind of amazing actually how many people she speaks to in the last week. One. After another. After another. Do you know why that is.

NS _ You said it. She had a lot of friends.

Y _ What is she like. Normally. I have never met her.

NS _ She's nice. Um. She slept a lot. Sometimes she was really hyper and laughed at her own jokes.

Y _ What about the other times.

NS _ Other times.

Y _ When she wasn't feeling hyper. What was she. Sad.

NS _ Not really. Just quiet.

Y _ When was the last time you saw her.

NS _ At mass.

Y _ And before this.

NS _ In our dorm.

Y _ Did you go to the mass together.

NS _ No.

Y _ Why not.

NS _ She had to make a phone call.

Y _ What phone call.

NS _ I don't know. She just said she had to . . . What.

Y _ Seven forty five. Emma walks from dorm to chapel. No phone call.

NS _ She probably used the phone on the way. In the human lounge.

Y _ Nope. No phone call . . . You look surprised. Is that what she told you . . . Neesha.

NS _ No. I was just getting confused.

Y _ Okay . . . A few people who spoke to her this afternoon said she was distressed. Did she seem that way to you.

NS _ No.

Y _ Do you have any idea what might be the cause of that distress.

NS _ No. She didn't say anything to me.

Y _ Is that unusual.

NS _ I guess not.

EVAN.

ZAZA WAS HALF right about the sweeps. They were easy to navigate. Twelve instructors and maintenance workers were assigned to each of the five schools. But they didn't walk with a codified pattern. Or at least they thought they didn't.

The staff members moved using a form of discrimination learning called win-stay, lose-shift. If a system sees an action generate a desired outcome, it will stay the course. If the strategy is unsuccessful, it will shift. It was the reason a game like rock-paper-scissors, despite its fifty-fifty mechanical probability, could be played with probabilistic skill. When a player ties or loses (66.6 percent odds), they rarely repeat that action, so playing the inverse action doubles an opponent's odds of success. As long as staff members thought they were being successful in their search—and they were, almost every time they checked a dorm—they wouldn't alter their strategy. They would continue in the same direction, making the safest place to avoid being seen exactly where they had just been.

Evan ran thirty feet down the second-floor hallway. A

flashlight came down the stairs and he ducked left, pausing for sixty seconds, then following behind it to the stairwell. He used the wall to guide himself to the third floor and turned the corner into his hallway, where he froze.

He'd failed to account for a variable. Emma was the one who was missing. There were ten gray suits outside her door. Evan swallowed and walked toward them.

He could hear Neesha answering questions inside her room. There were flashes exploding outward as staff members took pictures. Through the sliver of her door, he saw a huge shadow. Yanis was standing over Neesha, pressing her with questions.

"Evan Andrews."

Dr. Richardson was on the edge of the group. She was taller than most of them, and unlike the suits to her right and left, she wasn't wearing a mask or cover of any kind. The skin of her face was pulled back tightly over her skeletal structure. Her lips were barely visible and always pursed, which made her look to Evan like an amphibian. Every time she spoke, regardless of where she was looking, it felt like her voice was coming downward, from on high. "Where have you been? It's well past the announcement of the sweep."

"I—I was i-in the . . . the . . ."

She frowned. "Is that a stutter?"

He swallowed. "I was on a walk. I didn't realize it was a sweep."

"Really? You didn't notice the blaring sirens and bright red lights?" She nodded to his door and he unlocked it. She followed him and pointed to the bed. "*Sit.*"

Dr. Richardson closed the door behind them. He'd taken a class with her last year, everybody had to in their Year One, on foundations of psychology and morality. She'd described the work he did as "theoretically correct, but practically confused." She always seemed disappointed in him but he couldn't understand why.

"Where were you tonight, really?" she hissed.

"I—I told you. I was outside."

She didn't believe him. She scanned the room with her flashlight, jumping between the Utah Jazz basketball posters. He could see the tack on the corner of one had popped out, the top of the poster curling under against the wall, and his hands seized on the bed behind him.

"When was the last time you saw Emma?" she said, assessing his response out of the corner of her eye.

"Just leaving for mass."

"How did she look?"

"Normal."

"Did she say anything?"

"N-no."

"When did your stutter come back?"

"It's not back."

"It's psychogenic, remember. It doesn't have anything to do with your mechanics; it is *not* your body's natural state. You're choosing the blockage."

"I know."

"You just have to more consciously consider the connection between your thoughts and the way you express them."

"I know."

"The beautiful part about follies of our thoughts is that we have the power to change them."

"I know."

She smiled sadly down at him. "Then why do you still stutter?"

A passing gray maintenance suit bumped the door and for a moment, Emma's room was visible again. He could see the empty spot on her desk where her journal had once been.

Dr. Richardson pushed the door shut completely. "Is there anything you want me to know about?" she asked. She'd noticed the unrest in his hands. He was accidentally feeding her *S2—Subtext.*

"No."

"Your testimonial journal," she said, her back still turned. "You don't want me to read it?"

"No, you can read it."

"Students are so precious about their journals." She shook her head. "They forget, they're written *for* the staff. We're supposed to be using them to evaluate your progress. What would be the point if we couldn't read them?"

"You can."

"And yet, they also rarely tell us anything we don't already know."

Evan could feel his throat closing. Dr. Richardson was

getting closer to the walls and looking over every few seconds. She knew something she wasn't telling him. She was probing deeper with every new item she found; nothing in the closet but the same solid-colored, JCPenney zip-ups; nothing under the bed but a crate of art supplies and Post-it notes, nothing on the walls but his fragile basketball posters, starting to slip—

"John Stockton," she said.

"What?"

"You *love* John Stockton." She gestured with the beam of her flashlight. "The posters. It is not enough to see John Stockton once? You must see him five times? A John Stockton for every wall, and two for the desk?"

Evan nodded, his tongue still drowning in saliva.

"Why do you love him so much?"

"He's good at basketball."

"Does he have a stutter?"

"No, no. Just good at basketball."

She turned her flashlight onto the ground and crouched to his level. "Your progress is slipping here, Evan. Something is creating a blockage, something you can't even see yourself. And we have to find it and kill it; otherwise you won't be able to move forward. Have you been taking your supplements with lunch?"

"Yes."

"You know those aren't optional; we need those to keep your bodies healthy in the environment."

"Yes."

"You've been doing assessments with Dr. Edwards?"

"Yes."

She pulled a Post-it note and pen from her pocket, quick scratching and signing at the bottom, holding it out to him by a single finger. "Give this to him tomorrow. You're going to do assessments with me now, and we're going to fix whatever it is that's happening in you."

Robert, Evan Andrews is going to check in with me. Thanks, C.R.

"Let us know if you hear anything about Emma, okay? You're the light of the world, Evan."

"Thanks," he said, but she was already out the door. For a moment, Evan sat in silence, looking poster to poster, Stockton to Stockton, waiting for the final click of the door and for the sounds of the hallway to disappear.

In each photo, John Stockton was perfectly focused. Whether he was bouncing the basketball, or leaning forward to throw it, or high-fiving with Karl Malone, he always stared forward with singular, objective, uninhibited focus. John Stockton wasn't distracted by the noise of the world, the grinding of its motion, the expectations of his coaches, the opinions of his teammates, the size of his opponents. This was the source of his greatness—not what he saw, but his ability to see. Evan loved that about him, even if he'd never watched a basketball game in his life.

He went to the largest poster, on the wall across from his desk, and reached for the tacks at the top, pulling it down and rolling it into a small cylindrical container. He repeated this for the other four posters, carefully placing the tacks in a plastic casing. Taking a flashlight from the bottom drawer, he turned his attention to the far wall.

Sprawled about before him, interweaving and overlapping, was a system of string, Post-it notes, and photos from last year's registry. It stretched from one wall to the next, bending in the corners, weighed down by meticulous detail. First, in the corner above his desk, he found the photo of Zaza from last year's yearbook. There was only one note beneath it: *basketball stats*. Evan traced the line back to the center of the far wall, holding a single Post-it. *Day 37. 2:30p outside C-School dorm.* He added, *Day 40. 7:30p zaza dorm.* Nothing in the school buildings, nothing in the Human dorm, nothing suggesting a monetary exchange. Emma never read books, and she wasn't carrying any when she'd returned to her dorm earlier. Their interests were incompatible and showed no signs of a social friendship. Evan followed the line back to Zaza. Below *basketball stats*, he added *adidas jacket*.

Anyone at Redemption who interacted with Emma received a breakout section of the wall. There was so much detail in Neesha Shah's section of the map that she'd necessitated her own wall, near the door. He traced his finger to corresponding dates. *Day 37. 2:50p neesha dorm.* He added, *Day 40. 7:40p neesha dorm.* Every time she talked to Zaza, she talked to Neesha immediately after. A pattern.

He tacked the list of students at the center of the converging lines, each name aligning with one of the outward-branching strings. He copied the phone number from the top of the list onto a Post-it, and placed it on the *phone calls* section of the board. Zaza was right, Emma had made a dozen phone calls from Dr. Richardson's lobby. Now he knew the number she was calling.

Evan turned and, after double-locking the closed door, pulled open the top of his backpack and removed the soft, leather-bound testimonial journal. He took the Bible quote she'd scribbled in the magazine and pinned it in the center of the board, then sat, a flashlight in his mouth, and began to read, stopping only to notice the peaceful, focused look on Emma's face in the middle of the madness.

NEESHA.

ACROSS THE CEILING of her room, Neesha watched as the red lights clicked off and the yellow light of the back lawn started to leak through the window once again.

The school had cleared out Emma's side of the room; all the textbooks, piles of clothes, and photos on her wall had been loaded into trash bags and carried out by maintenance workers. The footsteps outside died down, the siren was turned off, and the school returned to its normal resting state.

Neesha lay alone, shivering under her covers. She hadn't slept in a room by herself since the third grade, when her family had to clear out their attic after she got chicken pox. She hated the feeling of it. Every sound was magnified; every change in the wind felt like the violins that brought in the start of the horror movie.

It was well after midnight, at least six hours since mass, and no one had seen Emma. The school had locked everything down, searched all possible areas, and still, the bed across the room was empty. Five hours ago, when Yanis the maintenance man had been in here with his MONKEY machine, she was sure it was some kind of miscommunication—Emma wandered too far for a cigarette, Emma ran off with Aiden, Emma was playing a weird prank. But five hours later, any hope of that had disappeared. Even before meeting Zaza in the woods, something about tonight had felt off. Now, two hours past midnight, it was evident something had happened, something terrible, and Neesha couldn't stop thinking about the worst possibility—that Emma *was* the something.

Emma had lied to her. There was no phone call before mass. Which meant there was no reason for Neesha to make the drop tonight, unless there was. Unless everything that had happened tonight, starting with Zaza, was part of Emma's plan: get Neesha involved, then disappear. If the school was closing in, now Neesha would be completely liable. Whatever punishment had been meant for Emma, it was coming for her now.

There was a soft knock on her door.

It was so quiet she tried to ignore it at first, but thirty seconds later, it happened again, four quick raps and then silence. She slid out from her bed and clicked the door open.

Zaza stood in the hallway, the hood of the same Adidas jacket thrown over his head.

"Can I come in?"

Her heartbeat doubled, surging with rage and pushing blood into her fingers. She turned to let him pass, and as she watched him enter, casually, as if nothing had happened, she felt the full chill of the night sweeping in with him.

As soon as the door latched shut behind him, she sprang, throwing her right palm upward at his nose.

"Ah, fuck!" Zaza went tumbling backward onto Emma's bed, clutching his face. "What's that about?"

"You're lucky I didn't kill you," she said, taking another step over him.

Blood seeped its way out around his hands, thick streams rushing down the bright yellow stripe on his sleeves. She watched for a moment as he struggled to plug it, helpless against the speed and strength. She pulled a few tissues from the desk and handed them over, keeping her distance.

"That's a myth, you know," he said, his voice more nasal than usual. "You can't kill someone like that. The skull bones are too strong."

"I'm sure you know that from the *zero* fights that you've been in."

"I think it might be broken." He sat up against the wall, tissues stuck from both nostrils like tusks. "Why are you hitting me?"

Neesha cleared her throat. "First, I want my money back, now."

His eyebrows bent. "Your money? The . . . wait, what do you mean *back*?"

"You know exactly what I mean."

"I don't." The tissues shook with his head. "I don't at all."

She stared at him for a long moment.

"You think *I* took it?" he asked. "Are you forgetting the part where I gave it to you—"

"I *know* you took it. I saw you busting ass out of the chapel."

"Everyone was busting ass out of the chapel—"

"Convenient, huh."

Zaza shifted on Emma's bed, some blood from his sleeves spilling over onto the mattress. "You think I took your money, then came over here three hours after curfew, so I could what . . . gloat about it?" Zaza ran his hand over his barely existent hair. "What else do you want?"

"What?"

"You said first. What do you want second?"

Neesha felt her fists clench again. "I want to know what Emma told you to do tonight."

Zaza's face collapsed to the center in confusion, his eyes almost crossing. "She . . . told me to meet her at the well? Ten minutes before mass? Then you showed up. That's it."

"Where is she now?"

He shook his head. "I have no idea. I don't even—I barely know her."

Neesha sat on her own bed across from him. She could taste her saliva, heavy and acidic. "Then what are you doing here?"

His eyes glanced back and forth. "I wanted to warn you about something. This kid came to my dorm during the sweep, Evan Andrews. Do you know who he is?"

She shook her head.

"Okay, well. He's very creepy. He knew she was missing before the sweep, and he knew she came to my dorm tonight."

"Why are you telling me?"

"Because he asked about you, too."

Neesha shrugged. "I'm a popular person."

"You're not taking this seriously. I think he was following her for a long time, and he definitely knows more than he was telling me." Zaza dropped his voice. "She was in a hurry earlier, when she stopped by. That's when she was asking for half the money."

"Why didn't you give it to her?"

"I didn't have it from Aiden yet. But something was weird about tonight. Don't you think?"

Neesha rocked on the bed, staring at the spot where earlier that night, Emma had come gliding into the room, faster than usual. *Can you please handle this one?* she'd said. *I need you tonight, Neesha.* The more times she heard it in her head, the more it sounded like bullshit. Something was wrong, she'd felt it the whole time, the rains coming at sunset to bring the flood, she should have listened.

Neesha exhaled. "Yeah. Something was weird."

"Do you think it has something to do with Apex?"

Neesha winced at the mention of the project, then nodded again.

"Okay. If you have any more, you should probably hide it. Or dump it."

"Yeah, right, and let someone else walk off with the Discovery—"

"Just until Emma's back."

The wind outside picked up, and she heard her mom again: *We're all with you now.* She pulled her shoes from under her bed, and a black hoodie from her closet.

"Where are you going?" Zaza asked.

"Take your shiny-ass coat off," she said, tossing him a second hoodie. "And follow me."

The only lights in the hallway this late at night were the exit signs at the ends of the halls. They ran quietly around the wide edge of the dormitories with their hoods up—Human to P-School to C-School—and turned inward to the academic building. She pulled a key from her back pocket.

"You got a key?"

"I'm an exceptional student," Neesha whispered, and they slipped inside.

The Chemical Sciences building was one of the only sites of disorder on Redemption's otherwise geometric campus. There were so many small offices, miniature laboratories, special packaging rooms, freezers, and holding spaces made out of converted storage pods that the hallways had to be built with sharp corners and random turns. There were overhead fluorescents, but they were hung so high that their light barely reached the ground. Instead, various shades of neon lights poked out of different classrooms and labs, occasionally staining the hallway red or blue. Creepiest of all, the school had adorned the hallways and laboratories with statues of dead-white-guy genius types throughout, by far the scariest-looking genre of human. Albert Einstein smiled at the entrance; René Descartes beckoned outside the bathroom, and Isaac Newton glared down with fury upon Dr. Yangborne's chemistry classroom.

Neesha wheeled an old cart from the very back of the closet, covered with a thick white cloth. She peeled back the cloth to reveal a harmless-looking setup of a few vacuum flasks, cardboard boxes, and an ancient hot plate. She took two Redemption Prep water bottles from the bottom of the cart and tossed them to Zaza. "We're bringing those back."

He popped the lid off one of them. "Whoa." It was full to the brim with tiny silver beads.

"That's a five-thousand-dollar water bottle."

Zaza examined the inside of the bottle, astonished. "What is it, even?"

"What's what?"

"This. Apex?"

Neesha's constant motion slowed. "We've been in class together for four years. You just bought five hundred of them. You don't know what it is?"

Zaza shrugged. "I do O-Chem, not drugs. And my nana didn't believe in medicine."

Neesha went back to work, unscrewing a vacuum flask from its stand and placing both softly in a cardboard box. "It's not anything, technically. It's a central nervous system stimulant. I borrowed the recipe from a drug that went to consumer trials a few years ago. It's like Ritalin, but more effective, targeted, and extended-release. . . ."

Zaza was staring back, his face blank.

"How did you get here?"

"I followed you."

"No, *here* here. Redemption. Everybody did some crazy thing, what did you do?"

"Oh." He smiled, clearly proud of himself. "I created a neutral taste agent that makes milk taste like Pepsi."

"Ew, why?"

"People hate milk, but it's good for you. And they love Pepsi."

"That's the dumbest thing I've ever heard. But okay. Remember how you felt when you first tried it, your milk-Pepsi thing—"

"Lacto-Cola."

"Yuck, but okay. Do you remember the breakthrough moment? Where you thought, *Oh my God, I can do this, I'm going to be able to do this for my entire life, every beverage combination I ever try will be this successful because I'm just that good at it?*"

"I guess."

"Okay, it's like that feeling, but for eight hours, about anything in the world. It's a focus drug and a mood booster. Math kids take it to do math, basketball players take it to play basketball. Emma called it Apex because it takes you straight to your peak, and it holds you there."

She held out a pill in front of him, and he recoiled.

"Anyway, a bunch of companies are trying to figure out a legal way to sell amphetamines as a drug to help kids who can't focus in school, and I cracked it."

"Amphetamines, like meth?"

She shrugged. "You say potato, I say extended-release."

Her hands flew expertly around the cart, breaking down the last few structures and disassembling the hot plate.

"Did Emma take it?" he asked quietly.

"Yes," Neesha said, plugging the hot plate into the wall. "Emma took it every day."

"Who else?"

She snorted.

"What?"

"Who else?" Neesha rolled her eyes. "There are nine hundred students at Redemption. We sold two thousand pills in our first week. Who else? *Everyone* else. *Everyone* is taking it."

"Why are you doing this?" Zaza's voice wavered.

"What do you mean?"

"I mean, you're basically guaranteed to get into Berkeley already, you know money's not going to be a problem for you . . . is it really worth making all this for three thousand dollars?"

She shrugged.

"Then why? What could possibly make this worth it?"

She tried to ignore the question, but he waited for an answer. "Because," she finally said. "With a drug this general, you need a pretty large sample size to prove its efficacy—"

"Wait—"

"—and I'm not going to get that kind of data from just feeding the drug to rats all the time, so I needed a way to prove to the judges that it can actually work, large-scale."

"Oh my God." Zaza looked like he was going to be sick. "You're running human trials."

"I mean—"

"We're your rats."

"I guess."

"Just for a *trophy*? Is it really worth the risk, just to win?"

Yes, she wanted to scream at him, and the fact that he couldn't understand that was exactly the reason he'd never win it. But instead she just said, "Sure."

He was quiet for a while, as she finished with the cart. She snuck a glance at him. He'd moved farther away and set the bottles on the table. He looked like he was going to hurl.

"Is it working?" he asked, still keeping a safe distance from the silver powder. "Your trials. Are they showing results?"

She smiled and pulled a manila folder from the bottom of the cart. "See for yourself."

She watched proudly as his eyes lit up with wonder. A half-point rise over the C-School's test average. A spike in neural activity above the B-School's baseline. The Robo kids had made incredible progress on their fiber-optic network; the basketball team was shaving seconds off their reaction times. "This is insane," Zaza muttered to himself. "This is *everybody*. You've caused an uptick for the entire school. In a week."

She smiled. "Might as well give me the trophy now."

"Yeah," Zaza mumbled into the folder. "Unless you go to jail first."

Her smile disappeared. She yanked the joint of the final stand so hard that its top metal piece went flying across the room, clattering across the ground.

"Does Yangborne know about it?"

"The trials? Of course not. The drug? Kind of. He loves the idea. His only suggestion is that I should call it *adderall.*"

"What's this part?" Zaza pointed to the page. "'Over-exposure,' what does that mean?"

Neesha slowed down. "Yeah, I mean, like any trial, it's had a couple of unintended consequences."

"Like . . ."

"Well, there's the shakes. Muscle hyperactivity. Twitchy fingers, clenching jaw, shaking."

Zaza waited. "And?"

"*And* some other types of concerns. When you start doing anything all the time, your body starts to count on it, and in the case of a drug this effective, people have gotten . . . kind of serious about it." She finished and returned the cardboard boxes to their place on the shelves. The only thing that remained of her Apex lab build were the water bottles on the desk.

Zaza was still staring intently at her. "What do you mean, serious?"

Neesha took the bottles and toyed with the caps. "I mean . . . there was a kid in the music school who played guitar until his hands were bleeding. Some of the basketball kids have gotten a little violent. A few people have stopped sleeping altogether."

"And you're comfortable with that? Making a kid bleed from playing the guitar?"

Neesha sighed. "That's a very authoritarian view of personal responsibility. I don't think it's fair to tell people what they're capable of or not capable of. We don't do that with other shit. Plus, that's not a part of the drug, that's just the way people are reacting to it. Most people are fine. It is possible to be *too* focused on something, you know.

"It makes you the most extreme version of yourself. And some people's most extreme versions don't work out very well."

PART III.

uppers.

Testimonial: Emmalynn Donahue

Year 1995–1996. Day 28.

THE FIRST MORNING of summer, when the sun is bright enough to cut through the fog and it just hangs in the air like it's waiting for me.

The first day of class, when everybody has a reason to introduce themselves.

The first sixty seconds of a high, the way it rushes up and reintroduces itself, the familiar feeling that everything is different, the unshakable certainty that everything is possible.

The way somebody smiles in the middle of something difficult, the nod to acknowledge that they see you next to them.

The smell of the mountain, the smell of the wild grass, the smell of the mud, the smell of the farm, the smell of the kitchen and the back porch and the barn, the smell of my room.

Dr. Richardson told me to make a list of all the things that I loved in the world, and that's the best that I can come up with.

She told me that my ability to see was the source of my poetry, and that I felt things other people couldn't feel because

I took the time to notice them.

But reading the list now, I can't feel any of those things. Lately, I can only feel the thoughts of those things, the ink meant to represent those things. I've stared so long at the letters that they've lost their meaning, and I'm stuck writing the idea of someone else's poetry.

The only thing I learned from writing them down is that all the things that I love point in one direction—away—and occur at one time—not now.

When I was a little girl and I felt this way, my mother told me to find my faith. She told me that I could give myself to God, when I couldn't hold the world on my own. When I was a little girl, I didn't know where to look for him.

Dr. Richardson says religion was my mom's way of dealing with things that she couldn't understand, like pain and sadness. She says everybody in the world does that, creates ways of dealing with things they don't understand, because once you've seen enough of this life, you realize it's easier to mute the world than it is to listen to it. But she said I didn't have to. I had the ability to be better. I wouldn't need to invest in systems to realize my life's meaning, because I realized the meaning of my life every time I looked around me. She says that ignoring the pain and sadness of the world, or wrapping them in the cellophane cover of religion, took me further from the world. Instead, I should let them have me. I should allow myself to feel the world.

And I want to feel the world. But the thing is—I've seen God. He's already speaking to me. And his voice isn't coming from the forests.

emma donahue investigation.

aiden mallet—year 4.

transcription by MONKEY voice-to-text software.

YANIS (School Administration) _ Please speak your full name aloud.

AIDEN MALLET (Student) _ Aiden Mallet.

Y _ Aiden Mallet the basketball star. So I hear.

AM _ I guess.

Y _ And friend of Emma.

AM _ Boyfriend of Emma.

Y _ Her file doesn't say anything about a boyfriend.

AM _ Yeah they probably don't put that stuff in our files.

Y _ They do.

AM _ Well it's probably not updated.

Y _ I have a long list of her friends. I've even got a list of your friends. Nico Ty On Peter Durk.

AM _ Those guys aren't my friends.

Y _ In whatever case. You're not in her file.

AM _ Then how did you know to talk to me?

Y _ I'm very smart. Also the school has cameras everywhere.

AM _ I always thought those were just for show.

Y _ Turns out they're not. So help me understand. What are you talking to her about before church.

AM _ Just about our relationship. I had some questions and . . . she always wants to be early for church so we didn't get to talk for very long. What do you guys think happened to her.

Y _ If you were leaving the school where would you go.

AM _ What. Is that . . . why are you asking me.

Y _ I just want to know.

AM _ Back to my parents house probably. Like anybody else.

Y _ Did Emma talk about her parents.

AM _ I don't know.

Y _ Did she have family nearby.

AM _ I don't know.

Y _ Did she have friends outside the school.

AM _ I . . . I don't know.

Y _ I thought you were her boyfriend . . . Did she talk about leaving.

AM _ The school.

Y _ Yes. In any capacity. Any description of what life might be like if she wasn't at the school.

AM _ We . . . yeah.

Y _ Aiden.

AM _ We used to talk about going to stay at my uncle's cabin. He had a place in Tahoe. We hadn't talked about it in a long time but . . . we did talk about that.

Y _ What was the plan.

AM _ We were . . . I don't really feel like I should be telling you this.

Y _ If she talked about transport. Or perhaps places she might go. It could help.

AM _ Um . . . I was gonna call my parents and tell them I needed them to send me a suit. Or something. Something that a driver would have to come all the way up to Redemption for. And then when he came in to bring it to me we were gonna offer him money. Not to do anything illegal but just to leave his trunk unlocked and use the bathroom for a few minutes. That was her idea. So he wouldn't have to do anything shady but we could still escape. Then . . . we were gonna get out wherever he stopped. Probably salt lake. And go to the Alamo car spot. She heard that sometimes they let you rent a car if you were seventeen as long as you had a credit card. And we were gonna rent a convertible. Or the nicest car they had. And drive all the way across Utah and Nevada. Just me and her. All the way to Tahoe. We were gonna live there except when my uncle and his family were using it we would get a motel. And she was gonna go to the grocery store every day to get new foods so she could make stuff. And write poetry. And I would just go to movies sometimes. And we wouldn't need any friends or anything. It could just be the two of us.

Y _ What about being a basketball star.

AM _ What about it.

Y _ They say you're going to go professional. And make millions of dollars.

AM _ So.

Y _ So if you run away you don't make millions of dollars.

AM _ Oh. Yeah. I mean we didn't go. So I guess it doesn't matter.

NEESHA.

NEESHA LEFT HER dorm just after 6:00 a.m., every day, so she could walk the long loop around the school at the perfect moment of morning, right when the sun was rising and the fog was lifting and the eerie blue of the complex was starting to glow golden, and there were no instructors outside to tell her she couldn't smoke a cigarette.

Neesha'd never smoked before Redemption. It was Emma's idea to smoke cigarettes, just like it was Emma's idea to sell Neesha's Discovery project to their classmates, and Emma who convinced her that human trials would help her win the trophy. It all stemmed from Emma; every misbehavior and anxiety was the result of this toxic and lucrative relationship.

She waited outside, gnawing her way nervously through the pack of Marlboros until the warning bell sounded. She took the long way to class, crossing as much of the back lawn as possible, close to the forest, before cutting inward to the C-School. As she passed the bench outside Human, she saw someone had dug up two branches from the forest and planted them in the mud, sticking straight up. It looked like an absentminded art project, but for whatever reason, she was unable to look away. She stopped, alone in front of a walking path to the forest, and stared. It felt like it had been left there for her. To warn her.

By the time she got to her pharma lab, everyone was buzzing about Emma's disappearance.

"I overheard her in church saying a prayer for something."

"You can't disappear from praying."

"Unless God beams you up."

"That's not how God works."

"I heard her say the other day she was super tired. Maybe that's what happened?"

"She fell asleep?"

Neesha steered clear, sinking into the farthest possible chair to avoid looking interested.

"She told me she didn't have a pen, when I asked her in homeroom last week, but she seemed really sad about it. Like, I remember thinking, 'I don't think this is about the pen.' I think she might have been depressed or something."

"Do you think she killed herself?"

"It's hard to say."

"That would explain why no one has heard from her. I feel like at least the school would have heard from her by now if she's not dead."

"No way, she didn't kill herself. She was selling Apex. It probably has something to do with that."

"Like someone from outside the school came and killed her?"

"She was on the phone a lot."

"Maybe someone inside the school killed her."

"Who in the school would kill somebody?"

"Aiden almost killed Eddy."

It was embarrassing, listening to these plebes talk about her with half-informed speculation. None of them actually knew Emma.

"I don't know. But I talked to the guy who's looking for her, and he's *big*. I don't think they'd get somebody that big if it wasn't serious. . . . Neesha, do you have any idea what happened?"

The last one to talk was Margaret Chun, a Year Four from Taipei who had invented some kind of device for a telephone, and then come to school and turned into Redemption's resident speakerphone. If Margaret knew something, everyone knew it.

Neesha sat up, realizing that she was tucked into the back corner, not reading or writing, just staring angrily at them. Behind Margaret, she saw Zaza sit up, too.

"No," she snapped. "Of course not. Why are you asking me?"

"Oh—" Margaret looked between a few other classmates. "Aren't you her roommate?"

"Oh . . . yeah, no, she didn't come back last night. That's all I know."

Margaret Chun licked her lips, checking to be sure Yangborne wasn't listening, then leaned closer. "Did she tell you anything about Apex?"

"I don't know what you're talking about, Margaret," she said, and flipped open a textbook to a random page.

Yangborne was extra manic today. He started class with a lecture on mirror neurons that sounded like it was being assembled as it was happening, scientific basis included. They had a joint experiment with the B-School that night, and he was always on edge on test days. All he ever wanted to talk about was the experiment. Two hours into the lecture, the dam finally broke. "And—and I don't mean to get off track here, but I think we've really got it this time, friends. I mean, this is not unrelated to the topic at hand, but I *really* think this is our moment, in open election communication. This is the breakthrough.

"And like I always say, one breakthrough in a hundred is good science. That's a high percentage, in our work. But I really think this is our day."

Eyes rolled back around the classroom. Yangborne said this every test day, at least a dozen times, totally unable to take his own advice and understand that if only one in a hundred experiments were supposed to work, then ninety-nine of the days *weren't* "our day."

"You may say I'm overconfident. But I'll tell you why. . . ." He paused. "I know it's irresponsible to talk about the Discovery this early, in October . . ."

Chairs around the room squeaked as everyone sat up, listening closer.

"But the reason for confidence tonight is in the incredibly hard work of one of our own."

Neesha swallowed. She'd submitted a version of Apex for

consideration, and even though her original rat tests hadn't gone well, no one else in the class was even close to a product.

Yangborne's eyes scanned the room, up to the back row, landing on her for a moment before falling back to the front-right corner. Leia beamed back at him.

"Leia, what are we going to give our subjects tonight to boost their neural activity?"

"Oxytocin," she said proudly.

Neesha felt like the wind had been knocked out of her. Oxytocin was a *naturally occurring* hormone. Leia didn't even know how to synthesize complex compounds.

"Oxytocin, indeed! To those of you in the back of the room who aren't familiar, oxytocin is a naturally occurring hormone in humans that boosts neural activity, acting as a kind of mailman for some of our most important neural activity. Its presence makes us more inclined to trust, be affectionate, and understand others.

"Humans started producing it when we started having children. We've found recently it releases during activities like maternal care, paternal care, kissing a baby's forehead, hugging. It really is a miracle hormone—if you've got people who aren't getting along, you hit them with a puff of this, and boom. They're understanding, they're listening, they're kissing, they love each other. Like MDMA without having to dance all the time."

"What's MDMA?" someone in the front asked.

"Doesn't matter. Point is, it's the most important chemical

in the human body. Many would say it's the reason humans ever evolved past the primate stage. We started caring for our children, started caring for other people's children, started caring for our brothers and sisters, started caring for random people, and before you know it, we've built a whole complex architecture of emotional perception we call *empathy*. And that has become the only reason we do anything, beyond survival."

The class wasn't nearly as excited as he wanted them to be, so Yangborne drummed his fingers on the desk a few times. "It's also the hormone your body releases during orgasm!"

"Except," Neesha said, raising her hand and speaking without waiting to be called on, "if it's *naturally* occurring, how come we're giving Leia credit for inventing it?"

The class laughed.

"Leia," Yangborne said with another gross little smile in her direction, "has created a booster that is effective with rats. It activates exactly the parts of their brain we want to be activating, and she's proven it with research. Well done, Leia."

A few people clapped. Leia buried her head, feigning like she was above the attention.

Neesha took few deep breaths to keep her face from flushing red. Not only was it ridiculous that Leia would get credit for something that was already actively existing in all their brains, but Apex stimulated way more neural activity, and she *had* the proof. The problem was, it wasn't with rats, and she couldn't show it yet.

"So be ready tonight. Wear a nice shirt, in case we have to take a picture." He nodded to the wall on the right, covered by framed photos of Redemption classes of old, surrounding successful experiments and discoveries. "We'll start at nine, come early if you want a seat—"

A loud buzz from the corner of the room interrupted him. Several students jumped. Yangborne made his way over to the radio dock on the wall and plugged it in, then flipped a switch. "Hello?"

There was a crackling, then a woman's voice. "Carl, do you have a class in right now?"

The school had a closed-circuit radio feed, physically wired into the building by the Robo students, that allowed the heads of the schools to communicate directly. They all had docks in their offices and classrooms, so occasionally, Yangborne would leave his on and transmitting while his boom box played country radio. Once during a lab session, Dr. Richardson came flying in and ripped his boom box from the wall, because it was broadcasting "Achy Breaky Heart" to the other offices.

"Just my Year Fours, go ahead."

"Would you mind talking to all your students about the sweep last night?" It was a high voice, either Dr. Richardson or Dr. Roux. "We decided we'd rather have it come directly from instructors, to help people with the news."

"Sure thing." He flipped the switch off, and the crackling stopped, then turned back to the class.

"I'm sure most of you already know this, but Emmalynn

Donahue from Human hasn't been seen since last night. If you know anything, anything at all, please go to the office in the GRC and tell them. I'm sure we'll know what happened quickly, and it'll be some kind of misunderstanding, but until then, if anyone needs help with it, we can do a support group. Okay? Okay, great." He smiled. "I'll see you tonight."

EVAN.

EVAN SAT ALONE outside Dr. Richardson's office, his feet propped on her waiting table. Through half-open eyes, he followed the lines across the paper in front of him, thinly covered by a piece of schoolwork, tumbling through the associations of Emma's final week and lining up details.

Zaza, Neesha, Aiden; before mass.

A violent mess in the chapel, with her boyfriend at the center of it.

Yanis immediately sent by the school to find her.

A phone call, from the booth ten feet away—to an unidentified number.

He hadn't slept. Her testimonial journal had presented him with forty days' worth of new data points, directly from the source itself, and he had to log them all before morning.

The writing in her journal was frustrating. There was little recounting of the particular details of her life, and almost no mention of classes or conversations. Sometimes he was able to glean details from the context of described interactions—

assessments with Dr. Richardson, late nights with Neesha—but most moments were omitted or left to biblical parable. There were still inexplicable behaviors, and huge gaps and variables in her pattern.

On the other hand, it was the Emma he knew, the Emma of May fourteenth, pure and true. It was exactly what he needed to know about her, and he knew her now better than he ever had before. The depth of her sadness. The amount of her time that was spent wallowing in past nightmares. He wasn't wrong. Emma was troubled, and she needed help. Now more than ever.

Dr. Richardson leaned out of her office. "Thanks for waiting, Evan. Come on in." He watched over her shoulder as she typed four numbers into the keypad.

Her office was plain and warm, with soft light coming from lamps in all four corners, a large desk in the center, and neutral-tone bookshelves along the walls. It was intentionally welcoming, obvious *S2—Subtext* suggesting this was a place where students could feel safe. There were photos everywhere of Dr. Richardson, shaking hands or holding microphones next to political and academic types, waving to cameras and accepting awards. He wasn't sure exactly what she'd done to earn her all this praise, but all the instructors at Redemption seemed overqualified.

She stared at him for sixty seconds, smiling as if she had learned everything she needed to know in one silent moment. Finally, she plopped open a thick folder on the desk.

"You wrote in a paper for Dr. Edwards that a creature whose

purpose has been voided is living a nonexistence worse than death. *'Only those with a mission, with a reason to have lived, will know true salvation.'"* She smiled. "That's very literal, Evan, and very biblical. Also, it's a very serious standard to apply to life. Do you really believe that's true?"

He nodded.

"Then what is your purpose?"

Evan's eyes flittered around the room before returning to her. He didn't look away or stutter. "This. Redemption is my purpose."

He could tell in the creases of her eyebrows that she wasn't satisfied by the answer, or she didn't believe him. "Most students say that. And if you don't succeed here? If you were, for some reason, to fail? What are we supposed to do with you then?"

"I . . . I won't fail."

She flipped over pages in the folder. He tried to make out what was written upside down, but she moved so fast through them, he only caught glimpses. A photo that looked like his family's living room. A photo of the chess computer. A newspaper article about his victory.

Whatever she was looking for, Dr. Richardson didn't find it. She readjusted in her chair. "Do you ever get sad here?"

It caught him off-balance. It was completely outside the pattern. There was no place in the conversation for a question like that. It had no visible *S2—Subtext*, no apparent *S3—Intention*, but it asked him to respond with *S4—Emotion*.

"Everyone gets sad," he said with no inflection. "But I don't, very often."

"About what?"

"School. Friends. Sad movies."

"Interesting," she said. "You don't seem to be a fan of these kinds of conversations. Is that fair to say?"

"I don't know."

"I understand. That's common, particularly for exceptional students. We have a lot of those here. That's on purpose, of course; we recruit the students we think are the most gifted, yourself included, so we can develop those gifts. That's the way we've operated for twenty years; it's the reason we have the results we do.

"But one of the unintended consequences of orienting students like that, toward the pursuit of being the best at what they *do*, is that they tend to underestimate the value of the way they *feel*. To be the best basketball player, the best debater, to win at chess—these goals are so urgent and defined, everything else feels like it just gets in the way. Feelings of stress or loneliness can seem like an obstacle to the more important thing we know we're destined for. So students ignore those feelings, over and over again, until eventually they've built mechanisms to shield themselves. And one of those mechanisms"—she flipped the folder shut—"is not talking about it."

She looked into his eyes. "Feeling alone, or scared, or empathetic—those feelings *are* who we are. They're the engine that makes the rest of it go. If we weren't constantly in pursuit of love, or afraid of the loss of it, we wouldn't have any reason for doing anything.

"And talking about them is how we make sense of them. The practice of trading empathies is what creates our moral base-line. After all, how am I, as one of the heads of this school, to understand the pain of stress on students, unless you express that pain? How am I supposed to know what's blocking your progress, if I don't know what's going on inside you?"

It was a rhetorical question. Evan let it hang in space for a moment.

"The lesson is this," she continued. "Don't disconnect from the forces that drive you from the inside. Listen to them. Experience them. Because if you don't control them, they will come back to control you, in terrible ways. Like a stutter."

She let it sit with him for a long moment. But he didn't flinch. "Okay."

"Good." She sat up. "The first step, of course, is you and I working together to understand what has shaped you into the person who sits before me. In order for that to happen, I need you to make me a promise. You have to be completely open. You have to tell me everything. No secrets, no rules, no punishment. Can you promise me that?"

Her lips curled upward. She could already see through his skin.

Evan nodded.

"Wonderful." She nodded. "Then I'll see you tomorrow."

He stalled in the lobby after the assessment, watching as the next student, a Year Four named Archie, disappeared behind the thick wooden door. She was right. He didn't like talking about sadness. But not because it was uncomfortable. And not because it wasn't important.

He didn't want to talk to her because as soon as you told someone something about yourself, it was no longer yours. In chess, signaling information was the quickest way to lose an advantage. Some argued information sharing was evolved, that the most advanced forms of civilization, reserved exclusively for ants and science fiction, used hive minds to share information simultaneously between all members of their species. In the human world, however, where there was no such thing as a parity of power, there was no such thing as a parity of information, either. Advantage could only be gained by keeping information in your own head, for yourself alone.

Checking to be sure the lobby was empty, he slipped inside the phone booth.

There was a slot in the front of the machine where you could feed dollars or coins, below an analog timer that ran counterclockwise, counting back the time you had left on your call. Evan pulled three one-dollar bills from his bag and inserted all three. The timer's needle swelled up to 180 seconds.

There was no direct dial on the phone system. Instead, you gave the number to the school's operator, and she placed the call for you.

"Operator." It was the same woman as always; her voice was bright and loud. "Is this a student call?"

"This is Evan Andrews."

"I'm sorry?"

"Evan Andrews, student number eight, eight, eight, four, five, two, three, two. I'd like to make an outgoing call."

"Oh, hi, Evan! Oh my gosh, it's been forever."

"Five months."

"Right, wow. Well, same number as always, or—"

"Different number." From his pocket, he pulled the list of names and read the phone number from the top.

The operator went to work. He hadn't used the phone system since May fourteenth. He used to sit down in the booth equipped with twenty-dollar bills his mother had mailed him. They would run through nine or ten in one sitting. Even after his mother fell asleep, he would insert another twenty. Just in case she were to wake up and wonder where he'd gone.

"Okay, I've got it for you here, Evan," the operator said, cheery. "Would you like me to save this number?"

"No, that's fine."

"Of course. I'll connect you, just hold on . . ."

On the wooden table in front of the phone, students etched in pencil markings, absentminded doodles and half-completed pictures, the result of active brains trapped in inactive states, stuck on the phone. In the bottom-left third of the wooden table, the drawings got more concentrated: religious symbols, cartoon drawings overlapping and adding on top of the ideas of the students before them; one particular monster had half the face of a human and half the face of a buffalo growing up from the back of a dragon, the work of three different artists. Near the bottom, curling off the top of the table as the wood rounded at its edge, was familiar handwriting. It was a short sentiment, with small doodles between the letters.

wait for me, with an anchor around the center *o*.

It was Emma.

"Can I just get your student number, for confirmation?" the operator asked again.

"You already have it," Evan said urgently.

"Looks like I didn't get it in there right. Sorry. Can you confirm it for me?"

Evan paused. This was wrong. She'd never gotten the number wrong before. "Alright," he said slowly. "It's eight, eight, eight, four, five, two, three—"

The door to the booth screamed open and a pair of hands grabbed him from behind, ripping him out and bringing the phone with him. He let go just in time to keep the wire from snapping against his face. The two massive hands that had taken control of his arms wrestled them behind his back. He fell to his knees, a stinging pain in his shoulder. He kept his head down, afraid a swing for his face was next.

It didn't come. The room settled, and the light from the booth reflected off three pairs of black boots, surrounding him. From the phone, now hanging a few feet from his face, he could hear the outgoing call.

"Hey, baby, what can I do for you?" a raspy voice answered.

Yanis, the maintenance man, picked the phone up and clicked it back on its base.

emma donahue investigation.

evan andrews—year 2.

transcription by MONKEY voice-to-text software.

YANIS (School Administration) _ Please speak your full name aloud.

EVAN ANDREWS (Student) _ Evan Magnolia Andrews.

Y _ Evan Andrews. We've met before. Do you remember this.

EA _ Yes.

Y _ You were in Emma's dorm. Getting homework. I remember. I'm starting to think maybe you were not there for homework.

EA _ I was.

Y _ So you have this knack. For being places you should not. I am sure you can tell me. Why did you call this phone number.

EA _ I was calling my friend.

Y _ Strange friends you have. Tell me this. How did you meet your friend.

EA _ I don't remember.

Y _ Have you made this call before.

EA _ No.

Y _ Did you make this call last night.

EA _ No.

Y _ Think very hard about answers Evan.

EA _ My shoulder hurts.

Y _ You can see the doctor when we finish. You told the operator to call a number that Emma don a hue has called before. Did you know that.

EA _ No.

Y _ You're showing up in her dorm room on the night she goes missing. And you are making phone calls to numbers she used to call. Those are two things I know. They are facts. Can we establish this so at least we come from a common understanding.

EA _ I . . . Okay.

Y _ Great. So now that we know those two things to be facts we can answer important questions. Such as why are you showing up in her dorm room and making phone calls to numbers she used to call.

EA _ I I want to know where she is.

Y _ Good. Me too. But why do you care so much.

EA _ Because she is my friend.

Y _ Were you close.

EA _ V v v very close.

Y _ Perfect. Thank you. See. It's an easy system. Question. Response. Smile. Gratitude. Trust. Relationship. Now we understand each other. So we can have real conversations. Did she tell you to call that number.

EA _ No.

Y _ Then how did you know.

EA _ I I just guessed.

Y _ How about this. I make you a deal. You tell me how you knew to go to that phone booth. And to call that number. And I will tell you who you were about to call . . . does that sound alright. Evan.

EA _ O okay.

Y _ Perfect.

EA _ Sh she told me she used to talk to someone outside the school. And made me swear not to tell.

Y _ And where did you find the phone number.

EA _ I uh wrih. Written in her room. When I was picking up homework.

Y _ Well. Would you look at that.

EA _ W what.

Y _ You told me truth and the world doesn't end. Now I know something that helps me find your friend. See how easy . . .

EA _ Who was she calling.

Y _ What. Oh. Right. A phone sex hotline.

EA _ What.

Y _ Yep. That's the number you called. A service called swingers.

EA _ What is . . .

Y _ What is a phone sex hotline.

EA _ Yes.

Y _ Oh boy. Well. It's a phone number for people to have simulated sex over the telephone with a professional on the other end. Phone sex of course. No actual sex. Just sex noises.

EA _ N no. No that's not it. She wouldn't.

Y _ I have no reason to lie to you Evan. That's how you know you can trust me. I want to believe the same about you.

EA _ Okay.

Y _ Is there anything else you want to tell us.

EA _ No.

Y _ You can't think of anything.

EA _ No.

Y _ Okay. I'll call a doctor.

Testimonial: Aiden Mallet.

Year 1995–1996. Day 24.

LAST NIGHT, EMMA didn't want to do anything except paint.

I went over to her room late at night (before curfew, of course) and instead of talking about anything, she pulled out a box of watercolors and gave me a piece of paper and told me to paint whatever I wanted. I painted a horse. It looks like shit.

She painted the backyard of a farm; I think the one from Kansas. She's much better at painting than I am, even if she says she's not.

She was talking a lot tonight, more than usual. It was one of those days where she wanted to talk about my life, so I told her about the Mavericks scout, and how when I want something, I picture it in a photograph, and pin it in my head until I have it. I told her the picture of me in an NBA jersey had been in my head since my dad and I put it there twelve years ago.

She asked what other photographs I had, and where they were now. Behind my desk, I told her, the photos with all my other teams, my AAU teams, holding championship trophies.

She asked if I ever looked at them and I said not really, why would I. She asked if I felt any closer to how I was supposed to feel, right now. I said no, but I probably would when I had the NBA picture.

Emma said that means I'm thinking about my dreams in the wrong way. She said I should shoot for the dreams that aren't just photographs. She said I should think about dreams as living, breathing things, instead of just checked boxes on a list that would one day get crumpled and thrown in the trash anyway. And I think she's right.

On days when she wants to talk, Emma is smarter than anyone I know.

All she wanted to do was paint and talk. She fell asleep on my shoulder, and I put her into her bed and put the blanket on top of her and left.

Then, when I saw her today, she didn't want to talk to me at all. I have no idea what I did. I went to her room before lunch and she said she was going to do an assessment. I tried to find her at dinner, but she spent dinner in her lounge, talking to basically everybody except for me. Then, when I finally caught up with her, she told me that I wasn't a priority right now. I asked if I did something to hurt her, and she said no, but she still wouldn't tell me why she didn't want to be around me.

Some days Emma needs me. She tells me how happy she is that I'm around, and how I make her feel safe and noticed. Today, she must have forgot.

AIDEN.

"AND YOU KNOW what you'll say to the scouts, if they come talk to you?"

"Uh-huh."

"Do you wanna role-play it? I could pretend I'm one of the scouts, and you could be you, and we could make sure you're ready for anything they throw at you."

"I'm fine, Dad. I've talked to people before."

"I just wanna make sure nothing you say distracts them from what you do on the court."

He held the phone several inches from his ear. His dad hadn't figured out that telephones transmitted his voice the whole way; he didn't need to close the distance with volume.

"How'd those motivation videos go?" his dad shouted. "The ones I sent Coach Bryant?"

"What videos?"

"The ones I made for him, pumping you up?"

"I don't know what you're talking about."

"Hm. Must not have used them yet. Well, what I say in there

is important—stay focused. Eat, breathe, sleep, basketball. I even asked if you could get out of some classes—"

"I need to take classes, Dad."

"Not when you're in the league, you don't. Trust me. This is big for us, okay?"

"Okay."

"Good." There was a long lull before his dad added, "Anything else going on you wanna talk about?"

Aiden hung on the line for a second. There were a million things he wanted to talk about. His girlfriend had gone missing, the man the school had assigned to look for her seemed to think he was some kind of a suspect, and wherever she was, she might not even be his girlfriend anymore.

"No, I'm good. I'll call you after the game."

When he got back to his dorm, Peter Novak was waiting outside, leaning against the exposed stone of the wall. "You look pissed," Peter said as he approached.

"I'm not," Aiden mumbled, going straight for the door.

Peter followed him in without asking permission. Aiden swapped his warm-up jersey for a cloth Redemption sweater and tucked his book bag in the back of his closet. Checking on Peter over his shoulder, he took the Apex from the front pocket and rolled it into a pair of socks.

Peter was more focused on the photos above Aiden's desk. "Holy fuck, buddy. Look at all this basketball. You ever do anything other than basketball? Friends? Girls?"

"I have a girlfriend, remember?"

"Right. You should put a picture of her up here."

Aiden dropped a few textbooks onto his desk. "Was there a reason you were here?"

Peter pulled his eyes from the photos and turned to sit on the desk, straight on top of Aiden's textbooks. "Right. So, I was thinking, about the whole Emma thing."

His chest tightened. "What about it?"

"I know something. That I didn't tell you. And I think you deserve to know it, now that she's missing and all."

Aiden froze, raising an eyebrow.

"She was being followed."

"What?"

"By a couple of people, I think."

"*What?*"

"I know, it sounds ridiculous. But I've got two classes with her, and a couple weeks ago, I started noticing these people hovering around, wearing black hoodies with the hoods up—"

"Everybody wears black hoodies. It's basically the uniform."

"Yeah, but these people were different. They were there for her, I could tell."

Aiden thought about it for a minute. "You know, I heard extreme paranoia is a symptom of Apex—"

"They were real," Peter insisted. "Not moving, not talking, just lurking around corners, watching her."

Aiden pulled one of the textbooks from under him. "I was with her all the time; pretty sure I'd have noticed. I think your brain might be fried."

"You were *with* her. They'd have been hiding from you too!"

Peter lowered his voice. "Do you know who Evan Andrews is?"

Aiden stopped digging through his bag for a second. "Yeah, sure."

"I saw him watching you two the other night. From a bench in front of the chapel."

Aiden swallowed. He did know Evan, and he had seen him around a lot lately.

"It's not just him, though. Something else is going on."

Peter reached in his back pocket and unfolded an old newspaper page, cut to a single article. The headline read: *Prep school student awaits trial for drug distribution.*

Aiden stared at it for a full minute. The date was September 26, 1995. That was three weeks ago. He tried to read the text of the article, but quickly realized he couldn't; it was just a series of obscure symbols where the words should be.

"Is Emma really on trial?" he asked, his voice cracking. "What newspaper is this from?"

Peter pulled it back. "That's the crazy part. It's not a real newspaper. Somebody just made it—I think it's a threat."

"A threat?"

"Someone printed a fake newspaper, saying this *could* happen, if she doesn't do what they want. Look here." He pointed to the last sentence of the article. It was just two words:

fifty pills.

"She's getting blackmailed?" Aiden asked. "By Evan Andrews?"

"No way," Peter said, shaking his head. "It's definitely more than just him. But he's got something to do with it."

"She would have told me about that."

"You think? And risk them finding out?" Peter spoke quickly, without any doubt. "Think about it. Did anything change recently? Did you notice her acting different?"

Aiden stopped. "When did you say that was?"

"The date on here is September twenty-sixth. Three weeks ago."

Aiden stood slowly and floated to the closet. His testimonial journal was tucked in the back of his sock drawer. He flipped forward a few pages, then back—

"September twenty-seventh. *'Emma didn't talk to me again today. Something's seriously wrong.'*" He looked up. "That was three weeks ago. And she's been like that ever since."

Peter exhaled slowly. "Damn."

Warm relief melted in his stomach. It wasn't about him, or anything he'd done.

They weren't breaking up; she was getting blackmailed.

"You're happy she was being blackmailed, and then disappeared?"

Aiden hadn't felt his mouth creeping into a smile. He swallowed it quickly. "No, sorry," he said. "It just . . . explains a lot. So, what do we do? How do we tell somebody?"

"Tell somebody, are you serious?"

"Yeah, I can go to Coach Bryant about it. Or Dr. Roux. . . ." Peter was glaring at him. "What?"

"I think you may have forgot for a moment that your girl-friend is a drug dealer."

"Oh . . . oh." He hadn't thought about what might happen to Emma if the school found out about Apex. She'd be gone, before they could even welcome her back.

"Which I think," Peter said seriously, "means we gotta find her first."

"We? What do you have to do with this?"

"I don't know how many times you're gonna make me remind you of this, man. I buy drugs from her. She gets busted, I get busted, everybody gets busted."

Aiden examined him, more critically now. He wore the same oversized coat and a thin black beanie. The hair popping out was curly, and his teeth were large and slightly crooked. Aiden barely knew anything about him. But everything he said made perfect sense.

"Okay." Aiden nodded. "How do we do that?"

Peter slid down into the desk chair on his level, already a step ahead. "First, we've gotta figure out who all was following her, or checking on her. The hoods."

"So we go talk to the kid, Evan Andrews."

Peter shook his head. "If we go to him right away, they'll know we're onto them. I've got a better idea," he said, dropping his voice a decibel. "You bought last night, right? Five hundred, you said? For the basketball team?"

Aiden pursed his lips. "Maybe."

"I got a proposition for you. Don't give it to the team."

"What?"

"Apex is your way in. Whoever was onto her, whoever took

her—you've got what they want. And you're the only one."

Aiden could already feel his heart racing. "What do we do with it?"

Peter stood and started to pace. "We gotta draw people out. Have a stakeout. Tell them we're selling and see who shows up."

"That's stupid," he argued, trying to catch up. "She's missing. Nobody's gonna show up if they know she won't be there."

Peter's confidence was unshaken. "Yeah, probably not most people, right? Just the ones who're really desperate? So desperate they might do something to her, only to find out she doesn't have any more Apex? That she sold it all to her boyfriend?"

It seemed almost like common sense as Peter said it. "Okay," he agreed. "Okay. So how do we do that?"

"Here." He clicked open the door and leaned out into the hallway. "Ay, Mischa!"

A tall kid Aiden didn't recognize met him outside the door. "I need you to get the word out on something." The kid nodded. "Tell people, they're selling the rest of the Apex, nine p.m. tonight, at the old basketball court. Don't tell them where you heard it. Got it?"

"Wait!" Aiden shouted, but Peter clicked the door shut.

"What?"

"I have a voluntary shootaround tonight."

"Oh." Peter ambled back into the room. "Don't go."

"I can't."

"But it's voluntary. It's right there in the name."

"Voluntary doesn't mean voluntary. Why don't we just do the stakeout a different time?"

"It's a little late for that. . . ."

"You just told him! Go catch him, tell him to change it!"

Peter looked to the door but didn't move. "Mischa runs track, man. Can't catch Mischa."

Aiden exhaled, rocking back in his chair.

"Look, if you don't wanna miss your practice, I get it. I'll do the stakeout and let you know who shows up."

Aiden's eyes settled on the wall behind his desk. In the center, there was a photo of an AAU basketball team he'd played on when he was thirteen. In it, he lay across the front of a group of ten kids, sprawled out and holding a trophy, with a tiny gold basketball player at the top, doing some kind of one-leg-up crossover. The trophy itself sat a foot in front of the photo, on his desk, next to a dozen like it.

His entire life, he'd been a basketball player. If that was going to continue, he couldn't be distracted. He needed to find her.

"Fuck that," he said, shaking his head. "I'll be there."

NEESHA.

HER WHOLE CLASS was tittering excitedly as they entered, Yangborne's boom box blaring country music. With the B-School students in the room, there weren't enough chairs, so students were standing between them, sitting on tables, leaning against walls. Several instructors from around the school—Dr. Roux from the P-School, Dr. Richardson from Human, and even Father Farke—were crowded in the back of the classroom, staring at a glass case in front.

Two rats sniffed around inside, one on either side of a solid granite block. From the third row, Neesha could barely separate their glassy marble eyes from the matted fur of their faces. Two patches were shaved into that fur, on the side of their tiny rat heads, where a simple electrical wire was fused in.

Dr. Yangborne killed the music and stood behind them, his hands placed lightly on either side. "Mice in a cage, the oldest of scientific experiments, today made revolutionary," he said to the whole room, emceeing the proceedings in a white lab coat. "Ladies and gentlemen, meet the most important rats in human history, Turner and Hooch."

The class snickered; they'd voted on the names last week. Neesha leaned forward onto her elbows, watching Turner sprint corner to corner to corner inside her cage.

"I've spent the morning teaching Turner a specific behavior task—touch lever, receive treat." He demonstrated. As soon as the light switched on, Turner ran for a plastic protrusion at the front. She leapt up, a tiny paw falling onto it, releasing a brown pellet from the tube behind her. She pounced immediately.

"Our implant connects Turner's motor cortex to an electronic signal, which will then be sent to"—he traced his hands along the wire to the computer between them—"a shared electron environment. Hooch knows nothing of lights or levers. He's simply living in his cage." He flipped the light in Hooch's cage on. Hooch stood still.

"If Turner's brain can communicate this behavior to Hooch's, without ever physically interacting, it will represent the most sophisticated linkage between two brains in history. But, of course, the linkage isn't the most complicated part of the experiment. More challenging is the translation of their brain signals. If you'll remember, from when we last tried this experiment, we weren't able to stimulate the right parts of the brain. Brain science students, we appreciate all of the work you did on the electronics side, I'm sure it will help, but today we're accelerating the experiment with a more . . . human solution."

He placed a small paper dish inside both of their cages, and immediately the rats leapt for it, lapping up the white, frothy liquid with their tiny tongues.

Yangborne beamed at Leia. "An impressive *discovery* from one of our own."

Neesha felt her lips curl into disgust as she stared at the glass case behind him. The Discovery Trophy was a holy relic. The people in the photos that lined the wall next to her were *real* scientists, actual innovators whose ideas changed the lives of millions, not hack students who passed off natural hormones as some kind of breakthrough for rats. But if tonight's experiment went well, Yangborne made it sound like he was ready to bash open the case and offer Leia the trophy. Her stomach backed up at the image.

Both rats finished the compound and began to chew through their paper trays.

"Well," Yangborne said, taking his time, smiling. "Should we try it?"

The room cheered. Neesha kept staring into the cage, watching as Turner returned to testing the limits of her environment, revisiting each corner only to find that it still had her trapped. Her circles grew tighter and more panicked until eventually she froze in the center.

Neesha shifted in her seat. Turner was staring straight at her.

Behind the rats, Yangborne turned the computer on, and both rats went stiff. "All future communication will exist across open electron environments," Yangborne shouted, over the hum of the machine. "This represents not a new technology, but a new framework for our species." He flipped the switch

on Turner's cage. The light came on, and she flew to the lever. "Civilizations more advanced than ours require it—no secrets, no individualism, just shared information and emotion. That evolution begins now—"

With force, he slammed forward the lever to the light on Hooch's cage.

Hooch stood perfectly still at the center.

He turned it off, then back on again several times, but it didn't change a thing. "His brain should be stimulated . . ."

But Hooch didn't care. He sat on his butt in the center, blinking and doing nothing else.

Eventually, Yangborne gave up, and switched off the computer. "I'm sorry to disappoint everyone." He spoke to the instructors huddled at the back. "Looks like our classes have a bit more work to do. But like I say, in science, if only one experiment in a hundred is successful . . ."

Slowly, everyone filtered out of the room, the B-School first, and the C-School after, mumbling to each other.

Neesha was among the last to file out and felt herself drawn toward the front. Yangborne still hovered at the case, wallowing silently as he stared at the rats.

"Mine would have worked," she mumbled in his direction without thinking.

Yangborne looked up. "I don't even know what yours is, Neesha."

"It's an amphetamine—"

"You say that. But I don't *know* that."

"You've seen the work—"

"You have no results," he said, voice raised, drawing the attention of a few lingering students. Zaza poked his head back in through the door. "You've shown no initiative to test your work. Until it's proven, it's *nothing.*"

Neesha felt a lump form in her throat. "Except I know it works."

He shook his head. "That's not science, Neesha. The work we do here is the light of the world. We don't get to slack off, and we don't get to speculate. I need you to do better."

Neesha didn't move, still hovering between the desks.

"I have results."

Yangborne was already moving to his desk. "I haven't authorized a single experiment for you yet."

"I did some outside of class."

He stopped. Everyone waiting in the doorway stopped. Yangborne looked her up and down. "You know that's not allowed," he said, but he didn't look angry. "I trust you were safe?"

She nodded.

He pursed his lips. "Well, as a matter of discipline," he said, using the word lightly, "I'll need to see them."

Neesha smiled. "Absolutely."

As soon as she had cleared the door of the C-School, into the lounge, Zaza rushed up on her from behind. "Are you serious?"

She rolled her eyes but slowed to let him to catch up. Over-assertive as he always was, it was strangely comforting to have someone freaking out more than her.

"Just curious," he said. "Do you remember a day, in the distant past, when we said no one should ever know you were involved with Apex?"

"Yesterday—"

"It was yesterday!" He smacked a passing Year Two in the forehead with an animated gesture. "Then, *today*, you decide it's cool to just let Yangborne in on your experiment? *Why?*"

Neesha shrugged but didn't answer.

"I already know. You told me last night. But, for the sake of argument, do you think maybe there's something more important than the Discovery Trophy? Like, not going to jail, for instance?"

"Jesus, you're dramatic."

"Nope, this is rational. This is what rational looks like."

"I'm not going to show him everything, just a little."

"And you don't think that comes back to you?"

She shrugged again.

"You don't think, with the school turning over every rock to try to find Emma, that it's going to come back to you?"

She shrugged again.

"Wow. You are taking this trophy way too serious—"

"Oh, I'm the one being too serious?"

"This is high school," he said, rounding the corner with her, following her down her dorm hallway. "There's gonna be plenty of trophies to discover—"

"God, you sound just like her."

"Like who?"

"Like *Emma*." She stopped in the middle of the hall. "She was always saying shit like that. 'Oh, why do you care so much about this?' 'Oh, you take this too seriously.' It's fucking exhausting, being told what's okay for me to care about and what's not."

Zaza rubbed his head. "Well. In this case, she was right."

"No." Neesha shook her head. "She was lying, mostly."

"Lying about what?"

"She wasn't saying that for *my* well-being. She was saying that because she didn't want me to focus on the actual experiment. She wanted me to focus on selling it, so we could make more money. And now she's gone, and she's left me here to take all the blame, like it wasn't her idea to sell Apex in the first place!"

She was done with the conversation and pivoted back toward her dorm. Zaza kept walking alongside but lowered his voice.

"Okay," he said. "I get it. I don't think that distinction's gonna matter to the school, but I get it. Can you at least promise me you won't tell Yangborne about it until Emma gets back? And you can figure out what's going on?"

She reached the entrance to her dorm and froze.

"*Please*, Neesha. At least promise me that?"

Neesha stared past him, her stomach backing up. She let her backpack drop to the ground.

"What are you . . ." Zaza turned with her to face the door. "Oh."

Scrawled at eye level with a red marker, in childlike handwriting, was a simple message:

she's going 2 die.

emma donahue investigation.

edward velasquez—year 4.

transcription by MONKEY voice-to-text software.

YANIS (Administration) _ Okay. Last one of the day. I'm excited to get to talk to you because it sounds like you had quite the night. State your name please . . . Edward Velasquez . . . Can you hear me. Can you understand me. Do you know what you're doing here. Do you know where you are.

EDWARD VELASQUEZ (Student) _ No.

Y _ Okay. But you know you are being spoken to.

EV _ No.

Y _ How about this. Repeat the word yes for me.

EV _ No.

Y _ Yes . . . Yes. Repeat this word. Yes. Yes. If you have any idea of what I'm saying at all just repeat the word yes.

EV _ No.

Y _ Jesus. What goes on in that brain . . . How about . . . Do you know this girl . . . You're staring does that mean that you know this girl. Yes you can touch it.

EV _ No.

Y _ Eddy please. Give me something to work with here.

EV _ No.

UNIDENTIFIED VOICE (Unknown) _ He won't.

Y _ Oh I'm sorry. I didn't hear you.

UNIDENTIFIED VOICE (Unknown) _ Sorry for dropping in without warning. How is it going.

Y _ He won't say anything other than no.

UNIDENTIFIED VOICE (Unknown) _ I know. It's tragic.

Y _ What happened.

UNIDENTIFIED VOICE (Unknown) _ Some kind of trauma but we have no idea. Wait what is this.

Y _ Oh it's called a MONKEY. It records what we're saying.

UNIDENTIFIED VOICE (Unknown) _ I know I use one too. I am just surprised my name is coming up as unidentified voice.

Y _ Yes you have to program the voices for each session.

UNIDENTIFIED VOICE (Unknown) _ Of course.

Y _ The school wanted us to record every conversation we have in this missing student search.

UNIDENTIFIED VOICE (Unknown) _ How is it going.

Y _ Not well. I don't know if it's this girl in particular or just how the students are here. But everyone seems to be very guarded and no one wants to answer questions about this directly. It seems like every time I say the name Emma.

EV _ It took her.

Y _ What. Eddy. What did you say. It took her. What took her.

EV _ The flood.

Y _ What did you say. Repeat that. Tell me what took her.

UNIDENTIFIED VOICE (Unknown) _ He said the flood.

Y _ What does that mean.

UNIDENTIFIED VOICE (Unknown) _ It's been a repeat phrase for him. Just started recently.

Y _ The flood. The flood. The flood.

EV _ It took her.

Y _ Who is her. Emma. Is it Emma. Eddy do you understand. Emma.

UNIDENTIFIED VOICE (Unknown) _ He doesn't understand.

EV _ The flood.

Y _ What is the flood.

UNIDENTIFIED VOICE (Unknown) _ That's what all of us are trying to figure out.

AIDEN.

AIDEN STARED, BAFFLED, at his own desk. "Why don't you just swallow them?"

"Faster if you snort it, man."

"I feel like it hits me fast when I swallow it."

"Not fast enough."

"It hurts my nose."

"Yeah, you'll get over that." Peter's head dove toward the table.

Peter boosted like an artist. He drew zigzag lines across Aiden's desk with the tiny silver balls, emptied from the pill's casing, cutting and sharpening them with his student ID and then—when they were angled just right—vacuuming them up in one swooping, ducking, floating motion across the desk, his nostril the crop plane, his Apex the crop. Except in reverse. Like, if the crop plane sucked the crops out of the fields. Or whatever.

"Alright, that's enough." Aiden eyed the bag of pills on the desk. "We should get to work."

"It's a focus drug, this is working."

"I think it's just making you focus on doing more Apex."

Twenty minutes before nine, they loaded a few notebooks, a Polaroid camera, and the bag of Apex into their backpacks and slogged across the back lawn. It had rained off and on since morning, so there was standing water on the court and it was weighing down the ball more with every dribble.

"You didn't need to bring that, you know," Peter said, nodding to the basketball.

"Gotta blend in," Aiden said, stroking a shot from the baseline, through the chain-link net.

"Blend in with what?" Peter asked. "Besides, we're not actually meeting anyone. We're hiding."

He pointed to the end of the stands that ran alongside the court, where a huge gap in the wood was blanketed by darkness. Aiden followed as Peter crawled his way in and swung himself up into the metal bracketing.

Once they were seated, Aiden pulled out his notebook. "I made a list of a few theories, based on what you told me earlier." He stretched back the binding of his composition notebook and held it to Peter's face. He'd spent hours filling in the document, using the terms he remembered from watching *Law & Order* with his dad.

"We've got to establish motive and opportunity for any potential perps." He turned the notebook to Peter. "Theory one, Evan Andrews; his motive is getting the drug. Theory two, someone else at the school; their motive is getting the drug.

Theory three, someone outside the school, their motive—"

"Wouldn't everybody's motive be getting the drug?"

"Theory *four*," he pressed on. "The school found out about it. And did something to her."

"Wow," Peter said. "And you said *I* was being paranoid—"

A hundred feet away, they heard the fence rattle. Someone was moving for the gate. Aiden checked his watch. It was eight forty-five.

The grinding of the fence got louder as the person struggled. From where they were sitting, they could see the entrance, but not the figure behind it. The rattling stopped, and the fence was still closed. It was silent.

Aiden craned his neck, sticking it outward through the hole in the bleachers. It looked like the hooded figure had disappeared from the entrance. But as he exhaled, he heard a soft crunch, then another, then another. Footsteps, getting louder as they got closer, making their way along the fence. They were slow and uneven, kicking up mud around them, snapping twigs as they got closer.

Aiden swallowed, watching as a hand, translucent in the light, slid along the fence toward them, its owner blocked by the bleachers. It sounded like they were mumbling, groaning under their breath.

"Shut up," Peter whispered, crouching farther back into the darkness. His leg was bouncing uncomfortably against the bench, making a metallic click.

The figure passed through a break in the bleachers, and

yellow light found its face.

"Eddy?" Aiden asked.

As soon as Eddy heard his name, he stopped.

"What are you doing here?"

Aiden stood, but the noise must have frightened Eddy because he spun immediately, running off-balance in the opposite direction.

"Eddy, what are you . . . ?" They watched him go to the other side of the fence, disappearing down the nearest path toward the school.

"Fucking weird, man," Peter whispered under his breath. "Well, write it down, I guess. Who knows what's got him all fucked up."

Aiden stared after the spot where Eddy had disappeared. "He freaked out last night, remember?"

"Yeah, I doubt he's forgot either, the way you fucking railed him."

"Somebody had to stop him," Aiden snapped back.

"Yeah," Peter muttered. "Tell yourself that . . ."

They were interrupted by the bottom of the fence sliding against the concrete. They both readied themselves, ducking to get a look at the far end of the court. It was another hooded figure, this one in blue jeans and black hoodie, the hood fully drawn over its face. It ambled to the center of the court and stopped in the middle circle.

"It's them," Aiden whispered.

"You got the bag ready, just in case?"

Aiden held it up.

They didn't have to wait long—two more people showed up, also wearing black hoods and moving slowly. One was short, and taking slow, purposeful steps, and another was thick. They didn't say anything as they followed in the same path to the center of the court.

"Fucking hell," Peter whispered. "They're not even talking to each other."

Three more people showed up in the exact same attire, walked the exact same path, and took their place around the rim of the center circle. None of them interacted. None of them looked surprised. None of them showed their faces.

"Here." Peter handed him the camera. "Get a picture."

Aiden nodded and leaned out of the break in the bleachers. He could hear Peter breathing excitedly behind him. He balanced himself, waiting for a few of the hooded figures to turn in his direction. The snap and hiss of the camera rang out across the court, but none of them moved. Aiden crouched back down into the hole. "What do we do now?"

Another set of footsteps approached the gate. Aiden watched for them, but no one entered. Instead, a mass of figures huddled behind the fence. They weren't wearing the black hoodies; they were in gray suits. Footsteps crunched around Aiden and Peter as the figures spread out around the fenced-in area. "Those aren't students," he whispered. "They're maintenance."

Peter's body language had changed. He was nervous now, gripping the bottom of the bleacher in front of them. "Why would they come out here?" he asked. "What are they doing?"

One of the maintenance workers had entered the court and was walking straight up to the group in the center. They noticed him approaching and began to shuffle, their heads snapping around anxiously. As they turned, Aiden noticed beneath one of their hoods a thick pair of wire-rimmed glasses.

"On my signal, we run," Peter whispered, nodding to a hole in the fence behind them. He'd picked this spot on purpose, Aiden realized. It came with an exit strategy.

"All of you." The maintenance worker on the court started to speak. "Stay exactly where you are. Put your hands on the ground—"

"Now!" Peter screamed. The hoods in the center of the court must have heard the voice and thought it was one of their own, because they scattered on his command. Around them, the gray suits sprang into action, blocking the exits, angling toward the other hooded students. Aiden stared in horror as a maintenance worker in the center sprang after the escaping hood with the glasses, reaching for his belt, and pointed a small device.

"Let's go!" Peter grabbed him and pulled, but just before he turned, he saw it. Tiny lines flew from the man's hand at the hooded figure, connecting with their back and gripping them in shock, sending them crashing and convulsing down to the wet ground.

Aiden took off, forcing his way through the fence, slicing the back of his neck against an exposed edge. He ignored it, sprinting away down the only path he could see in front of him. He could hear Peter a few steps behind, and another set of footsteps behind that. "Stop!" a voice barked, but Aiden was faster than any maintenance worker. He sprinted farther away from the court and into the darkness. He could still hear shouting over his shoulder, but it got quieter, and eventually the only footsteps he could hear were his own.

He slowed himself to a stop, turning to check his position. In the distance, he could see the yellow light at the top of the wooden cross, and even farther than that, the school. The first cut of the forest was only a few feet away. There were no flashlights near him, and all the sound was a million miles away.

He fell back onto a rock, panting. Whoever it was who showed up tonight, they weren't regular students. The way they dressed, the way they acted, Peter was right. They were organized.

And the men in the gray suits, they were dressed as maintenance workers, but that wasn't their job tonight. They looked more like riot control. One of them fired a taser at a student. He'd often thought the school had too many maintenance workers—they were always overstaffing functions and referring them to situations where they weren't necessary. Maybe some of them weren't maintenance workers at all. Maybe they were security. But why wouldn't the school just say that?

He reached for his bag, unsure of how to log all this information into his theories page. Did what happened tonight have something to do with Emma? Or was it something else, something much larger that he'd stumbled into? His hand found the corner of the bag and swept to the other corner, past his notebook.

The Apex was gone.

EVAN.

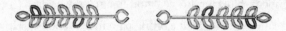

THE DRIP-DRIP-DRIP ON the window of late-arriving rain kept him awake, lying in his bed.

The vines of notes sprawled across his wall were starting to inch together, growing so thick with details that they threatened to fall inward, bringing the whole system down.

His clock ticked past 10:00 p.m. and the school's buzzer sounded for curfew. On a program he once watched on the Public Broadcasting System, it said after twenty-four hours, the odds of a missing person ever being found dropped from 75 percent to 10 percent. It said that 78 percent of missing persons who are killed are killed within the first twenty-four hours. Emma had been missing for twenty-six.

He pulled the skin of his eyelid off his eye and released it. It had been over thirty-six hours since he'd slept, but his eyes wouldn't stay closed. Even if they could, it wouldn't shut down the system. The second he left his brain to its own unconscious devices, he'd be flooded with images of her. Wandering scared across the campus. Locked in a closet. Despondent in the armchair in his living room. Lost in the forest. Alone on a hospital bed.

The school had given him medication for his arm, a separated shoulder, Dr. Simon said, and the edges of his vision were losing focus, blurring his real and imagined worlds.

He rolled over and felt a biting pain in his shoulder. He would be in a cast for eight to nine weeks. When he landed, there she was, staring outward from the middle of the wall. It was a photo she probably didn't even know existed, an outtake from a school photographer who had been covering the talent show on May fourteenth. She was biting her lip, nervously approaching the microphone. The photographer stepped in front of her, drawing her attention just long enough to freeze the moment forever. He stared back at her. She was still out there. She still needed his help.

He slid out of bed and pulled his spinning chair to the middle of the floor, moving with the details as he examined the wall.

He returned to the absolute basics. Emma had a predetermined pattern, an obvious rhythm to her life. She had lived in it with minimal interruption for almost three months. He'd built the board around this pattern. Thursdays were Compassion Lab, lunch, Groupthink lecture, assessment, dinner, evening mass, prayer, Aiden, sleep. For twelve Thursdays, she'd checked every box.

Then, two weeks ago, things started to change. The pattern had lost its consistency. She'd started sleeping, all the time. She doubled up on her assessments and skipped her meals. Less time with Aiden, more time with strangers. Still, she checked the boxes. She moved in rhythm.

Finally, last night, the pattern fully snapped. Instead of dinner, she made a phone call to a sex hotline. She dropped in on Zaza's dorm, and rushed from school to the church. She brushed off Aiden. She disappeared.

Someone knocked on his door.

He held his breath. Post-curfew, no one was supposed to be in the halls. He waited for them to go away but they knocked again.

He rolled out of bed and flew wall to wall, pinning up the posters. He shoved his clothes under his bed and Emma's journal with them, taking one deep breath before opening the door.

In the hallway, Neesha Shah was smiling.

"Hi," she said. "You're Evan, right?"

Every piece of information in his brain chased in a different direction, a thousand patterns trying to solve the *S3* riddle. Why was Emma's roommate at his door?

"Why are you here?" he asked.

"I had a question I wanted to ask you. Do you mind if I come in?"

"What question?"

"It's going to take a second, is it alright if I . . ." She nudged the door forward.

"Whoa, what happened?" she asked, and pointed to his cast. "I fell."

"That's it, you fell? Come on, dude, give me details."

Evan shook his head. "That's all."

She surveyed the room. "You've got a lot of Jazz posters

in here. I doubt John Stockton's mom has this many. Here's a harmless question: Do you feel pressure to surround yourself with traditional examples of masculinity, or do you really love the Utah Jazz that much?"

"I like the Jazz. What's your question?" He stepped between her and the most fragile poster as she reached out to touch it.

"Right," she said, leaning against his desk. "My friend Zaza, he was telling me that you were going around trying to find Emma."

He didn't answer.

"And I just wanted to know, how that's going?"

"Good," he said. "Why?"

"Just curious," she said. "She was my roommate, you know?"

"*Is* your roommate."

"Right. Yeah, is my roommate. Which is why I was kind of curious if you needed help?"

Evan stood taller. "Why?"

"Well, I figured she just ran away, and they were going to find her in a day or two, but then I got this message on my door, and . . ." She held something back, behind her teeth. "I just really need to find her. And I figured the fastest way was working together."

He heard the poster behind him starting to curl against the wall. If he helped Neesha, he risked sharing information, maybe even something he wasn't supposed to share. She wouldn't understand his methods.

But Neesha would have information of her own. And no strategy.

"Okay," he said. "We can do it."

"Awesome, that's so—"

He took two steps forward, pushing her toward the door.

"Oh, that's it?"

"It's late," he said.

"Right, I guess we start tomorrow." Neesha looked around the room, stalling in the doorway for a second.

"What?" he asked.

She looked to her own door across the hall and back. "Do you really think she's in danger?"

Evan balanced his theories on his tongue. "Probably. Yes."

"People keep saying she was skittish the night she went missing. Like somebody was following her. Do you think she was being skittish?"

"Do you?"

"I didn't think so." She sighed. "But after Yanis asked me, and Zaza asked me . . . I kept remembering things. Like, in the church, when the bells started, she basically jumped out of her skin. I didn't think it was weird at the time, but . . ."

Evan froze, holding the door in place. "Wait. What bells?"

"The chapel ones. For when the candle person lights the candles—"

"The acolyte."

"Sure."

Evan felt like his brain was shaking, fuzzy memories growing clearer. The interaction with Yanis at Emma's dorm was blurry in his memory. His brain had been so overcome by panic, so clouded by worst-case scenarios, that he'd failed to properly log the information in front of him, but as he played it back in his head, he remembered one thing, distinctly, cutting through his confusion: the bells.

"Okay, well. See you tomorrow," she said, and she disappeared into her own door across the hall.

Evan stumbled back into the room, a lump forming in his throat as he laid the timelines on top of each other.

If she jumped at the bells, that meant she was still in the chapel, where the entire school could see her. Which meant there was only one explanation—

Yanis was looking for her before she went missing.

PART IV.

rats in cages.

Testimonial: Emmalynn Donahue.
Year 1995–1996. Day 32.

I'm not sure what this is supposed to accomplish, but I'll give it a try—

I can hear Dad humming.

It's a Hank Williams Jr. song and I think it's the only song he remembers.

He hums it while he drives, bumping the truck along one of the dozens of roads that no one in the world knows, but they're the only thing he knows in the world. When I was a kid, he would steer into the bumps to send me flying, and we'd laugh as the suspension of the truck shook. Now I imagine he avoids the bumps as he drives the roads, every day.

I can hear he's tired; I imagine he spends most of his life tired, looking only for an every-so-often moment when he can relax, and just sit, and watch something that means nothing, like sports. I imagine him drinking a beer, because drinking a beer is the ultimate act of not having anywhere else to be, and I imagine him having several, because some days, he needs help convincing himself that he absolutely doesn't have anywhere else to be.

I can hear him at 2:00 a.m., shouting about the decision he has to make to people who have no sympathy, the closed door and the smell of fuel from the station next door. A "rambling man," like the song, a son of the blues. I imagine he has to make this decision often, to drive the roads he knows so well, so his family doesn't have to be without a father for the night; or to sleep in the truck, even though it's less than twenty-five degrees in Hayes.

I can hear him humming as he drives, no slower than usual, because to drive slower would be an admission that he's not himself. I can hear the truck on the other side of the narrow road. I imagine him completely sure of himself, not slowing down or pulling off because these are his roads and to slow down or pull off would be an admission that he doesn't know these roads and that he's not himself. But he can't avoid the bumps.

I feel the car rolling three times. I feel the paralyzing panic of screaming chaos, the car suspended in midair long enough to consider what the end result may be; long enough to worry about the cost of the truck and the cost of the insurance before the front right bumper makes contact with frozen ground; long enough to worry about his wife and his neck after that. I feel the moment of stillness, after the car finally rocks to a stop. I feel the cold, dark side of the highway. I feel the other man, clinging to life in the cab of his truck. I feel the wreckage, the smell of twisted metal, and the screaming of chickens. The truck was carrying chickens, and now the truck is on its side and the chickens are spread out across the highway.

I can hear my mother, calling me because she has to. "There's been an accident," she says, as though it's the twentieth time today she's said it. "Your father nearly killed himself. He isn't going to be able to move for a while. You're on your own out there."

And then I can feel nothing. I'm on my own out here.

There.

Done.

I'm not sure what that was supposed to accomplish, but I can feel it, all of it. I'm in the car, on my bed, in the ditch, in the truck, on my pillow, in the deeper reservoir of pain. I know this is the part of expanding that's supposed to feel like contracting; the part of moving forward that's supposed to feel like being dragged back into everything else. I know this is the part I'm supposed to master, to understand and choose to rise above.

I control my proximity. I know where I stand.

emma donahue investigation.

neesha shah—year 4.

transcription by MONKEY voice-to-text software.

YANIS (Administration) _ You didn't see anyone near your room tonight.

NEESHA SHAH (Student) _ I wasn't even near my room. I was in class.

Y _ At night.

NS _ It was a special session. We were testing an experiment we built in class.

Y _ Who knew you were in this class.

NS _ I don't know. Everyone. All you have to do is look in the window.

Y _ Tell me about the message.

NS _ I think it's pretty self explanatory.

Y _ Do you think they're talking about Emma.

NS _ Who else would they be talking about.

Y _ And you don't know anyone who would wish her harm.

NS _ No. Don't you guys have cameras or something.

Y _ We do.

NS _ Did you see who did it.

Y _ A short person wearing a black jumper with a hood.

NS _ Where did they come from.

Y _ They entered the school from a blind spot. Outside the D2 common room. Went straight for your door and straight back out.

NS _ So it could be anybody.

Y _ That's the problem yes. It could be anybody.

AIDEN.

AIDEN SPENT THE next three days on high alert. Ever since their stakeout, he could feel himself being followed, watched, from under hoods, in corners of the school he couldn't see. Twice, he'd tracked Peter down, in the Human Library, but Peter insisted the school was watching them and they were better off avoiding each other, so he took up the mantle of finding Emma on his own, studying the photo he'd taken and trying desperately to understand who they were, and what they wanted.

The only Apex he had left was a few pills that had clung to the bottom of his bag, so he rationed them, spilling them into twenty tiny piles in the corner of his desk and snorting one every two hours, as Peter had suggested.

He could already feel his last high wearing off as he stared out the massive window, watching as his classmates moved around the back lawn, circling each other in patterned chaos.

"Do you feel like you're being seen?"

Aiden whipped his head around. Dr. Roux, his mentor, was staring down the barrel of his nose at him, his eyebrows crowding toward the center of his face.

"What? No. I mean, yes." He shook his head, his brain rattling inside, trying to clear the cobwebs. He was in Dr. Roux's office, in the P-School. It was his weekly assessment. It was Sunday afternoon. He was fine. "I'm fine. Why? I mean, what?"

"We're talking about your performance in practice recently." Dr. Roux cleared his throat. "You've described some frustration with your teammates and coaches, and I'm asking if you feel seen by them. Recognized? Understood?"

"Oh, um. I don't know. I don't know what they think."

Dr. Roux noted it in the folder. "You understand your physical ability hasn't changed?"

"Um, okay."

"Your jump shot, your sprints, your weights—they're all tracking consistently. Which means your blockages are psychogenic."

"Psycho-what?"

"The problem is in your head. Slower reaction times, dismal free-throw percentage—these are problems are mental—a lack of focus—and they're killing you."

"They're not *killing* me. It's been a couple off practices."

Dr. Roux leaned forward. "The rest of your teammates are improving, rapidly. Every other player is showing better metrics. The team—hell, the entire school—has reached an evolution point, with very few exceptions. It's not enough to just tread water, anymore, Aiden. Failure to progress *is* failure."

"But I'm not failing!" Aiden felt himself squeezing the chair. "I'm still the best one out there, by far!"

Dr. Roux sat back, nodding. "I'm sure that's true. But we

need to address the problem of whatever's affecting you, and quickly. Let's get back to your teammates."

Aiden shrugged. "What about them? They're fine. Annoying, but fine."

"Have you considered their needs?"

"I've scored twenty-eight a game for two years. They should be considering my needs."

Dr. Roux nodded. "It sounds like you're having a difficult time empathizing with them."

"Or they're having a difficult time empathizing with me," Aiden snapped back, turning his attention to the window.

Dr. Roux studied the folder for a few more minutes. "Would you like a snack?"

"What?"

"Perhaps a cookie? Some milk?"

Dr. Roux offered Aiden a tray with a small, store-made chocolate chip cookie and a paper cup. He shrugged and took them both, downing the cookie in a single bite, then tossing the milk into the back of his throat. It was thick and warm, dripping into his system, warming his insides from the center. He felt his stomach turn over a few times.

"That tasted weird." He looked down into the cup.

"Well." Dr. Roux smiled. "Cow's milk is meant to provide the fat calves need to grow, far too much for human bodies. But you can't deny its appeal next to a warm cookie. Let's get back to the assessment."

Aiden returned to the window. He'd never noticed how green

the lawn was in the daytime, how patterned and strange its natural geometry looked from above. He found himself staring at separate students, wanting to know who they were, where they were going.

"Tell me," Dr. Roux said. "How are you feeling about Emma?"

"I'm . . . I'm feeling—" Aiden considered it, rolling his shoulders involuntarily, aware of how nice the stretching movement felt underneath his skin. "I miss her. I feel like I'm missing something, without her. I don't feel like myself when she's not around."

Dr. Roux leaned forward, excited. "Why do you think that is?"

"I don't know, I just . . ." In Dr. Roux's posture, he saw his father for a moment. It freaked him out. He clutched the edges of his chair to anchor himself back in reality.

"Aiden?"

"Uh, I feel like everybody around here sees me as this . . . basketball player guy. Like that's what I am, and what I'm good for."

"And how does Emma see you?"

"Like . . ." His eyes drifted back to the window, where his classmates' movements had become a dance; interconnected and sweeping and beautiful. They weren't secretive, they weren't watching him. They were all moving through the world just like he was, trying to get people to like them, trying to find their place, trying to get by. He didn't see a basketball boy and a theater girl and a science nerd and a plebe. He just saw one person after another. "Like just a person," he said.

"Just, any person?"

"Any person."

"And how do you see yourself?"

The people outside bobbed and weaved, in and out and around each other, circling the dirt paths, making room for a new dancer to come wobbling in from the edge of the window, his movements off-balance, but familiar—

He leaned forward. It was Eddy.

Aiden stood up. "I'm sorry, I have to go."

"Aiden, these assessments are mandatory, you can't just walk out—"

"I'm sorry." He threw his backpack over his shoulder. "I know you have to do your job and I'm making that impossible. But right now, I have to go."

Dr. Roux stared for a long moment. "Alright, but *please* journal today."

Aiden felt like his insides were exploding as he rushed down the stairs, through the P-School Lounge and out onto the back lawn. He pushed his way through a crowded path, parting students with his hands. He wanted to hug people, kiss people, but instead, he pushed past them, feeling their soft jackets and warm skin until Eddy appeared in front of him, disappearing into the chapel. Aiden followed him in without hesitating.

It was cool and damp inside, like the public library. The murals on the wall were bright, leaning forward out of their two-dimensional space. He'd never taken the time to look at them, but as he stared, he could feel them coming to life in all their strange splendor. In one enclave, a bearded man, Moses, huddled over a bush that burned like a fallen star, so radiant with heat that it almost looked metallic and smooth. In another, hippie Jesus handed the homeless men around him something that looked like Percocet. He wanted to go to it and take a Percocet from Jesus, but then he saw Eddy.

He sat alone in the center of the chapel. He wasn't looking anywhere, or doing anything, or talking to anyone. Aiden's footsteps were the only noise in the room as he approached.

"Eddy," he exhaled.

Eddy didn't turn around. His face was frozen forward, staring at the mural in the front of the church: the story of Noah and the ark.

Aiden sat a row ahead, resting his arms atop the pew between them. "I'm not sure if you remember me, but . . . wait, do you remember me?"

Eddy didn't say anything; he didn't have to. The outer rims of his eyeballs were swollen and purple; a cut across his forehead, hastily covered with a loose Band-Aid, still looked fresh and bloody. His hair was thrown over it, unwashed and sticking in strange places. He was younger than the picture of him in Aiden's head; his cheeks were soft; his eyes were buried and harmless.

"Oh my God." Aiden cringed. "I did this. I did this to you."

He couldn't stop himself. His hands levitated upward, straight for Eddy's face, sliding along his cheeks and grasping him by the neck. "I'm sorry," he whispered. "I hurt you. I half-nelsoned you and body-slammed you into the ground."

Eddy's body reacted, not away from his hands but toward

them. The tension in his neck released beneath Aiden's grip; the creases on his face dissolved into smooth skin; his hands floated upward to meet Aiden's, gripping onto the tops and squeezing.

"I don't know what I was doing," Aiden said, the words pouring out. "I thought I was being a hero, but . . . but I hurt you. I don't know what I was thinking."

Eddy squeezed him more powerfully, more lovingly, reassuring him he was on the right path. The murals danced around them; the air got warmer and softer.

He felt tears starting to form in the corners of his eyes. "This is supposed to be the best week of my life but all I can think about is how I want it to be over. And her. I thought I was helping Emma, but . . . but I was just helping myself, and I fucked that up too—"

Eddy's eyes snapped open.

"Eddy?"

"The flood," he whispered.

The words chased away immediately, evaporating to the ceiling of the chapel and plunging the room into a cold and incoherent silence. Eddy's hands hardened, suddenly unfamiliar, squeezing him tighter, trapping him there. He couldn't tell what was real.

"I don't—I don't understand. What do you mean?"

"The flood," he said again, louder and more viciously, accusing Aiden. *"The flood!"*

"Eddy, I don't understand—" He tried to pry his hands

loose, shaking them, but Eddy squeezed more violently. "Eddy, please!" he screamed, and tore his hands away.

He took off running up the center aisle, leaving Eddy alone in the chapel without looking back. He sprinted all the way across the back lawn, unsure of where he was going, or why.

"Aiden!" someone was shouting at him. He spun—it was a Year One plebe, a recruit from Bosnia who barely got scrimmage minutes. "Dude, practice started thirty minutes ago. They sent a bunch of people to come look for you."

"Thirty minutes? I just got in here like ten minutes ago." Aiden spun wildly; the sun was starting to set. "How did I . . ."

"Come on, dude. Coach's pissed."

His chest burned; he needed something to pick him back up. "I gotta run to my dorm—"

"No time, dude. He said get to the gym or you're not playing tomorrow."

NEESHA.

"FIRST OF ALL, your handwriting is terrible. Second, what's up with all these little pro-Emma editorial comments? *If anyone deserves heaven, it's Emma.* What the fuck is that? Neither of us even said that."

"She's very religious," Evan said quietly. "That's an objective judgment."

"It's not 'objective' where I come from." Neesha took a Sharpie and drew a line through it. "What does this say, under motive for someone outside the school? Kidnap apple . . . *kidnap-ably beautiful*? Is that seriously a reason to kidnap her?"

Evan nodded. "Yes."

In three days, she and Evan had turned her lifeless room into the headquarters of an all-out investigation. He was surprisingly equipped with arts and crafts supplies, as though preparing for exactly this kind of assignment. They'd stuck pink and green Post-its to the walls, surrounding every block-letter theory with a colorful array of details.

Despite her insistence that Emma had run away, and

desperate attempts to focus their search—Evan was still suggesting wild theories.

"When did you put this up?" she asked, pointing to the *AIDEN TOOK HER* theory.

"He has a motive," Evan mumbled.

"Says *you*."

"Says the pattern."

"*She*," Neesha read from a Post-it, "*changed her breakfast plans Wednesday morning.* Pretty sure that isn't some secret clue into her inner psyche—"

"It is."

"—and she's not about to break up with, objectively, the best-looking and, also, not for nothing, the *richest* guy at this school. And her best customer."

"I saw it."

"Okay, well, I saw him in church, and he didn't look like someone who had just been broken up with."

Evan shrugged. "Maybe he was acting."

Neesha glared at him for a long moment. Evan had spent a lot of time around Emma. They seemed to have schedules that fell perfectly together, putting them in the same place for breakfast, the same study halls, at the same events. But every time he recalled time they'd spent together, their interactions seemed to lack one major activity: talking. He couldn't remember the specific things she'd said to him. Maybe because she treated him like she treated everybody else—an object to be ignored until useful. A fan.

"I think we have to go back to potential exit strategies," Neesha said. "None of these theories feel developed, when the most logical answer is staring us in the face."

She pointed to the block letters in the center of the wall—*EMMA RAN AWAY*, and the three Post-its hanging below: *Emma lied about phone call, Neesha forced to do drop (setup)*, and *School was looking for Emma (Apex)*.

Evan looked away, the way he did every time she steered them back to this. "She wouldn't do that."

"I know that this is hard for you to hear," Neesha said. "But in all likelihood, she was getting out to save her own ass."

"What about the thing on your door?"

She winced. He was right; that was the one piece that didn't square with her theory, but she shrugged anyway. "It was a prank," she said, more confident than she felt. "That's what everyone else is saying, anyway. There's been so much weirdness lately, somebody probably was just trying to get some attention—"

"That's association fallacy," Evan said. "When two events of significance occur close—"

"I know what an association fallacy is, plebe," she spat back. "Like you associating your happy, super-fun friendship with Emma with her not wanting to run away."

Evan stared out the window. "Where would she go?"

Neesha sighed, her eyes wandering to the tape marks above Emma's bed where the photos no longer hung. "I feel like I don't know anything about her anymore."

They sat in silence, surrounded by information. It had taken them three days to get to this point, the moment of clarity where realizations should start to form; but now that everything they knew was within reach, she couldn't find anything to grab on to, or anywhere to begin. She could feel the school closing in on Apex. Day after day, more of their customers were being brought in to speak in front of Yanis; it was only a matter of time before one of them squealed, and the school found out what she was selling, and the school found out where she was getting it from. Neesha had started spending almost all of her time with Evan, but for all of the obsessive questioning, they weren't any closer to finding Emma.

Obsessive questioning; the phrase reminded her of Yangborne on test days. "We need to get more scientific about this," she said. "Run an experiment. Test our best theory. Hypothetically . . . let's say you're Emma, and you decided you wanted to leave Redemption. How would you do it?"

Evan shrugged. "Through the forest."

"Exactly. The center gate would be way too hard to get over—"

"And cameras."

"—so you go out into the forest, *around* the gate." Neesha mapped the grounds in her head. "Where would she go?"

She noticed Evan shift uncomfortably.

"What?"

"She had a favorite loop," he said. "Around the Human building."

"By the bench, that's right! And there's a path. That's has to be it."

"But . . . she couldn't just leave," Evan argued.

"What do you mean?"

"People notice her. They would notice if she was gone."

"Exactly." Neesha could feel the argument building steam. "So she would need to throw people off the scent. She goes somewhere public, shows up just long enough to be seen—"

"In the only other place with no cameras," Evan finished her thought. Both of their eyes drifted out the window, across the back lawn, where the top of the chapel and the wooden cross were visible in the distance.

Neesha smiled. "So how do we test that?" she asked, then answered for herself. "We do it ourselves. Tonight. We break out of school."

Evan was quiet. She could tell he was weighing it by the way his fingers seized at the top of his pants, one of his many ticks. He was a strange-looking kid, kind of like she imagined Marilyn Manson would look if he grew up in the *Leave It to Beaver* neighborhood. He wore an oversized button-up underneath his hoodie and spent most of his time with the hood drawn over his long brown hair. His mannerisms were strangely damp—from the way he talked to the way he cracked his fingers one by one as he processed information.

Really, he was exactly the kind of person Emma would pretend to care about, so they'd throw their loyalty at her. They'd probably had a few conversations, she'd probably asked him for help on some homework or something, and now he thought they were in love. Which made it impossible for him to believe she would abandon him.

"Okay," he said finally. "Okay. We'll do it."

Neesha stared at him. "Can I ask you something?"

"Okay."

"And will you promise to give me an answer?"

"What?"

"Why do you want to find her so bad?"

Testimonial: Evan Andrews.

Year 1994–1995. Day 322.

Mom taught me to play chess when I was six years old.

She's told me the story a hundred times: she noticed that instead of building the pirate ship Lego set that I got for Christmas, I was organizing them by size, shape, and color, placing them on a gradient and stacking them into the sky. Our first chess set was carved out of wood and small enough to fit on the TV dinner stand in our living room. She taught me the names of the pieces by inventing characters for them: Ricky Rook sees the world in straight lines, but to Bobby Bishop, everything is slanted. All the Johnny Pawns only know how to march and kill. King Dad can't see very far ahead, so he moves one square at a time, but Queen Mom sees everything, so she can go wherever she wants.

My first competition was the Spring Hill High School Chess Club fall tournament when I was ten. I won my first three matches but then in the finals, I forgot about controlling the center and Sandra Diver beat me in fifteen moves. I cried afterward but Mom said that I should be proud because they'd never even had a ten-year-old compete in their competition before. She took me to get ice cream and told me part of winning is losing, just like how part of waking up is being asleep in the first place. She said it was the most important pattern of all.

That was the year that I got in my first fight at school and Mom became my teacher for everything. In the morning, we would do classes in the kitchen—first English, then world history, then poetry, then math, because that one was the easiest—then in the afternoons we would watch television and play chess. Sometimes, I could beat her because she was distracted by *Days of Our Lives*. By the time I was ten, she could only beat me once every two hundred times we played, but she still wanted to play every day.

Some days, Mom would cry. She would tell me about all the places she used to live, and poems she used to write. She said she used to have friends, and go to parties, but now she just had a "split-level house in bumfuck nowhere." She said her life was different now, but I always made her feel better. Playing chess made her feel better. One Sunday, Pastor Tim said people who didn't have a true mission were wandering in the desert and would never know true salvation. Mom leaned over and told me I had a mission: I was the cure to her sick.

When I was eleven years old, the Spring Hill High School Chess Club fall tournament was on a Saturday, and I thought about it every day for the entire summer. I practiced a defense of the center so many times that I knew every permutation by heart. I even washed my chess shirt—a black T-shirt with a pawn on it that said *PWNED*—and took two showers, so that if they took my picture for the newspaper, I would be clean. If losing was a part of winning, today was going to be the winning part. But we didn't get to go to the competition, because Mom didn't feel like driving that day.

Soon after that, Dad bought us a computer to help with school, and it had a chess game on it. When that got too easy, Dad bought us an internet website that let me play chess against other masters all around the world, and before too long, RickyRook123 had the most points of anyone on the internet. QueenMom123 barely had any points but it was okay because she didn't really like playing on the internet, she just liked playing against me.

One day, instead of doing school or playing chess, Mom woke me up early and drove us to the ocean. She said it was more important than school, and it was okay if we didn't do math or chess today. We sat on the beach staring at the waves for almost two hours, Mom pointing out all the different ships and guessing where they were going. "That one is going to Paris," she said, "with a brig full of bananas," even though I don't think she knew anything about the ships. She told me that one day I was going to be one of the people on those ships. I told her I wasn't interested, but she said it was okay, that it was inevitable. Eventually, the waves have to go back out into the ocean, because they can't stay trapped in the same pattern, lapping into the same shore forever. I told her she was going to be one of those ships too, but she said probably not. She said now she was a crab, living under a rock in the dirty part of Rye Beach. When we got home, my father was waiting in the living room with two police officers. She didn't tell him where we were going and he got scared. Mom slept for three days after that.

By that time, we'd mostly stopped going to competitions, and we only did school some days when Mom wasn't too tired. On the days where she did school, Mom usually didn't feel like math or history, so we just read poetry and played chess. A few days after my birthday when I was twelve, a woman named Miss Sandra came to our house to watch us do school. Mom pretended to do the classes like we used to, but by lunch, she said she needed to go to sleep and Miss Sandra should leave. Two weeks later, I started going to Spring Hill Middle School.

I only went there for four days before they changed me to Spring Hill High School, even though I was only twelve. It was scary at first, because the kids were bigger and they didn't like me very much, but every day when I got home, Mom was waiting with the chessboard on the TV dinner stand and *Days of Our Lives* on the television.

I got better at school. After I turned thirteen, I didn't get in any more fights. I got an A in my calculus class and I was elected the treasurer of the chess club in an uncontested election. One day, Sandra Diver asked if I wanted to come to the Taco Bell with the rest of the chess club. Mom was crying when I got home that night. She said she was happy that I went to the Taco Bell, but sad that she didn't have anyone to play chess with.

She started sleeping even more. Some days I would come home from school, and she would already be asleep. Some days we would start playing chess and she would quit halfway through. I started to make more friends at school. Mom started to cry a lot.

Clinical depression is a disease that affects someone's brain and makes them feel sad, even when they want to feel happy. Sometimes, it makes them want to drive to the ocean and sometimes, it makes them want to sleep for the entire day. It's nobody's fault, it just happens. There's no pattern to it, and there's no way to make it go away.

But Mom had a cure. I was her cure.

When I was thirteen, we got a call from Redemption Prep. They saw some of my chess competitions and wanted me to come to school there. We met with Dr. Richardson at a coffee shop in Burlington and two months later, we got on the airplane to Utah.

Dad called tonight to tell me Mom's in the hospital, but that I don't have to worry. He asked if I wanted to come home, but tomorrow is my Analytical Reasoning test and it's illogical to get on an airplane just to look at someone in the hospital. My summer vacation starts tomorrow, and we decided as a family that I would stay at school, instead of paying for two flights.

He said it wasn't a big deal and that I should stay and do my test. But now I'm afraid he only said that because he can't see very far ahead. He can't see that we're breaking the most important pattern of all, and now Mom's lying in a hospital bed with no cure, and I'm in the middle of the ocean, alone.

EVAN.

SOMETIMES WHEN DR. Richardson was talking for a long time, she would stand up and start walking around the room.

"Pain is the most obvious and immediate emotional center in the body. I tell you something painful, such as, you're failing a class, and immediately, it conjures in you something that you can't understand. Consider the saddest day of your life. Did anything else matter on that day? Could you move? What other physically indefinable concept has the ability to render you motionless, besides pain?

"Now think about that day, *today*. Try to live in it for a moment. You can't, really, right? It's not all-consuming, as it once was. Now you're able to see it proportionally, as we see all things. No pain is too great, when compared to the scale of a lifetime.

"But the pain of that moment still exists, right? The only difference between the fact of that pain then, and the fact of that pain now, is your proximity to it. The point is this. We choose where we stand, emotionally. You have the ability to control that reaction, if only you can remember it."

It sounded like a threat. But Dr. Richardson sat up, smiling. "Let's do an exercise. Tell me, what was the most painful day in your life? Can you take yourself there now?"

Evan didn't say anything. She was right; if there had been worse days of his life, he was distantly removed from them now. The only pain he felt currently was Emma's pain, and that was the one pain he couldn't talk about.

"Your mother passed away, five months ago."

"Yes."

"You wrote in your journal at the time that your mother often told you that you were the only thing in the world that made her feel better. Then you left, and less than a year later, she was gone."

Evan blinked a few times. He'd thrown away those pages of his journal in the garbage can by the front gate, ensuring that he'd never see them again. How had they ended up in Dr. Richardson's folder?

"Every day, you would come home, and the two of you would play chess. For people who suffer from clinical depression, patterns like this are incredibly important. I refer to them as anchors, processes and people that can keep them exactly where they are, even when things around them get stormy. But do you know what happens when those anchors go away? Do you have any idea what happens to a ship when its anchor is snapped off?

"Of course you do, you experienced it. It's not like you believe your mother passed away from natural causes?"

Dr. Richardson watched him in the reflection of one of her photos. Her nose was angled like a bird of prey, preparing to dive. She wanted something out of him. She was pushing him for *S4—Emotional* feedback. She wanted him to be sad, or angry, or in pain. Instead, he ignored her.

"You weren't there, Evan. You stayed at school for the summer, and now she's gone. So place yourself in that hospital room. Look at her. Don't look away. What would you say to her?"

Evan stared at the folder on her desk, left open next to where her elbows met the table. There was a photo he'd never seen before, of his mother on a hospital bed. How would Dr. Richardson have gotten a photo that he didn't have? Why would they have kept it in his folder?

"I need an answer, Evan. That's how we get better. That's how we learn to control these things; we talk about them. We put ourselves in the moment, and then we remember our proximity. We control where we stand. I'm not letting you leave until you answer the question. What would you say to her?"

Dr. Richardson waited with her mouth half-open, but he had nothing for her. He couldn't place himself in that room. He couldn't even think about that room. There had been a time, just after May fourteenth, when all he thought about was his mother's absence. But now his pattern had normalized without her. His existence was possible with the absence of her. The gaps had been filled. And he couldn't go back to before that was true.

"Evan?"

"I—I . . ." He found his reprieve again. One thing had made all of it better. In one moment he'd realized he could be forgiven, given a new mission and a new path to salvation. And from that day forward, he never felt the pain again.

"Yes?"

Evan swallowed. "I'd read her a poem."

NEESHA.

SHE WENT TO the chapel early, an hour before she'd agreed to meet Evan, so she could have a few cigarettes alone to clear her head.

It had been four days, and no one had heard from Emma. The school was still searching; there were extra maintenance workers around all the time and occasionally, she'd wake up and see a dozen flashlights moving along the paths of the back lawn. Most students had decided it was no longer possible she'd just gone home, or left. In fact, everyone else at the school had, for the most part, stopped gossiping about her, because to them, there was only one logical explanation: the reason they hadn't heard from Emma was because Emma was dead.

"Neesha!" a voice called out of the fog. She scanned the area, expecting Evan to magically be three steps behind her yet again, but he wasn't.

"Hello?" she asked into the abyss.

Before she could react, Zaza was breaking the fog.

"What are you doing here?" she asked abruptly, smashing the cigarette.

He pointed back toward the school. "I saw you in the window. You looked sad."

"You could see that from your window?"

He didn't answer, instead dropping next to her on the step. "Waiting for someone?"

"Sure."

"Well, tell me when they're coming and I'll disappear."

"Don't feel like you have to wait to make that move—"

He was unaffected. "So I was thinking . . ."

"What?"

He shifted uncomfortably. "Why not go home?"

She snorted. "Yeah, right."

"I'm serious. I mean, if you think that's what Emma did, then why wouldn't you do it too? Just to be safe, maybe until it blows over?"

"I'm not going home," she said.

Evidently he didn't understand the finality in her voice, because he asked again. "Why not? Does your family not like you, or . . . ?"

"No," she mumbled into her knee. "Because there's not enough beds."

"What?"

"My little cousin took the one I was sleeping on—there wouldn't be a bed for me."

Zaza rolled his eyes. "Sleep on the floor."

"I can't."

He waited for her to continue. "Because . . ."

"Because on the day that I won my Little Genius award, the one that got me in here, they threw me a party, and said they couldn't wait until they never had to work again. Because when we were moving to Salt Lake, any time someone asked my mom why we were moving, she said, 'So our daughter can be rich and famous.'"

"Wow, sounds awful."

"It *is* awful, you're just not really hearing it. She wasn't saying it for other people, she was saying it for *me*. So I would know that I was the reason we moved. And now she hates it here."

"They tell you that?"

"No, she'd never say that, but I can tell. She hates the weather, she hates the grocery store, she hates my little niece's teacher who teaches them math with a guitar—"

Zaza burst out laughing, then swallowed it.

"Sure, yeah, funny for you. But my whole family came to this country so I could go here, and if I fuck it up, or I don't make all of that worth it, then why the hell did I even come here. . . ."

She trailed off into silence and they listened to the forest for a long while, the volume of the croaking bugs building in intensity.

"I'm sorry I made it seem stupid, what you were doing," Zaza said. "I think I just worry more than you, about the worst, *worst*-case scenarios."

She rolled her eyes. "How about just trusting me that I can make decisions for myself?"

Zaza exhaled. "Yeah, that too. I'm sorry for not trusting you."

His eyes drifted out to the forest, and she used the chance to sneak a look at him. The conversation was over, and still he sat next to her. He knew everything about her operation, but it hadn't scared him off. Either he was a very good liar, a sadistic criminal mastermind who got off on proximity to his victims, or, the increasingly likely option, he genuinely cared about what happened to her.

"So if you're not gonna go home," he asked, "then what are you gonna do?"

Neesha took a deep breath, balancing herself against the mountain. "I'm gonna find her. Before they find me."

AIDEN.

BY THE TIME Aiden got to practice, Coach Bryant was already screaming at the team. "Faster reactions, full-body commitments today. Anyone who doesn't improve their time is running!"

Behind him, two assistants were setting up their reactive agility drills, a system of light bulbs on top of eight thin, padded poles. It was a technology Redemption borrowed from air force training exercises—the poles lit up, different colors indicating different commands: green for move to the pole, blue for move to the pole and shoot, yellow for pass to the pole, and red for engage your opponent, one on one. It was one of their many drills aimed at training the processing centers of their brains, and based on Redemption's track record, it worked.

"Dirk and . . ." Coach Bryant glared. "Aiden. Nice of you to join us. You're up. Let's go."

Aiden jogged to the three-point line, taking the right side of the court, while Dirk set up on the left. An assistant bounced him a ball. "On red, Dirk, it's your possession. Aiden, you're on D."

The programming started slow, lighting poles up green on opposite sides, keeping them moving. He and Dirk flew to their respective poles, choreographed and perfectly spaced in their steps. It was their fourth year of the drills; the patterns and spacing were a part of their muscles now. Assistants watched from behind the hoop, standing over a Macintosh computer with a handheld clicker to log their times.

The lights began to accelerate, one after the other. "Faster!" Coach Bryant shouted. "Neither of you are strong enough for the league, you have to beat them to the move."

To his left, bright green. Aiden charged around it as a yellow lit up in the corner. He slammed a chest pass off it within a second, catching the ricochet and pulling up as a pole to his left turned blue. He shot, his ball clearing the rim a quarter second after Dirk's and rimming out.

"Come on!" Balls were back in their hands, the sequencing starting over. Green, a loop, yellow, a pass, green, another loop, green, another loop—he could feel his body wearing down, the sharp turns tearing into his most gentle tendons, over and over and over again—green, a loop, blue, a shot, yellow, a pass— he felt himself moving faster but the poles said otherwise, a yellow flashing before he had a chance to clear the last green, the cut from the fence on the back of his neck suddenly feeling inflamed—green, a loop, green, a loop, green, a loop—his jaw was clenching so hard his teeth started to grind—green, a loop, green, a loop, back and forth and back and forth and—

All eight of the bulbs lit up red.

He turned to locate Dirk, but Dirk was already attacking from the baseline. He dropped his ball and charged, on a course to intersect him three feet before the basket. Dirk had to cross-over to avoid a pole, confusing his footwork. Aiden beat him to the plant, to the launch, threw his body up in Dirk's direct line, screaming with force, arms straight up to stop the ball toward the hoop—but there was no ball.

Dirk adjusted, his delayed step allowing him to change directions in the air, sailing past Aiden and dropping the ball in for a layup. The only contact Aiden made was swiping his shoulder on the way by, a foul.

The team erupted. "Yes, Dirk, that's what I'm talking about!" Coach Bryant shouted.

"That's bullshit—that was a fucking travel!" Aiden screamed.

"Not a travel," Dirk protested, his accent even thicker with a mouth guard in. "It's called Eurostep. Sarunas Marciulionis does this for Lithuania."

"That's the most made-up shit I ever heard!"

"Sit down, Aiden," Coach Bryant said. "Maybe if you cut his line quicker, he wouldn't be able to get that position on you. Rocco, let's hear times."

"Dirk, point-seven-seven-eight seconds."

Coach Bryant slapped his clipboard and guys clapped Dirk's back as he fell to the ground. Running the exercise in .778 was less than a tenth of a second off the record pace—*his* record pace.

"Aiden." Rocco looked at the computer, then looked at Coach

Bryant, then back to the computer. "Point-nine-two-one." The team was quiet.

"Two more, let's go!"

The rest of the practice was more of the same. His agility drills fell from a .921 to a 1.012. In the scrimmage, he was the last to make his ten consecutive free throws. He swapped teams with Taion to match up on Dirk, then watched as Dirk put up forty points, beating Aiden nearly every time he went to the hoop with his ridiculous delayed step. "Do better tomorrow," Coach Bryant said to him as Aiden dragged himself to the locker room.

Back in his dorm, he dropped his bag to the floor and snorted the last three piles of Apex, immediately spreading his detective work on the desk in front of him. If she was still missing tomorrow, this was only going to get worse. He needed to focus.

Emma was being hunted by the hoods. All the other theories were out, he slashed them with his pen and held the Polaroid up to his nose. No faces were visible in the photo, but he did know who one of them was. He glared at one of the short hoods in the front, his blood pressure rising, and stormed out of his dorm.

He had to ask a few students in the B-School, but he found Peter's dorm and slammed on it. A student Aiden didn't recognize answered the door; there were six of them around the dorm, surrounding Peter in the center.

"Aiden—" he said. Peter was surprised.

"Follow me," he growled directly to Peter, ignoring the rest.

"Yeah, I don't know if that's a good idea, you look pretty cooked—"

"Get the fuck out of your chair, get a jacket, and follow me."

It worked. Peter stood up slowly, watching Aiden the entire time. Once his door was shut behind him, Aiden marched them to the Human Lounge and out onto the back lawn, settling on a lonely bench.

"What's this about?" Peter asked.

"It's time."

"Time for what?"

Aiden swallowed. "Evan Andrews."

Peter took a deep breath. "Whoa, this is not the time to show our hand—"

"Then when is the time?" he almost screamed. "I'm losing my fucking mind! You promised you were gonna help me find her, and I haven't seen you in three days! I'm done with waiting—someone said that kid goes out to the cross every night. We're gonna find him, and we're gonna get some answers."

Peter looked frightened, for once unsure of himself. "Look," he said calmly. "Your body doesn't have the amount of amphetamine it's used to, and you're going through withdrawal—"

He tried to put a hand on Aiden's shoulder, but Aiden snapped it away. "Don't fucking lecture me, bro. Just help me, please." Aiden felt himself gasping for air between his sentences. "My game is tomorrow, and if I don't find her, I'm gonna fuck my whole life up. I have to know what's going on. I have to know who sent her that newspaper article."

Peter was silent. His hands retreated to his pockets, and

he wouldn't meet Aiden's eye contact. "Okay," he said finally. "Okay. I'll tell you. I did."

"You did what?"

Peter looked back to the school, then to Aiden. They were alone. "I sent her that article. Well, I didn't actually get to send it to her, but I made it."

Aiden set a hand on the bench to balance himself. "Made it?"

"I've been buying Apex for the debate team. We have three teams going to Stanford in two weeks, and we're cramming, but the school's research tools suck. Without Apex, we're not gonna be ready, but we ran outta money. So I was gonna show her that, let her know I was fully within my authority to rat on her, and see if I could get some for free. One of the debaters heard her tell you to meet at the court, so I went. Then when you showed up, I . . . changed my focus."

Aiden's mouth felt dry. "To me?"

Peter nodded. "Yeah."

"So . . . the hoods, last night—"

"The debate team."

"And Evan Andrews?"

"That part's real, actually." He couldn't tell if Peter was proud or ashamed. "He was following her, but I'm not sure it has anything to do with Apex."

Aiden could feel the world spinning around him. "And you stole the bag?"

Peter nodded.

"You've been lying to me this entire time? For Apex?"

"Yeah," Peter said, stretching the word out. "But it's not like—"

"Yes it is!" Aiden felt his chest puffing like a motor engine. "Whatever you were about to say, whatever you think it isn't, I guarantee you, it is. You just don't understand it because you have no sense of right or wrong, or—fucking anything!"

"Oh?"

"You were gonna threaten to ruin my girlfriend's life, just so you could get free drugs. Think about how insane that is? Then you lied about it to me—actually, no, you did more than that! You pretended *somebody else* was doing it, forced me to miss basketball practice—"

"I didn't—"

Aiden motored on, raising his voice to talk over Peter. "—and made me run in fucking circles, for what? You ruined my life, just so you could get a little bit of Apex?"

Peter didn't look remorseful at all. "I didn't force you to do anything."

"In what fucking world is that even human? You don't give a shit about Emma—and you definitely don't give a shit about me, you shitty, druggie, degenerate asshole!"

The words echoed across the empty back lawn, hanging in the air for a long minute. Aiden felt like he was coming up from underwater, gasping for air, clenching every part of his body that could be clenched.

Peter just shuffled his feet, waiting.

"Okay," Aiden finally said. "I didn't mean all of that—"

"Yeah you did," Peter said. "But it's good. You've been think-ing it for a while, yeah?"

Aiden kept clutching at his chest. His heart felt like it was going to stop.

"Thing is," Peter continued, "I'm alright with my choices. You didn't say any shit I didn't already know. At least I can say that, right?"

Aiden tried to balance again and failed, hyperactivity in his mouth and fingers and knees. "I wish I could be like you. And just not give a shit about other people."

Peter glared at him. "You know, I actually kinda like this moment, seeing you all pissed, 'cause for once it didn't work like you were thinking it was gonna."

"That's bullshit—"

"Naw, man, think about it. *Really* think about it. You're so used to getting everything you want, just 'cause of who you are—basketball, money, fuck, even Emma—you don't have a fucking clue what to do when you lose it. You don't even know what it feels like to want something. And that makes you think that's how life's supposed to be? Naw, man, you're born lucky. You're a fucking haircut. You're candy shit."

"Are you serious? I worked for everything—"

"Naw, man. You took the path of least resistance. You got trainers, coaches, opportunities—you think you worked for it, but you just did what was right there in front of you. And the saddest part is, you're completely oblivious. You don't even know enough to know how fucking stupid you sound when you say, 'I work for my shit.' Kids here, man, they grew up in slums, trying to learn math by candles so they can fight a million other people to be the one that gets to come be a scientist? *That's* successful. You're not even close."

Aiden felt like his throat had swollen closed.

"I took your drugs 'cause it was easy. I'm trying to find Emma so I don't have to go back to my old life." He swallowed. "We don't find her, worst thing that happens to you is you gotta look sad on the news. You *think* me lying is some problem to you, you want to be pissed about it, it doesn't change one fucking thing. You're candy shit, man. And you don't even know."

They were still alone on the back lawn. Aiden hung his head, staring at nothing. His arms, his chest, the rest of his body swayed below him with the wind.

He couldn't believe what an idiot he'd been. He'd betrayed every certainty in his life—basketball, his dad, his teammates— for a fucking hustle. He'd spent hours thinking about her, panicking about the danger she was in, when all of it was complete fiction. He'd blown up his entire life, for a hustle.

In the silence, the door to their right opened, and a short figure slipped out of the door to the Human Lounge. They both watched as he walked quickly past them, directly toward the chapel and the cross.

It was Evan.

"Okay, buddy," Peter said to him softly, watching Evan disappear into the fog. "We gotta come back from that now—"

Aiden spat on the ground at his feet. "Gimme it. Now."

Peter pulled the bag of Apex from his pocket and dropped it into Aiden's palm. It was half as full as it had been three days ago. Aiden threw it in his coat and marched away from the school.

"What're you doing?"

Aiden ignored him, allowing the buzzing in his head to take control as he stalked after the hood in front of him.

NEESHA.

ZAZA DIDN'T GET to finish his sentence. Footsteps started to creep up from the fog in front of them. "Are you meeting someone?" he asked.

"Yes," she blurted. "You should go."

"Shit." He looked around. "I'll hide." He ran up the stairs and moved behind a pillar just as Evan entered the clearing.

"Okay, let's go," Neesha said to Evan, starting toward the forest before Zaza could notice Evan.

"Wait," Evan said, trying to stop her.

"What?"

"We need a signal to warn one another. Do you know *SOS* in Morse code?" he asked.

"Why would we need to communicate in Morse code?"

"In case we find trouble. It's three short beeps, three long beeps, and three short beeps."

"Why can't I just say 'help'? Come on, we have to go—"

Evan stared doing the noises with his mouth, sharp repetitive beeps, and she turned just in time to see Zaza stepping out from behind his pillar.

Evan froze.

For a second, it looked like Zaza might hit Evan, but then Zaza turned his attention to her.

"I'm sorry, what the fuck is this?"

She swayed nervously. "We're working on something."

"You're meeting *him*? Is that why you're out here? Neesha, *this* is the kid I told you about! The one who—" He swallowed the rest of the sentence. "Look, whatever this kid has convinced you—"

"Has nothing to do with you," she finished for him.

"It's not safe! He was stalking her!"

"No, he wasn't!" she screamed. "He's been helping me, and he's gonna help me find her!"

"Neesha," Zaza said, lowering his voice to pretend like he was rational. "This is not a good idea. Now is not the time to be out looking for her—"

"Do you fucking hear yourself? You're doing it *again*! I'm not going to apologize to you for wanting to do something about my situation. You know what you are? You're inert."

"What?"

"You wedge yourself into compounds, and then you just sit there, inactive. You'd rather quietly exist than try to do anything to change the world around you. You're a scared, inert little boy, and I'm not like that."

"You're—" Zaza started to boil up, his hand rubbing across his head faster and faster, but he couldn't even sputter out a comeback. "I'm not—"

"See?" she said. "Nothing."

He spun and began to walk away but turned back after three steps. "They use the inert gases to prevent *toxic* chemicals from creating harmful reactions, you know that, right?"

"Give it a rest, dude. The metaphor is dead."

Zaza's mouth hung open. He looked ready to apologize, ready to shove his tail between his legs, but he was interrupted by the sound of footsteps galloping up one of the center paths, quietly at first. Neesha thought it might just be some students passing in the distance, but the footsteps quickly got louder, and by the time the three of them fully appreciated their size, speed, and direction, Aiden Mallet was ripping out of the fog, grabbing Evan by the back of his hoodie, and throwing him to the ground.

"No!" Neesha shouted, but it was too late. Aiden collapsed on top of Evan like a wrestler, pinning his whole body from the midsection, ruthlessly controlling his arms and staring into his face. "What did you do to her?" Aiden shouted, spit dangling. "Where is she?"

"I—I—I don't know!"

"Aiden!" Zaza tried to intervene, but Aiden was in his own world.

"Wrong answer!" Aiden swung his head forward, straight for Evan's cranium, connecting with his skull and rocking both of them backward. Neesha screamed. She'd always assumed people could only head-butt like that in movies and judging by Aiden's cross-eyed reaction, she might have been right. A small pool of blood formed on Evan's forehead. He was shrieking as Aiden geared up to hit him again. Before he could, however, another large body came screaming out of the fog, pile-driving Aiden off Evan and into the clearing in front of the church.

The figure stood up, over Aiden, and in the yellow light, she recognized Peter Novak. "Chill, man! Jesus!"

Both of them rolled to a standing position, glaring at each other, Evan crumpled on the ground between them.

AIDEN.

"I DON'T CARE if you're not gonna help me, but for God's sake, get the fuck out of my way!"

"You're out of control, buddy," Peter said, inching over in front of Evan, placing himself between Evan and Aiden. "We don't know this kid had anything to do with it—"

"He was following her, you said that," Aiden growled, flexing his fingers. "So I just want to know"—he turned his attention to Evan—"what he knows?"

"I—I don't know anything," Evan stammered.

"Yes, we do!" Aiden had barely noticed Neesha, Emma's roommate, standing on the steps of the chapel. "We know she ran away!"

There were confused looks around the circle.

"Zaza?" Aiden noticed the team's statistician behind her on the steps.

"How do you know she ran away?" Peter asked Neesha.

"Evan?" Neesha looked to him, still cowering on the ground.

He cleared his throat. "The school was looking for her before she went missing. They sent maintenance guys to her dorm during mass."

Aiden's head spun as the five of them stumbled outward into a circle, each defending their own position.

"So"—he turned to Neesha—"what are you doing out here?"

She shifted uncomfortably, and he realized he'd never said more than three words to her. "We're gonna test our theory. That she ran away."

"You mean, you're gonna run away?" Peter asked.

"Just to see if it's possible."

An image of Emma clicked in Aiden's head. "The long way around, past that bench, by Human Sciences?"

"Exactly."

He swallowed, the inside of his mouth suddenly thick with saliva. "We had our first kiss on that bench."

"This is a horrible idea," Zaza said, poking his head into the circle.

"What are you doing here?" Aiden asked him.

"Uh, I was here to talk to Neesha."

"And this guy," Aiden said, completing his turn, all the way around to where Evan was cowering out of the light. "Who's here because . . ."

"I have to find her," Evan whispered.

Aiden nodded, his eyes flashing to every face around him. "I guess we've all got that in common."

They held in another moment of stalemate.

"Well," Neesha said finally. "This was nice, but if you'll

excuse me and Evan, we're gonna find Emma." She started down the path away from the church. Evan caught up to walk lockstep with her.

"No *fucking* way!" Zaza shouted at her from behind. "Do you have any idea what's out there? That shit goes for *miles*, and if you don't know how to get back to a path, you're lost in there. So unless you've got a really serious plan—unless *she* had a plan—that's not where she went."

No one even looked at him. Aiden looked to Peter. "I'm going with them," he challenged, and Peter didn't back down.

"After you," Peter said, and fell in line behind Aiden and Neesha.

"Oh, absolutely, one hundred percent fuck this," Zaza said. "Fuck this, fuck this, fuck this," he mumbled to himself, walking a wide circle around the clearing before falling into line behind them.

EVAN.

"WE'RE PRETTY DEEP," Zaza announced. It was the fifth time he had quantified their progress. "Are we sure she would go this deep?"

The first hour of walking had been uphill. Evan had to take small steps to scale the uneven terrain, allowing Peter and Aiden to push past him. Now, a mile and a half in, the altitude had flattened and the forest had thickened. Evan had to lift his feet high to step over fallen logs and jagged rock faces, but the group continued on, conversation thinning with their breath, no one complaining other than Zaza.

Every time there was a clearing, Evan rushed back to the front. If they found her tonight, he was going to be the first to see her. Every one hundred yards, he tied yellow strings around the trunks of trees to mark their path. Five people was too many social signals to process at once, so he stayed quiet, ignored questions, and focused on the picture of Emma that hovered just ahead of him in his mind's eye.

"Definitely never been in this far before," Aiden said. "Not even for capture the flag."

"You know a group of kids got killed in here, right?" Peter asked the group from behind, casually. "Just after the school opened, in these very woods—"

"I don't buy it," Aiden said.

"I don't care if you buy it, it happened. It all started seventy years ago—"

"Redemption opened twenty years ago," Neesha corrected him.

Peter ignored her. "At the time, they hadn't figured out exactly what kind of a school they were gonna be yet. They were experimenting with a lot of different ideas, teaching all kinds of crazy subjects. Sure, normal stuff, like biology and chemistry, but they also were experimenting with much darker shit. Telekinesis, torture techniques, mind control—"

"You're making this impossible to believe," Neesha interrupted again.

"Christ, have none of you ever heard a *story* before? Just let it breathe." The leaves crunched under his feet. "As I was about to say, the school knew what they were teaching was bullshit— nobody actually knew how to do mind control—but people believed crazy shit back then. They could recruit gullible plebes to come study. That was, until one student changed everything. We'll call him . . . Evan."

Evan felt the hair on the back of his neck stand up.

"Evan wasn't like the other kids. For one thing, he was way taller—seven feet, at least. He was weird, closed off, but superintelligent. Strangest of all, he spent most of his time in the forest, practicing techniques from class. A rumor started to go around school. Maybe Evan isn't like us; maybe he's an alien.

"One day in class, his teacher is in the middle of a lesson when she turns around to put some coffee on. She's talking back over her shoulder, and before she knows it, she's pouring the hot coffee all over herself. She tries to stop, but she can't—Evan's controlling her mind."

Neesha groaned. "If you're going to tell a story about mind control, the twist should be way scarier than coffee."

"What happened then?" Evan asked quietly. He knew it was just a story, but he had no trouble picturing it in the halls and classrooms of Redemption.

"The school starts to run all kinds of tests on Evan. They give him growth hormones to stunt his development, they try to shock it out of him with electricity, but none of it works. The best they can do is put a light in his brain, that starts to blink when he's controlling someone—"

"A light in his brain?" Neesha asked.

"Dude, this is super off the rails," Zaza added.

"Shut up, I'm getting there. One day in the middle of mass, one of the female students, this popular Year Four—Emma, we'll call her—stands up outta nowhere. Everybody's confused, quiet—until she holds up a brick and starts smashing it against her skull. People freak out, her friends are grabbing her, trying to stop it, but she's possessed by the force of God. She keeps smashing till her skull falls in, and she dies. And hiding in the back of the church, there's Evan, controlling her mind."

Evan glared at Peter. It felt like an accusation, Peter using the names he did. He'd never hurt Emma, even as a fictional character in a made-up story. Still, the pit of his stomach turned as if he had.

"The school realizes they've gotta do something about this, but what can they do? They can't have him bashing kids' heads in with bricks, but they also can't kill him, or they'll have killed the greatest scientific advancement of this century. So the best they can do, they decide, is to contain him. They put an electric shock fence around the school, like a bark collar for dogs, and send him into the forest to live on his own. And they never heard from him again. Or rather, they never saw him."

A big gust of wind sent a swirl of leaves flying around them. The fog was turning into real moisture. Evan could feel it gathering on the front of his jacket.

"Twenty years later, the school's thriving. There's hundreds of kids here, they're only teaching real science. That's when this group of Year Ones—the Neeshas—decide to go camping. Nobody's worried about it, right? Nobody's been in the woods for years, why would there be anything scary out there?

"As they're sitting there in their tent, one of them hears something, something big, a huge—" He snapped a thick branch with his hands and all four of them jumped. Everyone was really listening now. "In the distance, she sees a little red light, hovering toward them, fifteen feet off the ground.

"Without warning, she takes an iron rod from their tent

and starts attacking her friends. She slugs one of them over the head so hard it knocks her out cold. The other two go sprinting toward the school, but only one makes it onto the back lawn in time. Everybody comes outside; they can hear her screaming, 'Please, help me, help me!' but as soon as she hits the clearing— bam. She drops to the ground, writhing in pain. Instructors try to help, but they can't figure out what's going wrong. Nothing's touching her, but she's being tortured in her mind. The pain gets so intense, her eyes roll back, and just before the color drains from her face, she says it: 'The light. It's in his brain.' And she's gone. Not a single, physical sign on her body that she's been hurt, but she's dead on the ground in front of them.

"After that, there was a ten-year ban, no going out into the forest. It's been so long now, nobody even believes it anymore. But the instructors, the ones who've been here the longest, they swear some nights they can still see a tiny light, blinking deep in the forest."

It was silent for a moment. The story was impossible. Peter had gotten even basic facts of the school wrong, but it still gave Evan a creeping feeling about being in the woods this late, about all the strange patterns of the school that weren't explained. Eventually, Neesha couldn't hold her tongue anymore.

"Yes, okay, spooky, but you're basically just butchering failed science experiments to make a story. The technique you're referencing, using light to control neural activity? It's called optogenetics, and it's never even worked. We tried in Pharma."

Peter sighed. "You had to fucking kill it."

"So, the guy is fifteen feet tall?" Aiden asked.

"Yeah, he's an alien."

"Oh, yeah, you didn't make that very clear."

Evan froze. The rest of the group stopped behind him. At the farthest reach of his flashlight, the trees stopped.

"I think it's the timber line," Neesha suggested. "The end of the forest."

They started again, slowly, reaching the edge of the forest and emerging into a clearing, nothing but black rock in every direction, as far as they could see.

"Are we past the front gate yet?" Aiden asked.

"I think the gate is that way." Neesha pointed. "So it must be farther."

"No," Peter argued. "We've gone at least two miles. We should be way past it."

They stood in silence. With no trees left to block it, the wind whipped their faces and necks. Neesha took another step into the clearing. "I guess we keep going—ahh!"

Her scream rippled across the mountain. When Evan's flashlight found her, she was terrified, pointing off in the distance. Fifteen feet in the air, a tiny red light was blinking.

NEESHA.

THEY STARED AT the light, but it didn't get any closer, hovering perfectly still.

"I made that up," Peter said quickly. "It was the best I could remember the story, but I made most of that shit up, including the part about the light."

She scanned the area. "Look." She pointed. Fifty feet along a horizontal line, another red light blinked. She checked in the other direction—another light. "It's a fence," she said.

She crept forward. The beam of her flashlight landed on stone pillars and chain-link fence in between. She traced the fence upward; it didn't stop for twenty feet, nearly disappearing into the sky. At the top, there were rows of spikes, angled in both directions to prevent anyone from climbing in, or climbing out. Every twenty feet or so, there were stone pillars, resolute against the mountain, anchoring the fence.

"What the fuck?" Peter whispered. "Who would put a fence out here?"

"They would." Evan's flashlight landed on one of the stone

pillars. Etched into its stone, covered in debris and surrounded by thick-growing vines, was the Redemption crest, its book of knowledge at the top, shining light into the heavens.

Step by step, they approached it. "We should climb it," Neesha suggested. When she was a kid, the park near their home was one of the only places her parents would let her go without supervision. She used to spend entire afternoons racing against friends to the tops of the trees and fences.

"No way." Zaza waved his flashlight at the top. "They've got spikes."

"I'll climb around them." She reached for the fence. "I used to do it all the time at this park back home—"

"Hold on." Zaza stopped her hand. "Why are you even trying to get over it? Then you're on the other side?"

"To prove it's possible!" Neesha answered.

"I'm sure it's possible, but it doesn't get us any closer to finding her."

"I don't think you understand science—"

"I don't think you understand probability."

She noticed Evan pulling his journal from his bag and starting to flip through it.

"Why would they even put a fence two miles into the forest?" Peter asked. "If you're trying to keep animals out, why not make it closer to the school?"

"Maybe it's somebody else's fence?" Aiden guessed.

"It doesn't really matter at this point," Neesha said. "It's here. Either Emma got over it, or she didn't. I'm climbing to the other side—you guys can stay here and have a tea party, I don't care. I'm finding her."

"I'm not letting you hurt yourself!" Zaza grabbed for her arm, but she swung wildly, fighting him off and jerking her body away from him. As her arms swung back, her right arm caught inside Evan's sling, yanking it forward and throwing his journal out of his hands and toward the fence. The leather binding met the chain with a light tap, but as it connected, it began to sizzle. Sparks exploded off the impact and steam released up the fence line. The journal landed on the ground in front of them with a thud.

Neesha leaned over slowly and picked it up by the part that still resembled leather. The other half had melted, warping its shape, and still sizzled with the burn of electricity.

All of them stared at the fence. "That's . . . a very extreme charge," Neesha said. Her heart began to beat warm and loud in her ears.

"The whole thing is electrified?" Zaza asked breathlessly.

On top of the fence, bright red and yellow siren lights started to spin.

PART V.

recruits.

Testimonial: Emmalynn Donahue.

Year 1995–1996. Day 33.

I don't have a home in this world anymore.

Sinful girl.

I didn't know my mother was capable of saying something like that about anyone. I guess I was twelve the last time we were in the same room. I probably know the censored version of her. The version that was trying to raise a gentle daughter.

I wonder what the last four years have been for her. I wonder who she talks to, if not to me. I wonder if my dad gives her any support. I can understand how she thinks I've abandoned her, but this.

Sinful girl.

Wicked girl.

Abandoned her family for a life of excess.

She says it to a video camera. That's the worst part; someone offers her a chance to record an opinion of her daughter, and this is how she responds. I left her behind; I did it to her. I don't love her and that's for the better, because she doesn't need me anyway.

She's drinking. I can tell she's been drinking even if she isn't holding anything in the video. My dad isn't in the video. Maybe he's the one recording, but I doubt it. He's probably laid up in bed.

For four years I was able to swim, knowing that no matter how far out I got, there was always a shore to return to. But at an exact point between them, the Atlantic becomes the Pacific, which means you could enter an entirely new ocean, and you wouldn't know until you came up to look for shore.

I knew we talked less and less. I wanted to tell her more, but I knew it was painful for her to hear what I was doing. I knew we talked about nothing, and eventually there was nothing to talk about.

I had the money. That's the worst part; we always said we didn't talk because we couldn't afford it, but for three months, I've been rich. I could have called her whenever. I could have saved our relationship but I didn't.

Wicked girl.

Deep breaths. Deep breaths. Deep breaths. Understand her needs. She needs to be comfortable where she is. She needs to be okay with her life. She needs to take care of my dad.

I control where I stand. I can forgive her. I can care for her. But how can I care for her if I can't come home.

Might as well not come home. Like she wanted me to hear it.

She did want me to hear it. That's why she's talking to a camera. This is her telling me. I don't have a home in this world anymore.

emma donahue investigation.

ahmad galbia—year 4.

transcription by MONKEY voice-to-text software.

YANIS (School Administration) _ Please speak your full name aloud.

AHMAD GALBIA (Student) _ Ahmad Galbia.

Y _ Zaza right.

AG _ Right.

Y _ Okay Zaza. Simple question. Why did you go into the woods last night.

AG _ Honestly. I have no idea.

emma donahue investigation.

neesha shah—year 4.

transcription by MONKEY voice-to-text software.

NS _ We were on a walk.

Y _ Two and a half miles into the forest. Why.

NS _ I was looking for my missing friend.

Y _ Emma.

NS _ Are other people missing.

Y _ Why did you want to find her.

NS _ Are you serious . . . because somebody has to.

Y _ She is your friend.

NS _ Yes.

Y _ You were nervous about your friend so you went to check the woods for her.

NS _ Okay.

Y _ And you thought the best moment for that was midnight. Why didn't you ask us about this.

NS _ Yeah right.

Y _ I am serious. Why sneak off instead of asking for help.

NS _ Because this school is insane about the rules.

Y _ But I'm not the school.

NS _ You're not.

Y _ No. I'm the person they put in charge of finding your friend. If you would have asked. First I could have told you that we've swept those woods twice a day every day since Thursday and haven't found anything . . . and second you wouldn't have to face a mandatory punishment hearing from a school that is. As you say. Insane about rules . . . do you understand.

NS _ Punishment.

Y _ I've been told they are considering explosion. Not explosion. Explosion. No. Expulsion. There. Got it that time.

emma donahue investigation.

ahmad galbia—year 4.

transcription by MONKEY voice-to-text software.

AG _ Can I ask you a question.

Y _ Okay.

AG _ Why is there a twenty foot electric fence two miles into the woods.

emma donahue investigation.
aiden mallet—year 4.
transcription by MONKEY voice-to-text software.

Y _ The night before this big basketball game. You decide to stay out all night. Going into the woods.

AM _ Am I going to get in trouble.

Y _ Don't worry about that right now. I'm trying to understand what would make you think this is a good idea . . . Aiden.

AM _ I need to find her.

Y _ I understand. But you are willing to risk your basketball career for it.

AM _ Am I going to get in trouble.

Y _ Of course not. You have a game today. I just don't understand what felt so urgent. Why last night. Why the night before a game.

AM _ Can I go.

Y _ Is there anything you're not telling me.

AM _ No.

Y _ Okay. Then you're free to go.

emma donahue investigation.

evan andrews—year 2.

transcription by MONKEY voice-to-text software.

Y _ How did you come to be in the woods with Neesha.

EA _ We're friends.

Y _ Are you.

EA _ Yeah.

Y _ Who are your other friends.

EA _ Emma.

Y _ Right. Emma. Who else . . . Evan.

EA _ Zaza.

Y _ Zaza said he's spoken to you twice. Including last night. How long have you known Neesha.

EA _ Not long.

Y _ What about Emma. Your good friend Emma.

EA _ W we weren't good friends.

Y _ Evan. Because she is my friend. I want to find her. Yanis. Were you close. Evan. V v v very close.

EA _ It it was complicated.

Y _ That doesn't sound complicated . . . Did you know that the school hired ten security video people to come in to help with finding Emma.

EA _ Okay.

Y _ Why so many that was what I asked. Turns out if you get trained in this there's a way to take pieces of video and put labels on to organize. So we can go through all of it like no big deal. In no time. So when I come in to them with a question like what were the last ten times Evan and Emma interacted they all start typing in keywords and whipping the mouse around . . . And their keywords and data on the bottom will tell them that Evan and Emma are in the same camera all the time. Great I say. Lots of context. So we started watching some of the clips and you know what we found out. About your relationship with Emma.

EA _ What.

Y _ There isn't one. In the last two months we couldn't find a single instance of you actually speaking with her. Plenty of being in the same place. None of you talking.

EA _ That that that's spying.

Y _ Is that bad . . . that is a serious question. I want you to answer. What is the negative value associated with watching someone when they don't know you're watching them . . . Evan. What is it.

EA _ It it violates privacy.

Y _ Okay. So I know things about you that you don't want me to know. Is that bad.

EA _ I it's illegal. I'm a student.

Y _ What if I'm using those things for good. What if I'm using those things to try to make life better for. I don't know. Emma. Then it would be a good value right.

EA _ O okay.

Y _ But you only know that it's a good value because I tell you why I was doing it. I am being very transparent. I want to find

Emma. Do you understand what I am saying here.

EA _ Y yes

Y _ Then convince me it is a good thing. Tell me why you were watching her.

emma donahue investigation.

neesha shah—year 4.

transcription by MONKEY voice-to-text software.

Y _ Final question.

NS _ Look. I don't know anything. I am not hiding anything. I was just trying to find my friend and I thought this would be the best way. I'm sorry we tried on our own and if I could do it over again I would not. But I've told you everything else that I know.

Y _ Okay . . . I believe you.

NS _ Does that mean. You'll make sure I don't get expelled.

Y _ I can recommend a lighter punishment. But I make no guarantee. Your hearing is Thursday.

NS _ Okay.

Y _ And in the meantime. Don't go doing stuff like that on your own anymore. If you have an idea come to us and tell us.

NS _ Okay.

Y _ You promise.

NS _ Okay.

Y _ Oh. I did have one last question. Just to confirm the account he gave. What was Evan Andrews doing in your dorm room on the night of evening mass.

NS _ You mean his dorm.

Y _ No. I mean your dorm. Last Thursday. The night Emma went missing. What was he doing there.

EVAN.

HE HAD ONLY been out of the questioning room for twenty seconds when the buzzer sounded. It echoed like a gunshot across campus. Dr. Richardson's voice came on the loud-speaker.

"Attention, students. Peace be with you. We would first like to thank all staff and students for their cooperation with our search efforts for Year Four student Emmalynn Donahue. We're very relieved to report that Miss Donahue has been located and is safe with her family back in Kansas. While we regret the panic that was caused by this search, our primary concern, as always, is for the safety of our students. One important lesson students can learn from this experience: if you need anything, or desire to make plans off-campus, please let the staff know.

"Anyone in need of emotional support can attend the support group in the guidance office this evening at five p.m. Thank you."

Evan swallowed the bile building in his throat as he stared at the speaker. Emma hated her family. She never talked to them. They never sent her letters anymore. The only times she referenced her dad was to remember him crashing his car drunk. Every time she dreamt about her mom, it was a nightmare. Dr. Richardson was lying.

Evan put his head down and walked to the C-School. If his timing was right, Neesha would be between Advanced Biometrics and her dorm. He walked the route three times, each trip expanding to include more variables—hallways, the labs, the libraries, the lounge, the girls' bathroom. But Neesha wasn't anywhere she was supposed to be.

Finally, he saw curly black hair, spilling out of a hood, face-down on a table in the library. Without saying anything to draw attention, he slid in across from her.

"Th-there's no way she's gone."

The black curls didn't move.

"The school is lying. She hates her family. They never talked. She wouldn't go home."

Still nothing.

"I'm serious," he said. He dropped his voice another decibel. "She used to say—"

Without a word or even a look in his direction, Neesha took her head off the book she'd been resting it on and packed it into her bag below the table.

"Where are you going?"

She stood up, zipping her bag shut. He reached for her arm.

"*Don't touch me*," she said, peeling his hand off. "Ever."

"But she's not gone!"

Neesha ignored him.

"We still need to find her—"

Her bag was over her shoulder.

"Is something wrong with you?"

She spun and lurched back at him, hissing, "*You*. You are what is wrong with me."

It felt like his stomach disappeared, leaving only empty space in his gut. "What?"

"They threatened to kick me out," she whispered, but it sounded like she was accusing him. "They said there's going to be a hearing because of this, and I could get expelled."

"But she's—"

"Evan." She glared at him, so intensely that he felt like she was seeing some secret part of him that wasn't there. Or something that was there but he didn't know about. "They said she's fine. She ran away, and she's at home. It's over."

"But they're lying—"

"I'm not going to keep ruining my life because you can't control your imagination. I'll talk to her when she feels like talking to me."

"What about the fence?"

She rolled her eyes. "It's a fence. Probably for bears or whatever."

"What about the drugs?"

"What drugs," she mumbled, and walked away.

"She's still missing!" Evan called after her. Several students at the tables around them turned, but he ignored them. "She hates her family, you have to trust me!"

Neesha stopped in her tracks. "I'm sorry," she said to the students at the table next to them. "He hasn't taken his meds yet today." They laughed and went back to their books. Slowly, she sat back down across from him.

"I'm going to explain this to you. And then we are never going to speak again. Remember how you told me that you were close friends with Emma, and that you talked all the time, but you could never tell me anything you talked about?"

"I—I didn't say we were *friends*—"

"Remember how I vouched for you? How I swore on my life that you actually knew her, because you told me you did?"

"I n-never said specifically—"

"What were you doing in our dorm during mass, Evan? What aren't you telling me?"

His mouth hung open. He lost control of his bottom lip, his hands, his heart. Systems started to crash in his head. Nothing about this was right. Nothing about it made sense. None of it was in Neesha's pattern. The eight steps whirled into one, pieces of his necessary social machinery snapping off and skidding against each other. "I—I did—haven't lied. I . . ." She let him sputter out. "I never lied."

Neesha nodded. "Yeah. I got that. You avoided every question, so you could say you *technically* never lied. This might not compute in your fucked-up little computer brain, but that *technically* makes you an asshole. Making it seem like you were friends, when you probably never said a word to her? *That's* a lie. Sneaking into my dorm and not telling me? *That's* a lie."

Evan swallowed.

"And I'm sure there's more you're not telling me, about Emma, about yourself."

Evan swallowed. "N-nothing. Nothing."

She stared at him for a long moment. *"That's a fucking lie."*

She stood up again to leave. "Wait," he tried, but she didn't. Without thinking, Evan reached into his bag and dropped the leather-bound book on the table in front of her.

TESTIMONIAL JOURNAL: EMMALYNN DONAHUE

Neesha slammed her backpack over it, staring at the spot where the text had just been.

It sat on the table between them for a full minute.

"Why would you do that?" she whispered, eyes darting doorway to doorway, her shoulders angled to shield the table from the lone camera behind her.

"That's why I was in your dorm. I just wanted to read her—"

"I *just* told you," she said, her body shaking, "I don't want anything to do with this. Why would you show me this?"

Evan swallowed. "Read it. She's not at home."

Nothing happened for a full sixty seconds. Neesha didn't move; the kids next to them didn't stop whispering; the clock didn't even turn.

Finally, Neesha shook her head, cradling her backpack in her arms. "Naw," she said. "Naw, I'm good here. Good luck, Evan." She walked off without looking back.

Evan watched her go, through the double doors, then all the way around the room, through the library's glass windows. Neesha had exhausted her value. She'd told him everything she knew and given him every clue she had. She wasn't going to be helpful in finding Emma, especially if she couldn't understand that the school was lying. Still, it felt like he'd just lost something. His stomach ached. His heart hurt.

His eyes returned to the table. It was empty. Neesha had taken the journal.

AIDEN.

ON TUESDAY NIGHT, the Redemption campus was drowning in basketball enthusiasm. They hung banners of their alumni, bussed in a four-piece orchestra from Salt Lake to play over the loudspeakers, and lit the ten-foot Redemption logo on the school's front arches with purple and gold neon. An hour before the game, every student at the school had already loaded into the gym, passing liquor around in water bottles, filling the stands front to back. As Aiden stepped onto the floor for shootaround, he noticed a cap in the staff section—*Dallas Mavericks*.

The McDonald's All Americans had been bussed in that morning, a team of superstars assembled from high schools across the country. Their raw talent was overwhelming, most impressive among them a sharp-shooting two guard from Florida named Justus McNeil. Aiden had played him twice in AAU; he could shoot with almost no load time, which meant Aiden had to deny every pass and get him rattled early. That was the recipe that held him to eight points the last time.

Before the game, Dr. Richardson took a microphone at the center of the court. "I'd like to take this moment to welcome the McDonald's All American basketball stars to our temple of excellence. It's a thrilling opportunity, to witness such an impressive level of talent and competition in our home gym. May the best team win, and may all of you be blessed."

The gym was shaking as the starting fives stepped onto the court. The McDonald's All Americans were in bright yellow jerseys with red trim and red arches on the top; Redemption wore their home purple, the school's crest across their chests.

As usual, Dirk won the tip. He worked a right-side isolation, drawing the defense's eyes, and Aiden saw an opportunity to cut along the baseline. He moved for the hoop, gathering a pass and attacking the rim in one fluid motion; he soared for the hoop, his arms outstretched—

A buzzer exploded in his ears, and his whole body twitched, an electric shock from above. He collapsed to the ground, covering his face to hide as the ball fell on top of him.

When he opened his eyes, Dirk was standing over him, offering a hand. "You good?" he shouted down. The referee was signaling toward the scorer's table. Someone had accidentally triggered the buzzer.

"I'm good." Aiden helped himself up.

They backed down the court on defense. "I got him," Dirk said, pointing to Justus, but Aiden waved him off. "No way." Aiden put his mouth guard in and blinked, the world going dark for a full second. When it came back, Justus was already into his first move, crossing right. Aiden compensated too hard, dropping a step and giving him a few feet of space. It was all Justus needed—step back, fluid stroke, good for three. The gym deflated.

Aiden's body wasn't right. It was like his muscles were trying to fight their way out, prickling against the inside of his skin, demanding his attention. His breathing wouldn't go flat; it kept cresting and peaking, then falling again. He couldn't get the feeling of eyeballs off his back; every time he looked up into the staff section—a sea of black suits—one of them was staring at him. By the middle of the second quarter, he heard his number from the bench. "Forty-five, you're out! Let's go!"

The game came down to the final two minutes, with Redemption down eight, trading threes for fouls to cut the deficit. When Justus missed two free throws with seven seconds left, Dirk came away with the rebound, down two with no time-outs. He dribbled straight to the corner, faking a drive, then a pass, and stepping back for a fadeaway three in the corner. He dropped it, effortlessly. Everyone in the stands charged the court, his teammates piling on top of him.

Aiden had sat the entire second half. Coach Bryant hadn't looked at him once.

Aiden bolted to his locker as the gym celebrated. He loaded everything into his duffel and slid out the back door before any of his teammates made it off the court. There was a team meeting after the game, but the team meetings only mattered for the people who played. Which, as of tonight, wasn't him.

He kept his head down on the way back to his dorm. Passing through the Human Lounge, he saw a phone booth in the corner and pulled a twenty from his pocket.

His dad was always excited to hear from him. "How'd the game go?"

"Good. Yeah, good. I mean—"

"Was the scout there? What'd he say?"

"Uh, no. Not yet, it just ended." Aiden held his face stiff as he spoke.

"Should I be getting ready to buy some Dallas apparel? Are we Mavs fans now?"

"Yeah, we, uh—" He turned away as a few students entered the common room, talking loudly. "I didn't get to talk to any of them."

"How many'd you go for? Cool thirty? That McNeil kid can't guard you for shit."

"I don't remember. I was just thinking . . . do you still have those offer letters? From the other high schools?"

"Um." His dad took a long beat. "I don't think so, why?"

"No, just—I know we had a bunch of offers. I wasn't sure if there was maybe something that looked cool."

He could hear his dad whispering to his mom, over the receiver. "No, buddy. It doesn't really work like that."

"Could we try to find something?"

"Am I missing something here? You've still got five months left in the season, you can't just leave now."

"I know, it's just . . ." Aiden watched as partying students, still revved up by Dirk's amazing finish, spilled into the lounge, singing and drinking. "I just feel like this isn't the right place for me anymore."

"The right place for you? Are you saying you wanna quit?"

"I don't know—"

"The world doesn't work like that, Aiden. You committed to playing there. Our family committed to you playing there. You don't get to upend your life when you 'just feel' like it's not working out."

"Do you think maybe I could just come home, then? Until we find something?"

"Aiden, we invested in this. The trainers, the coaches—that wasn't a gift, that was an investment. This is supposed to be your season. I don't understand, what happened?"

Aiden fought to keep his face in place, turning to stare at the wall. "It's . . . fine. It's nothing. Nothing happened. I'm good."

He heard his father rustling off the phone, consulting his mom. He was pretty sure they were in the kitchen, but he could barely picture what their kitchen looked like anymore. When he moved out, they were in the process of remodeling everything, upgrading the whole bottom level. It was probably a different place now.

"I'm sorry, bud," his dad said. "There's nothing we can do. You gotta tough it out."

Aiden put his hand in front of the receiver to block any sound from his mouth.

"Can I send you something? Maybe you're just missing home-cooked food. We could have a driver bring you something from Chili's?"

"No, I'm pretty sure they wouldn't even be able to find us out here anyway."

"Okay. Well, we're looking forward to reading about the game. I'll talk to you later, okay?"

He slammed the phone onto the cradle.

Back in his dorm, he dumped his bag out on the bed and snatched the bag of Apex as it fell. It was entirely his now. He poured a few pills out onto the desk, too many probably, but why would it matter?

His eyes shot around the room in search of a card but got stuck on the photos behind his desk. This was the record of his entire life—a dozen photos from a dozen teams, all of them placing him directly in the center. He was a winner. That was what his dad always said.

On the bed, among the pages from his backpack, was his horse painting he'd drawn one night in her room, their last good night together. She'd doodled at the top, *a revelation from a true artist*, dotting the *i*'s with hearts.

That was how Emma saw him. Not a basketball player, but a shitty painter.

He dropped the painting on the desk and looked at the kid in the photos, smiling comfortably, exactly where he belonged. It looked nothing like the face that reflected back in the glass of the frame.

Maybe Peter was right. Maybe he had been handed all of this. How could he call himself a winner if there was never a chance he was going to lose?

He noticed another page on his bed: his theories from the

first few days of looking for Emma. He smoothed it out. The hoods, he now knew, were Peter and the debate team; the runaway theory was impossible; the plebe kid wasn't working for anybody other than himself.

He hovered over theory four: the school took her. *They got us all here*, Peter had said once; Aiden had written it word-for-word in the margins. *For what?*

Aiden stood up, sucking in a deep breath of air with his nose, suddenly feeling frantic. His eyes bounced around the room for a moment, then in one swooping arm motion, he cleared the trophies, along with the bag of Apex, off his desk and onto the floor.

From his drawer, he grabbed a pen and a fresh sheet of paper.

NEESHA.

THE HALLWAYS OF the dorm outside her room were silent while the entire school partied in the gym. Neesha lay alone on Emma's mattress, watching the small hand on the clock wind backward, counting down to the end of her life. In sixty hours, three thousand six hundred rotations of the small hand, she was going to be expelled from Redemption. Her research, her work, past and present, her dreams, her goals for the future, the lab she was going to own, the discoveries she was going to make— all of it would incinerate in a violent reaction, torching quickly and disappearing into odorless vapor until there was no sign it had ever been there in the first place. It was over.

Emma's plan had worked. She'd made it home safely, leaving Neesha to be blamed for every sale of Apex. Neesha had fallen into every trap. By Thursday morning, Yangborne would realize that only her compound could be responsible for the presence of amphetamines around the school; they'd all understand why she was so desperate to find Emma, and they'd hold her fully responsible.

And yet lying here in this horrible state of suspended animation, she wished for the first time that she could have Emma back. Even if it was bullshit, and Emma's plan had been to manipulate her all along, Emma always knew what to say in the worst moments. She had perspective.

In her backpack, Neesha found the testimonial journal, still untouched. The creases along the spine were thick and defined; it smelled more like Emma than any of her pillows did anymore. She pulled back the first page and read.

For over an hour, she read alone, rocking back and forth slowly, her face the moon hanging over the world of the journal. She was halfway through the entry on Day 15 when she felt her face starting to get hot and tears welling in the corners of her eyes. By the time Emma started therapy, Neesha was crying, uncontrollably.

For the last week, she'd assumed everything about Emma had been a performance, false sadness to manipulate Neesha into helping sell Apex, but here in Emma's private world, it was clear it wasn't. Emma was sad. Truly, profoundly sad. And insecure, and lonely, and deeply invested in the lives of the people around her. Emma needed someone to reach out. And she'd been sitting there for forty days.

Zaza came to her door after the game with a water bottle, half-full, presumably of vodka. She hid the journal under her pillow and tried to wipe her face before answering, but as soon as he saw her, his eyes got wide. "Holy shit."

"What?" she tried to snarl, but the word caught in her throat.

"Nothing, I've just never seen you . . ." He rubbed the top of his head. "Your face is a little red. Can I come in?"

She fell back onto her bed, leaving the door open for him.

"I heard about the hearing," he said, offering her the water bottle. "That sucks. Do you think they know anything about . . ."

The liquor stung her lips, the roof of her mouth, and her tongue. She drank anyway, forcing down two full swallows. "Yep," she said. "And if they don't yet, they will by then."

He leaned back in her desk chair. "You can fight it," he said. "Appeal to their thirst for excellence. Say you were only doing it to win the trophy."

"I was only doing it to win the trophy."

"Well then tell them that."

She shrugged. "It's not gonna matter."

He sat up. "Don't cry about it, Neesha. That's what an *inert* person would do." He smiled, intentionally turning her words on her. "You're not inert. Fight it."

"I'm not crying about it," she muttered.

"Oh." He sat back. "Then . . . what are you crying about?"

Her first instinct was to lie or find some excuse to avoid having to tell him anything, but her excuses had run out and all that was left in their place was a confusion she was desperate to share, so instead, she pulled the journal from below the pillow.

"Is that . . . Emma's?"

She nodded.

"Where did you find that?"

"Evan had it."

"God, I fucking hate that kid," he said. "What, uh . . . what's it say?"

Neesha flipped it open on her lap and shrugged. "Not much about anything. The story of a girl who was sad and trying a million different ways to make it better. And her roommate who didn't do anything about it."

Zaza grinned. "Sounds kinda cheesy."

The crease found the last entry, the day she'd disappeared. She'd written a single sentence: *out into the world, 2 find my place.*

Neesha read it again and sniveled. "I was so obsessed with that fucking trophy. She was sitting here, the entire time, painfully sad, and I wasn't noticing, because all I cared about was my shit. She probably only even wanted to sell it so I'd focus on something else for a change, but I never . . ."

She read the entry again. *out into the world, 2 find my place.*

"You never what?"

Neesha stood, dropping the journal on the bed and floating to the door, pulling it open to see the front. The school had sent a maintenance worker to scrub off the Magic Marker, but a faint outline remained, faded against the metallic blue door. *she's going 2 die.*

Not *to die. 2.*

"What are you doing?" Zaza asked, following her out.

Neesha stared into it, finally seeing what had been right in front of her all along. The branches, the threatening message on her door, the final entry in the journal. It was a simple code, a binary. "1" was yes, "2" was no. "1" was good, "2" was bad. "1" was safe, "2" was—

"Evan was right," Neesha said, gripping the door to keep her balance. "She's still here. Emma never left."

EVAN.

HE LAY IN bed, focusing on his eyelids. They popped open every forty to sixty seconds, and the harder he concentrated on keeping them shut, the worse it got. He pictured Emma, heard her reading, "eternally, endlessly," his breathing started to even out, "you tried to make a place for me." It had been at least two minutes, or maybe three minutes, they were naturally closed now, he could feel himself drifting—

The electric fence snapped. His eyes shot open.

He needed to rest. It had been seventy-two, ninety-some-thing, a hundred and twenty hours since he'd slept. He'd logged at least twelve more hours in a sleeping position, but inside his immobile body, his brain still whirled.

She hadn't escaped. She wasn't at home. The only reason the school would make an announcement like that was if they wanted people to stop looking. Whoever had her was moving into their endgame.

He could hear other students outside partying. The game had ended two hours ago but enough Years Ones had tried alco-hol for the first time tonight that no one was going to sleep.

Even the professors were still awake and celebrating. He could hear kids laughing like there was nothing wrong. Like they weren't stuck here. Like something wasn't coming for them.

No one was even talking about the fence anymore. No one took it seriously. Other students heard, and they assumed it was exaggerated. Some plebe in his Compassion Lab said he'd seen it before and it wasn't that bad. And Neesha seemed to want to pretend that it had never happened, and that Evan didn't exist.

Even more ignorantly, everyone believed the school about Emma. They believed she just walked away, somehow got past the fence, and was sitting at home in Kansas. Without ever telling any of them she was going to leave. Without even packing a single thing.

He heard a door slam across the hall and clutched his blanket above him tighter. Sleep wasn't coming. His brain wouldn't stop. He shot out of bed and threw on a black hoodie.

S5—Rationale, S5—Rationale, S5—Rationale; he could feel his *S4—Emotions* about Neesha and the school getting the best of him; he was losing control of the *S8—Consequences* of reckless behavior. He needed to control his actions, but how could he when nothing he was doing was having any effect on the world around him. Something was causing the system to break down. What was causing the system to break down?

He went straight to Dr. Richardson's office and slammed on the door with his open palm. Nothing happened. He tried again, harder and faster, his hand starting to glow hot with pain. He hit it harder, again and again and again, but there was no sound behind the door. He glared down at the keypad. With a deep breath, he punched in the code he'd seen Dr. Richardson enter twice. The perimeter glowed green.

The smell of her room rushed out first. He took a few steps inside, but the room wasn't empty. Dr. Richardson scurried back behind her desk from somewhere on the right side of the room. "Evan!" she almost screamed. "How did you get in here?"

He took another step into the room and froze. Eddy was sitting in the chair in front of the desk. He didn't turn around.

"I need to talk to you," Evan said.

Dr. Richardson glared. "We're in the middle of a session. How would you feel if someone barged in on the middle of one of our sessions?"

Evan stared at the back of Eddy's head. He wasn't moving. "I want to talk about my feelings. I need to talk to you about Emma."

Dr. Richardson narrowed her gaze. "Evan, are you feeling alright? You look like you're experiencing a tremendous amount of anger—"

"I'm fine, I just need to talk. I'm ready to be honest—"

"Evan," she cut him off. "I don't believe you're fine, and I can't speak to you until you calm down."

"She's n-not at home," he explained. "The school is lying."

"Evan." She wasn't even listening to him. "Identify the anger. Locate where it's coming from and control it."

"Y-y-you're not listening," he screamed. "She wouldn't go home and the school is looking for her, something happened that they're not saying! They're ly-ly-lying . . ."

She let him grind himself to a stop. "You're out of control, Evan," she said. "I won't tolerate that in my office."

"But—"

"Emma's fine. I spoke to her myself."

Electric flashes went off in his brain, one after another. "B-but . . . why? Why did she go home?"

Dr. Richardson checked on Eddy. He still hadn't moved. Evan noticed that the items all over her cabinets on the right side of the room were rearranged; a few of the framed photos were facing downward. "Over the last few months, Emma and I spent a lot of time together. I'm not sure if you spoke to her much about it, but she wasn't very happy at Redemption."

"I know, but she had to—she had so much t-to . . . I—I—I was gonna—"

"She wasn't feeling well, Evan. People who aren't well sometimes do things that don't make sense," she said. "If they could control their emotions, that might not happen as often. Emma will be back. Now leave my office, immediately. I'm in the middle of a session."

She took three steps toward him and closed the door in his face.

He stood with his nose to the metal for a minute, but behind the door it was completely silent. He settled into a chair in her lobby and waited.

It got later. No one came in, but he could still hear the party raging in the Human Lounge. He looked at the phone booth to his right. There was no one for him to call. There hadn't been for months. He was alone.

What if Emma actually had gone home?

He looked at the magazines on the table. He'd seen all of them before.

What if she decided that this place wasn't good enough for her and just left? What if she didn't need saving from something else, and all the monsters that she was seeing around the campus were actually just hers, and the only person she needed saving from was herself? And he'd failed. He wasn't there, and now she was gone.

He picked up the *Holy Life* magazine. It was worn, read a hundred times, with the story about some pastor in North Carolina on the front. He froze as he flipped it open. There was an Emma doodle on the back page.

This time, it was the story of Peter's instruction from the Lord: *On the rock, I will build my home; and the Gates of Hades will not overcome it. —Thessalonians 9:30.*

It was jotted down, with the spirit of an absentminded illustration, a roof over the central two letters in "home," the way people draw when they forget their drawing, but the work was precise—the angle of the roof was perfected and intentional. Evan read the verse aloud several times over, the words getting louder in his head. He shook it, shaking the cobwebs, jarring the memory loose. *On the rock, I will build my—*

He sat up.

He could hear the words in a voice. Not his own, not Emma's—

Flesh and blood hath not revealed it to thee. The voice was just above his head, smiling down, two feet, close enough to feel. *But my father is in Heaven.* The fifth row. The red satin cushion on the pew. The leftover sting of last night's cold. His mother's bony hand. "Isn't that amazing, Evan? Simon thought he'd figured it out on his own." It was warm like she always was. "But it was him the whole time—" She was smiling like she always did. *On the rock I will build my—*

Evan sat up.

There's a pattern to everything, if you just stand far enough away from it.

AIDEN.

HE SKIPPED PRACTICE the next day, but when Coach Bryant sent the same Year One to find him, he told the kid to get lost. He'd filled one page, then another, then another with his thoughts, scratching them in as fast as his brain could find them, until finally, that afternoon, something clicked.

There was only one person he could tell about it. "You didn't come here for debate," Aiden said as soon as he intercepted Peter in the B-School Lounge.

"Good to see you too, buddy," Peter mumbled, continuing past him. Evidently, he was still upset from the fight where Aiden had called him a degenerate, or maybe from the purple swelling Aiden had placed on his right eye.

But Aiden didn't give up. "You told me that the first night, the school didn't recruit you to debate. You said they found you after the article came out about you speaking twelve languages."

"Big discovery, man. Great stuff."

"They found us through newspapers," Aiden said. "People wrote stories about us, and then they recruited us."

Peter kept walking, passing into the GRC. "Why does that matter?"

"Because it doesn't make sense. Why would they want someone who speaks twelve languages?"

"'Cause that's how recruiting works? You get the best people?"

"What about him?" Aiden pointed across the lounge to a seven-foot-tall Year One, Nico Cruz. Nico was on the basketball team, but he was horrible.

"I don't know, maybe he paid them?"

"You said it yourself. They got us all here, there *has* to be a specific reason. What is it?"

Peter didn't have an answer. He stared past Aiden, while behind him, a group of basketball players followed Dirk across the lounge. Only one, a Year Two in the back, looked over in Aiden's direction; the rest intentionally ignored him.

"Dirk definitely came here for basketball," Aiden mumbled, watching them.

"I've got it," Peter interrupted him. "I know how we can find out."

Peter marched out and Aiden followed, not stopping until they were seated in front of one of the Macintosh computers along the back wall of the B-School library. The school owned a few, and as far as Aiden could tell, their primary purpose was for Year Ones to play Pong, so they didn't have to sit alone at lunch.

"A few of the debaters use this thing. They said the school's just got it in." He punched a few buttons on the keyboard din front of the Macintosh. "You're not gonna believe what we can do with this."

The machine made an awful hissing, popping, groaning, pinging sound.

"Ah, fuck." Aiden covered his ears. "What's happening?"

"That's what it sounds like when it's working," Peter said, rubbing the top. "That's the World Wide Web. All of the information in the world, suddenly available, in only ninety seconds."

On the screen, a large text box appeared, and Peter typed in a few letters. The screen beckoned again, a larger text box this time. "Newspapers sometimes put their stuff on here."

"And then we . . . go to it?" Aiden asked. "We just have to type in the code or whatever?"

"It's even easier than that. It'll find it for us." One by one, Peter punched the letters N-I-C-O C-R-U-Z—the machine whirred to life.

He leaned into the screen, staring up and down. *Nico Cruz dot com, the home of Mexican Superstar Nico Cruz—the Nico Cruz fan club—Nico Cruz and Mariah Carey Seen on a Boat Together—*

"Holy shit," Aiden said. "Nico's secretly famous. Why wouldn't he tell us all of this stuff?"

Peter cleared his throat. "I think that's a different Nico Cruz."

He pointed to the photo with Mariah Carey; the short Mexican man didn't look anything like Nico. "Oh. Okay."

"Where's he from again?" Peter asked.

"Nova Scotia." Peter typed that in, after Nico's name, and the machine whirled again. Sixty seconds later, there was one main line of text at the top of the screen—

WORLD'S TALLEST TEENAGER AND HIS LIFE IN NOVA SCOTIA

Peter fell back into his chair.

Aiden swallowed, continuing to stare at it. "Why would they want that?"

He pulled the keyboard toward himself and pushed in E-V-A-N A-N-D-R-E-W-S—and the computer answered again.

VERMONT BOY BECOMES SECOND PERSON TO BEAT COMPUTER IN CHESS

"I thought that was Bobby Fischer."

Peter shook his head. "Evan's the second one, but that makes sense. Of course you would want a kid with a brain like that."

"So much that you'd pay for him to live and go to school? For any of these people—are they really worth it, just for simple recruiting?"

Peter spun the keyboard back toward himself. E-M-M-A D-O-N-A-H-U-E—

THE SUN AND THE SKY: AN EIGHTH-GRADE POETRY BOOK SELLS ONE THOUSAND COPIES

Aiden ripped a piece of paper from a textbook on a table next to them. "So that's . . . an actor, a poet, a chess player, a giant, and a guy who speaks twelve languages."

Peter nodded. "Yeah, man. That doesn't really look like normal recruiting."

"It doesn't look like anything."

Peter stared at the list for another long moment. Slowly, using just his index fingers, he punched in: E-D-D-Y V-E-L-A-S-Q-U-E-Z.

The machine whirred, producing another full page of results in only sixty seconds. They scanned for a few moments, past a click about a Realtor in Cleveland, and a click about a minor league baseball player, but none of the results had anything to do with their Eddy.

"Wait, go back to the typing part," Aiden said, leaning over him. In the search bar, he deleted the "-dy" of Eddy, and typed "W-A-R-D." "Okay." He nodded. "Go."

Peter pressed go, and as soon as the first result showed up, Aiden felt his mouth go dry.

BOY THEOLOGIAN: TWELVE-YEAR-OLD EDWARD VELASQUEZ IS A BIBLICAL SCHOLAR

Neither of them said anything as Peter clicked through to the article. Evidently, at age twelve, the Edward Velasquez of the World Wide Web had memorized the Bible and could recall every individual verse on command. Aiden could hear Peter muttering incoherently to himself in his right ear as they read, offering a few "what the fucks?" as they tried to reconcile the article with the Eddy who exploded in church. Finally, when the page ran out, they both sat back and settled on the same question.

Peter asked it out loud. "What the fuck happened to him?"

Aiden shook his head, instead studying the article again. It didn't look anything like a newspaper; rather, all of the articles had looked somewhat similar. "It's amazing that all of this is on the World Wide Web already," he said. *"All* these newspapers use it? Even the one in Nova Scotia? That's crazy."

"Yeah, I guess—oh, no. Wait." Peter pointed to the corner of the screen. "This isn't a newspaper site. They're all coming from the same website. They're all posted . . ." He made a click at the top, and the main box went white. "It's loading, this page must be a bear."

Slowly, the web page started to fill in from the top, line by line. The colors of the page came in dark—black, with red running down the side. Aiden started to get a sinking feeling as he watched it, like even though he was the one watching the website, really the website was watching him. The design came first; the logo, the Redemption crest in the corner. They started to make out the tops of the letters labeling the page; they were less than a third of the way complete when Peter was able to decipher the word at the top of the page: *RECRUITS*. As soon as the title was fully loaded, a new word popped up, just below the logo where REDEMPTION PREPARATORY ACADEMY was supposed to be, in bold letters—*GRIOU*.

"Excuse me."

They spun. Secretary Phillips was wearing a full robe, standing at the end of the last aisle of books, staring down at the computer.

"Students only have World Wide Web privileges in class, and it's almost curfew. Please turn off that computer immediately."

"Are you serious—" Peter tried to protest.

"Now." Secretary Phillips took another step toward them, a small pointer brandished like a weapon below the sleeve of her robe. "Don't make me call maintenance."

Peter did as she asked, and they gathered their stuff in a rush, their heads down. Secretary Phillips followed them all the way out of the library, watching as they went.

PART VI.

light of the world.

NEESHA.

"THIS IS AN important part of the healing process," Neesha told him. "Punishment empowers the victim to forgive. An eye for an eye. You understand?"

Evan squirmed in front of her. "I know. Consequence."

"Right," she said. "If I could, I would punish you socially by just ignoring you forever, but we don't have that kind of time—"

"I understand."

Without hesitation, Neesha drew her right arm back and swung it open-handed across Evan's face. The skin connected with a sharp and satisfying clap, and Evan fell back onto Emma's bed.

"Wow." Zaza watched from the corner. "That felt good."

Evan sat up quickly, ignoring his cheek, where the pale skin had flushed bright red. "Do you forgive me?"

She nodded. "You were right. Emma didn't go home. She's still here."

Evan opened his bag and handed her a small, folded piece of glossy magazine paper. "I found this in her locker."

It was a doodle, one of hundreds she'd seen Emma draw into the corners of her textbooks, homework, and journals. This one was a Bible verse: *Put on the full armor of God, so that you will be able to sit firm against the devil. —Matthew 7:20.*

"Emma does this everywhere, I don't get it."

When she looked up, Evan was locked onto her with an off-balance stare. "It's wrong," he said. "It's not in Matthew."

"Do you seriously have the Bible memorized?"

"No. But it's not a story about Jesus," he said. His voice was quiet and excited.

"Why would that matter?"

"Read it out loud."

"Matthew. Matthew, seven twenty. Seven twenty . . ." She readjusted on her chair, her eyebrows taking the slow dive from confused to concerned. "P.m. Seven twenty p.m. Matthew. Seven twenty p.m. Ma . . . Monday."

Evan nodded and her heart leapt.

"Seven twenty p.m. Monday. But where would she . . ." She squinted at the image. There was a tiny drawing, the lines of a basketball sketched into the *o*'s. "A basketball? The basketball court?"

Evan pointed to the end of the sentence. "I looked up the verse. She got one of the words wrong. God doesn't sit firm against the devil. He stands."

The words hit Neesha in the gut.

"The stands, at the outdoor court," Zaza said. "It's a meeting place."

Neesha held up the clip. "She did this everywhere. I've seen these—she was leaving clues. She must have assumed that someone was going to find this, and . . ." She stopped herself. "And we missed it. I missed the meeting place. This was three days ago."

But Evan was already shaking his head. "Except you said it yourself. Emma draws those everywhere." He took another *Holy Life* from his bag. "I was thinking last night about the phone calls. It didn't make sense with her pattern. Why would she call sex people? And why would she go out of her way to use that phone booth? It didn't make sense. Unless there was another reason."

Neesha thought for a moment. "Like leaving behind a message."

He opened to a page near the back, where Emma had scribbled: *On the rock, I will build my home; and the Gates of Hades will not overcome it. —Thessalonians 9:30.*

Neesha looked at him. "I'm assuming that's not from Thessalonians?"

Zaza looked over her shoulder. "Thursday at nine thirty? The night she went missing?"

Evan shifted in his seat. "That's the last part I couldn't understand. When I called the sex people, Yanis kept asking me how many times I did it, even though I only called once. Which means someone else was still calling the number."

"Someone like Emma," Neesha said. "She wrote a message on my door, too. Which means—" She held up the magazine.

"This is for tonight, right after mass." She felt a lump form in her throat. "We're gonna meet Emma tonight."

"Maybe," Evan said.

"Maybe?"

Evan was quiet.

"Or we're going to meet whoever Emma was supposed to be meeting," Zaza said, still staring at the magazine clipping.

Neesha returned to studying the message: *On the rock, I will build my home.* There were small, upside-down arches over the word *home*, with a line jutting directly from their center. "What are those things, like, a wave . . . on a stick? The pool?"

Evan shook his head, smiling for the first time. "It's not a wave. It's a cross. And Peter doesn't build a house. He builds a church."

AIDEN.

"I DON'T GET IT."

Katie, the girl with the wire-rimmed glasses, sighed. It was dark in the back of the B-School Library, and Aiden had to squint to see her. With evening mass starting in twenty minutes, they had to cower out of the light to avoid drawing any attention. "The fact that these professors control the means of production, and students don't own the products of their own labor, makes us an exploited class."

"But we chose to come to school here."

"Forced autonomy is not autonomy. The idea is, a system is corrupted when—"

"We don't have time for Marx, Katie," Peter said. "Let's just say, what the school is doing to us is bad."

Katie shrugged. "Sure. 'Bad.' Breakdown of social order. Same thing."

"I've got something." One of the debaters, Lauren, piped up from behind them. She held a flimsy square of newspaper. "*Black Rock Gazette*, 1960. '*The Black Rock fire department was dispatched after signs of smoke were reported at the Griou Research Center in Wah Wah Springs . . . before the department could locate the facility, the fire was dealt with . . .'"* She read ahead. "Shit. It's nothing."

"No, that's good," Peter said. "That's a record that it actually existed. Save it for background." Peter crouched over a plastic bin. There were twenty-four of them, laid out end to end and zip-tied together, lined with spindle folders and packed full of thousands, maybe millions, of fragile old documents.

"What is this?" Aiden asked, circling it.

"The Clips," Peter explained. "Twenty years ago, one of the debaters here realized Redemption wasn't recording *any* modern history—no newspapers, magazines, nothing. It was basically cut off from the world. So he started saving everything he could get his hands on, and filing it by hand in these tubs. And the debate team's been updating it ever since."

Seven members of the team sat on their knees around the Clips, frantically pulling items from the folders and speed-reading as they went. In the time it had taken Aiden to learn their names, the debaters had already sifted through years of documents, compiling every piece of public information possible to create a timeline of Redemption's history.

"If you guys need any help—" Aiden started.

"We're good." Perfectly in unison, like a choir.

"Princeton Journal, 1955," Mika read. *"'Four professors have departed for the Griou Research Center . . .'* There's a picture of them all. Dr. Yangborne was kind of sexy . . . forty years ago."

The computer monitor, five feet from Aiden, started screeching. One of the debaters sat at the computer, fingers ready.

"Does anybody use actual books anymore?" Aiden asked.

"Yes." Peter rolled his eyes. "Jayme does."

"I heard that," a voice called back from between the stacks.

"Okay." Peter stood, shaking out both legs. "Can we go over what we know? I don't feel like we've found anything useful yet."

The room was silent.

"Okay, I'll go first," Peter said. "The Griou Research Center opened in 1955. It became an elite high school in 1975, and they added the extra buildings—we know that because we've got the first yearbook. What else?"

"It's French?" Mika offered. "Or French-inspired? Puy Griou is a mountain in France."

"The recruiting is making no sense," said Mischa, a German boy whose facial hair Aiden recognized from his photo of the hoods, sitting backward on a chair in the far corner. "You know Peteo? He gets recruited for having the world's roundest head. And Luca Martinez sings onstage with Madonna. That's it. No science at all. No reason."

"I guess . . ." Lauren looked back to her article. "There was a fire in the sixties? But the fire department couldn't find them?"

"It was started by Princeton," Mika added. "Princeton started it, as a research facility—"

"For what?" Aiden asked.

The group was silent.

"What do you mean?" Mischa asked.

"I mean, why start a facility all the way out here? Why start a high school out here? What's it all for?"

"For research," Peter answered, slowly but matter-of-fact.

Aiden shrugged. "Then where's the research?"

It was quiet for another moment, before Frank, the kid at the computer, answered. "There is none."

Everyone turned to him.

"I'm on the Princeton website; they don't list anything about it. They have a web page for all their satellite facilities, past and present—Griou Research Center isn't on here. There are no published papers with the names of any of the instructors. There's a page for Redemption, but—there's nothing on the internet that says 'Griou,' except this *one* website you guys found, which has news articles about students and no more context."

"Okay," Peter said, pacing the room. "What if the research they're doing is secret? There's some reason they don't publish it—"

"What kind of research doesn't get published?" Mika asked.

"Or . . ." Peter stopped. "It's not a research center at all. It's here for another reason." He looked around. *"We're* here for another reason."

Mischa's face lit up. "Like a cult or something?"

"It's already a cult," Katie said. "Christianity is a cult, especially when they force it down our throats like this."

Peter stopped in front of Mika, picking up the article she'd found to read it more closely, then looking around to the group. "I thought the school always said it was five professors? It's five schools. This article says it was four—"

"I found it!" Jayme's voice sang out from between the stacks. "I found it, I *fucking* found it! I knew it. I knew they'd have it! And now I have them!" Jayme came charging out, a stack of old pages in her arms. *"Real books until I fucking die!"*

She dropped them on top of the tubs, and the debaters crowded around.

"What is this?" Peter asked, thumbing through them. Upside down, Aiden could see angular drawings, with scales and numbers, units of measurements surrounding them.

"Building documents," Jayme said. As soon as she said it, he saw it. In the top left corner, it read: GRIOU RESEARCH CENTER. The entire team crowded around and started offering their opinions—

"These are . . . horrible. That's not even a blueprint?"

"Could you actually make a building with that?"

"It looks like it's calling for the whole thing to get made from stone; since when do people in America build with stone?"

"Have you seen the walls in the GRC?"

"Look—the research center wasn't the only building they built."

"How old is this design?"

Their eyes all chased to the bottom of the drawings. Peter said it aloud.

"1851."

The room was silent. The whole library was silent.

"So . . . it's not forty years old." Peter did the math in his head. "It's a hundred and forty years old?"

"What's this?" Jayme flipped the page; there was a design for another building that was just as old. "It's called the Reception Room."

She held it up and everyone leaned closer. It was a small room, with pillars and low walls.

"An office?" Mischa tried.

The next page was a map of the grounds of the school, which placed both buildings. The Reception Room was north of the school, distant from the main building.

"It's so small," Peter said. "Is it possible we've just never really noticed it out there?"

They sat in silence. Jayme turned the map all the way upside down, flipping it right-side up for Aiden.

"Oh," he said. "It's the chapel."

EVAN.

HE SAT IN the third row for evening mass. His classmates looked at him more than usual, but he squeezed his hands together and avoided them. He could feel the instructors watching them, cold water on his neck, staring down at the rats in their maze.

Neesha and Zaza sat in the back row with their heads down. There was no sign of Peter or Aiden.

Father Farke took the pulpit, as always. "Weeks like this," he said, "it's important to remember that we are at our strongest when we are sharing all that we have and all we believe with each other. The foundation of this school, and our illustrious history, is built on trust, an understanding of each other's needs, and an ability to see one another where we stand.

"When Jesus refers to himself as the light of the world, he immediately offers us the opportunity to follow, not so we may grasp for that light, but so that we may *become* it, not just in the world, but in the *kósmou*, meaning 'cosmos,' the entire universe as an orderly and intentional system. 'I am the light of the world, he who follow me shall not walk in darkness' is a challenge to which we can and *must* rise. I see, in all of you, the light of the cosmos shining through. Arise, and fulfill your potential."

When the service was over, Evan, Neesha, and Zaza waited by the benches for the area to clear, then snuck to the base of the cross. They chose a collection of rocks fifty feet away, where they'd be able to see anyone approaching, and watched as the last remaining students dissipated. Following them, most instructors and members of the clergy made the slow walk back to the staff building. Father Farke was the last to leave, hovering in the clearing outside the church. He stared up at the cross and whispered a silent prayer.

"You don't think there's any way this is a setup, right?" Zaza whispered. He sounded scared. "Like, the school leaves a message, then waits to see who shows up?"

"I don't think they're that smart," Neesha said. "Besides, what are we guilty of?"

"I don't know . . . thinking the school is lying?"

"We'll tell them Evan made us do it. And they'll believe us."

Both of them continued ignoring him as they waited.

"Okay, you guys stay here," Neesha said, ten minutes before nine thirty. "I'm going to check the perimeter. If you guys hear anything, let me know."

Evan could feel Zaza watching him as Neesha walked away. He tried not to look over, but as soon as Neesha's footsteps had disappeared around the back of the chapel—

"You might have fooled her for a minute. And she might still be entertaining you for God knows what reason. But I know exactly what you are, plebe." From the sound of Zaza's voice, Evan could tell Zaza was still staring straight at him. "I used to know guys like you, back in Santa Rosa. The creepy, obsessive kind. And you know where most of them are now? Prison."

Evan didn't say anything. Zaza's *S3—Intention* wasn't to help him. No matter what Evan said, the *S8—Consequence* couldn't work in his favor. He spoke with the conviction of a person who had made up his mind.

"Here's what I don't get," he continued, ignoring Evan ignoring him. "How come you can't just yank one off to the idea of her every night, and then leave it alone? Why do you have to take this obsession of yours and make it everybody else's problem? Get in her space, fuck everything up—can't you see how it's just hurting everybody?"

Evan checked his watch: 9:22 p.m.

"And honestly, man, it's hurting you more than anything. You're spending your entire life deciding to feel good about yourself or not based on the opinion of one person, who *doesn't even know you well enough* to have an opinion of you? Is that really a way to live?"

He leaned back like he was done. But he wasn't. "Finally, sorry, not trying to pile on or anything, but last question— what's your plan, or endgame, or whatever, anyway? What do you think is actually gonna come from your peeping and following and . . . stealing her journal and shit? What if she was to turn around and notice you one day—what happens?"

Evan checked for Neesha's return but she was nowhere to be seen.

"Whatever, man. I hope you find what you're looking for. And I really hope that in the process, you don't get Neesha expelled. And honestly, for your sake, I hope you never, ever have a conversation with Emma, 'cause I don't think there's any way that ends well for—"

"Most people are sad."

"What?"

"Most people are sad," Evan said. "And lonely. To those people, there's no such thing as good love or bad love. All love is significant."

Zaza was slow to respond. "Who told you that?" he asked.

"My mom." He swallowed. "Something bad was going to happen to Emma. She didn't have anyone to talk to about it and I could see that it was coming because it happened to my mom.

"If she turned around I would have said hi. I followed her because I wanted to know more about her. I stole her journal because I thought it would help me understand. I had a plan to introduce myself, but then I never got the chance.

"I wanted her to talk to me and like me, but I didn't care that much as long as she was okay. I wanted to be her friend or maybe her boyfriend so I could help her. I didn't want to yank anything off; I don't even know what that is. I just didn't want anything bad to happen to her. I promised myself that I would help her. I watched her because it seemed like nobody else was."

Zaza absorbed it. "All love is important?" he finally asked, and Evan nodded. "Yeah . . . I guess I'd tell you that if you were my kid, too."

"Five minutes," Neesha said, returning. "And nobody even close to the area."

His mom had said that. Many, many times. There was a sermon once where the pastor had talked about imbalances of love; either a love that was given more strongly than the love that was reciprocated, or a love that was given by a person who seemed more worthwhile than the person receiving it and vice versa. But Mom had said she didn't believe in that, and if you start believing in that, it becomes the root of everything that hurts you. She said you could measure and quantify every other part of the world, but when it came to love, there were no scales. The well wishes of a grocery store cashier aren't made less important because some people write love letters; Zaza saying that someone was cute made that person no more or less cute than Evan saying it. All love is significant.

At exactly nine thirty, the door to the church closed, echoing across the back lawn. They stared at the spot.

It took a moment for anything to interrupt the light spilling out from the top of the cross, but slowly, a figure did, creeping in silhouette toward the platform.

"Hello?" Neesha called.

Whoever it was didn't respond, inching closer to them, limping.

"Emma?" Neesha whispered, but there was no response. Evan took a deep breath and began to walk toward the approaching figure. Neither of them said anything as the distance closed, but it sounded like it was mumbling to itself, whispering incantations.

Evan stepped closer still, less than five feet from where the noise had come from. He pulled his flashlight from his belt and shined it, feet first, scanning up the body in front of him.

"Eddy?"

He was wearing the same light blue jeans, metal band T-shirt, and gray sweatshirt that he always wore. He looked as surprised as they were.

"What's he doing here?" Zaza asked, as though any of them would have an answer.

As soon as Evan's flashlight hit Eddy's face, Eddy started blinking, shrinking away from the beam, a moan softly whimpering out of his mouth.

"Eddy, why are you here?" Every time Evan tried to advance, Eddy cowered backward. Evan checked his watch—it was *exactly* nine thirty, just like the code had said. "What are you doing?"

Neesha walked over, stepping between them. Slowly, she reached out her hand and held it there. After staring for a moment, Eddy reached back.

"The flood," he whispered to Neesha. "Th-the flood."

In the bounce of the flashlight, Evan could see that he was squeezing Neesha's hand tight, crumpling her fingers together and turning their tips pale.

Her eyes stayed focused on his face. "What flood?"

"I-it took her," he said quietly. "The flood."

Every time Evan had observed Eddy, his face seemed incapable of registering a response, like his programming was controlled by a far-off system, a virus, that kept him in his own world. But he was actually listening to Neesha.

"What is the flood?" Zaza asked again. "Another code? Something in the Bible?"

Neesha wasn't listening to any of them. She was staring back into Eddy's eyes. "It's not a code. It's a place."

AIDEN.

HE LED PETER around a sloping path toward the chapel, both keeping their heads low. The rest of the students had mostly filtered back to the dorms, but three times, Aiden and Peter had to reverse course quickly to avoid passing maintenance workers in the fog. It was clear there were extra workers patrolling the lawn tonight.

Neither of them spoke, but they both were breathing heavy. "Hey," he whispered. "Sorry I called you a degenerate."

"Shh." Peter sprinted forward, his head below the cut of the grass, stopping at the mouth of a wide path to the chapel.

Aiden caught up. "Seriously, I don't know what I was thinking. I was calling you a shitty person and a failure, meanwhile, I don't even think I *like* basketball—"

"Seriously, shut up," Peter spat back under his breath. "No time for a gushy redemption scene." He turned around. "But thank you."

They sprinted to the main doors, pausing for a second before slipping inside. It wasn't an instructor or a secretary that greeted them.

It was Zaza, cowering in the doorway.

"Are you serious?" he asked.

"What luck!" Peter shouted, pushing past him. "You guys again?" Inside, Evan and Neesha stood huddled in the back. "Wait . . ."

"What are you doing here?" Neesha asked.

"We just read this old blueprint—" Aiden noticed Eddy behind her. He pointed. "He wasn't always like this! When he came to school here, he had the whole Bible memorized."

"A theologian," Peter said, jumping in. "*Not* messed up in the head."

"Jesus." Zaza took a step back. "How much Apex did you guys take?"

"That's all you get from that?" Aiden shouted. "Look, the school is up to something, we've got crazy proof! There was a room here called the Reception Room, and . . ." He took stock of his surroundings. "Why are you guys here?"

"He told us to," Neesha said, nodding to Eddy.

"He *told you*?"

"I know, it sounds ridiculous," she said. "But he kept saying it, so I figured he wanted us to come . . ."

The group followed her eyes as her sentence ran out, into the ground and up the center aisle of the church. Without a word, lost in the crossing glances, Eddy had begun walking forward toward the moonlight entering the front enclave. Neesha's eyes followed behind him, lifting to the enormous portrait at the front of the chapel, glowing blue in the reflection of moonlight off the pews. "The flood."

As Eddy reached the front, he continued around the pulpit and behind it, disappearing underneath what looked like additional pipes for the organ.

They watched the spot where he had disappeared without a word. Ten seconds later, a shadow, a figure, with a walk that wasn't Eddy's, came out from behind the organ.

Aiden felt like the air had been sucked out of him. It was Emma.

EVAN.

AIDEN WAS THE first to rush over to her and wrap her in an enormous hug.

"Oh my God!" Evan could hear him smothering Emma. "Where have you been? God, I've been losing my mind." Aiden held her for a few more seconds before she took herself back, smiling at him but not saying anything, pulling away to take in the small group surrounding her.

She was wearing an oversized black sweatshirt, and leggings, torn at the bottom to reveal a patch of skin on her lower leg; the only skin visible, other than her face. The circles under her eyes were deep red, maybe from not sleeping or maybe from crying or maybe both. But her face still glowed at the front of the church.

Evan took a few steps back, behind Peter. He didn't want to force their moment onto her.

Emma turned to Neesha next. "You found me," she said softly, falling into an embrace. Evan watched Neesha's face begin to shake, and then fully cry.

When they pulled apart, Emma was crying too. She scanned the faces around the room. She buried herself in Zaza's arms and he offered her a *"Holy shit"* in return, patting the top of her head. Next, she turned to Eddy and lowered herself to meet his line of sight. "You did it," she whispered.

"We found him back here, by the cross," Zaza explained.

"No." Emma shook her head, still focused directly on Eddy's eyes. "He found you."

She backed away, radiating outward to the rest of the room, passing over Evan's face to Peter's, then returning to Evan's.

Evan's eyes locked onto Emma's. She froze and just looked at him. Nothing worked. Thoughts stopped. Body still.

Emma's breathing began to pick up. "What the fuck is he doing here?" she whispered.

His heart froze. She was talking about him.

Zaza took a few steps over to her. "Evan?"

The wheels began to spin too fast. *Information*, she knew who he was. *Subtext*, she was angry. *Subtext*, she knows everything. *Consequence*—

Neesha was staring at him, too. "That's Evan. He helped us find you."

Emma looked around wildly. "Are you serious? He was following me!"

Aiden took a step toward him. "I told you, he's fucked up—"

"Why would you bring him here?" Emma was shaking. He was making her shake.

"No, I know." Neesha stumbled. "You don't really know him, but . . ."

"He was spying on me!" Emma threw her hood over her head, blocking any view of her face.

All Evan could see of Emma was the up-and-down of her deep breaths, the movement of her hoodie. She was whispering something into Neesha's ear. *"With them . . . know where I am,"* was all he heard.

His breathing went manic. He could feel his windpipe closing.

It didn't make sense. He didn't deserve this reaction. He was helping. He hadn't lied. Everything he'd done, he'd done to help her. All he'd ever done was show her that he loved her, in exactly the ways that people love each other.

Everyone was staring at him. They hated him. Everyone thought he was a bad guy. Now he was going to have to escape the people he'd thought were his friends. Now he'd never see Emma again. He wanted to scream something, yell at someone, but his mouth was short-circuiting with a perpetual "I—I—"

His eyes landed on Neesha. "Yeah." She was looking at him like she was in pain. "He wasn't working for anybody. He's the one who found you. And he led all of us here."

Emma turned to Neesha, slightly back to him, enough to see the outline of her profile. "But . . ."

Neesha continued before Emma could figure out her question. "He solved your Bible messages."

Zaza leaned in, his hands in his pockets. "I can confirm that. He's super weird, but . . . he's harmless."

Emma buried her face into the sleeves of her hoodie. Evan stared at the back of her hood, the place where her face should be.

"You were following me, just . . . for fun?" she asked into her sleeve.

Evan felt his lungs find their rhythm again and took his first true breaths since entering the church. "It—" He paused for a moment, planning his sentence. "It j-just seemed like you needed someone."

Emma took a deep breath, scrunching her face together, then released it with an audible exhale. "God, that's so weird."

"Let us take care of you." Aiden stepped toward her, but she jumped back.

"No—I'm sorry."

Aiden looked crushed.

Her eyes shot frantically around the church again. "No one knows you guys are here, right?"

Every head nodded.

"You?" Zaza asked.

"No one except Eddy."

"Is it safe for us to be here?" Zaza asked. "People might be looking for us. Should we hide out until there's a better time—"

"Fuck that," Aiden said. "We're here now. I'm not letting you disappear again."

Peter nodded. Neesha stared forward at Emma.

"Zaza's right." Emma bit her lip. Evan had forgotten she did that. "I can't really explain why, but . . . it's better for you guys if you go back."

"Come on." Aiden groaned. "Is it that bad?"

Everyone's heads turned back to Emma once more. "I can't tell you . . . because—"

"Say it," Aiden said.

"I can't tell you . . . because once I tell you, you won't be able to go back."

It was silent in the church.

Aiden raised his head and walked a small loop around Neesha, past Evan, past Peter, and past Emma, to the front of the church. He stopped in the very front pew, turned to look directly at Emma, and sat down.

AIDEN.

THEY SAT ON the floor in the center nave of the church.

Even though all six were hidden from the front door by pews, to be safe they set up a small, cascading security system to protect Emma. Neesha and Zaza would sit in the center aisle, ready at a moment's notice to assume some kind of praying position; they might be able to kill suspicion there. Next were Peter and Evan, who could roll under a pew, who would play the alcohol angle: they'd just come into the church to drink. After that, Aiden would try to charm them, and if not, he was willing to drop a teacher in a minute. He wasn't going to let anyone get to Emma, even if it did seem like she'd forgotten how to be close to him. Finally, Emma and Eddy sat against the altar, ready to slide back beneath it and drop the cover.

Emma talked just louder than the wind whipping the roof of the chapel.

"I'm not sure how to tell—"

"Everything," Neesha insisted.

"Um. Okay. I've been here four years, and I haven't left that entire time. And that's always been okay, because . . . I felt like there was some reward coming, like the school always promised it was going to get better. And this summer, I realized that wasn't going to happen. I got really detached, I stopped talking to people, I kept trying to write poetry and failing and . . . I don't know. I ended up just writing in my journal, all the time.

"I didn't think anything was gonna come of it, but I could tell I was . . . slipping. When the school year started, I tried to get it together. I started taking Apex." She nodded to Neesha. "And that helped for a little bit, but then I started taking it all the time. I thought having a boyfriend might help, but . . . nothing was working."

Aiden shifted in his pew but didn't say anything. The pit in his stomach turned to stone. That was how she felt about their relationship. It was a part of the "nothing."

"On Day Twenty, Dr. Richardson approached me. She said I'd been doing really interesting work in class, and she wanted to talk more about it. And I didn't understand that, because my grades were terrible, I wasn't writing anything other than my journal, so I didn't know what she was talking about. It ended up being therapy." Emma said the last word cautiously. "She said I was depressed, and I needed help."

Emma shifted uncomfortably against the altar. "Dr. Richardson seemed to be really interested in it, like it was really important, and it felt good, to have someone caring that much. So I started going, every day, sometimes twice a day. And it was helping, honestly. I'd never talked that much about how I felt. But the further we went, the better I got . . . the more she'd push it.

"On Day Thirty-Two, she asked if we could try to re-create some of the experiences I talked about. I didn't really get it, so I said okay, but . . ." Emma choked up. "She'd gotten tapes . . . of my family, from back home. My dog. Old teachers . . . everything I had talked about, even some stuff that I hadn't."

Aiden felt cold air against his spine. His dad had asked him about videos he'd made for Coach Bryant. Which meant they were building files for everyone.

"She'd play them and force me to watch. When I tried to leave, she wouldn't let me. So I had to just sit there and listen, and . . . she kept telling me that instead of trying to overcome them, I should try to get myself back to that place. So I could experience it again, so I could understand what sadness was. She said I had to know my emotions before I could control them."

Every time she'd pause, the room would sit perfectly still. Aiden tried to focus on what she was saying, to take it seriously, but when it was silent for long enough, he couldn't stop himself from drifting to the best moments they'd spent together—lying on her bed, sitting on the bleachers at the court—none of it had been real. He'd been an experiment for her, and a failed one at that. He held his face steady while she continued.

"I'd see Eddy," she said, "every time I was leaving. He always had a counseling session after mine, but I couldn't understand what he and Dr. Richardson talked about. He couldn't communicate, so what good was therapy? But just from the way he acted when he saw her, the way he was around her, in that room . . . I knew she was doing something worse to him.

"I started staying late after my sessions, so I could try to see Eddy. I figured if I could talk to one other person who knew what I was going through, it would help me . . . I don't know. And it did." She looked over at Eddy; he didn't look back. "He couldn't talk, but I knew he could hear me, and he was trying so hard. He'd grab my hand, and I could tell from the way he squeezed it . . . that he was trying to tell me he could understand.

"It was weird, like he couldn't figure out how to say or do anything with his face, but he knew what was going on. He kept motioning to my textbooks, so one day I opened one of mine up, and I started writing, and he started squeezing my arm, with the number of letters in every word. So I wrote, *touch my shoulder*, and he did."

"He can read?" Aiden asked.

Emma nodded. "Then one day Dr. Richardson came out of her office and she saw us together, and she *freaked*. She said we should never speak, and should try to avoid being in the same place, because we'd ruin each other's progress. That was when I knew that what she was doing to him was messed up. That he wasn't like this when he came to school. She made him like this, and I could tell that Eddy was warning me—she was gonna start doing it to me too.

"So we had to find a secret way of talking to each other, something Dr. Richardson wouldn't notice or understand. I realized, pretty early in my assessments—she didn't know *any-thing* about the Bible. So I started scribbling Bible verses in the margins of magazines, with clues about where and what time to meet—and then I'd leave them on her table."

"Wait," Aiden interrupted. "You want us to believe he still has the Bible memorized?"

"He does," she snapped. "And I don't care what you believe."

Aiden sat back.

"My therapy kept getting worse. Dr. Richardson would call me in three, four times a day, usually pulling me out of class. I knew it wasn't normal, but I couldn't talk to anybody about it. I tried to write about it, but she could read my journal, so . . . there was nowhere for me to hide.

"Last week, I collapsed in her office, after she showed me a video of my mom talking about me . . ." Emma choked, then caught herself. "Talking about me like I wasn't there, or like I didn't exist anymore. It was a real video. I don't know where she got it. And then . . . when the video was done, she just picked up with it, laying into me, like she was my mom, and . . ." Emma stopped herself and swallowed, hard. "She apologized after, but . . . she didn't mean it. I knew I'd stopped getting better, but she seemed to just be happier and happier. I told her I wanted to stop, but . . . she said I was making too much progress. And we couldn't go back now."

Emma cleared her throat. "I knew she wasn't going to stop. That whatever she was doing, it wasn't regular therapy. So I decided I had to get out. I figured if I had enough money I could pay some of the maintenance workers to let me go," she said, turning to Neesha, "so that's when I told you that we should try selling Apex." She turned to Aiden. "And I convinced you to start buying."

Aiden's whole body tensed. Their relationship was worse than nothing. It was another hustle.

"Dr. Richardson could tell I was up to something, so I started noticing maintenance workers hovering around me, all the time. Last week, that tall guy showed up—"

"Yanis," Neesha said.

"Right. I think she brought him in just to keep an eye on me. I realized none of these guys are maintenance, and they never were. They're security."

"I was fucking right," Aiden whispered.

"Then, on Day Forty, I passed Eddy on his way into a session, and he grabbed my wrist. I don't know how I knew what he meant, but . . . I did. I waited thirty minutes, and then I doubled back. Eddy had propped the door to Dr. Richardson's office open, so I went in. I didn't see them, but I could hear him, whimpering, from somewhere inside of the office.

"There was another room—a room I didn't know about. The door was hidden behind some of the books in her office, but it was cracked open. I looked in, and . . . I saw the next stage of the therapy."

Aiden leaned closer. His palms were sweating.

"Eddy was sitting on a chair, in the middle of the room. There was a bunch of tubes running straight into his head, and . . . there were computers, and machines in a big cabinet where Dr. Richardson was sitting. Behind her, hooked up to the tubes, there was this . . . big, white, metal . . . funnel, going all the way up to the ceiling. I tried to stop myself, but . . . I gasped, and she saw me.

"She didn't even look surprised or anything, almost like she knew I was going to be coming. She said it was a more advanced form of therapy, one the school itself had developed, that depended on reading some kind of . . . brain activity, or something."

"Neural impulses," Neesha whispered.

Emma shook her head. "I'm sorry, I don't know."

Zaza sat up. "What was the machine for?"

"She said it was the reason they built the school in the first place. *This* was the purpose of the Griou Research Center, but it wasn't always called that. It was the Alo—I don't remember, something with an *A*. She didn't tell me what it meant."

"So it's not the GRC." Evan put it together immediately. "It's the ARC. The arc."

No one said a thing, but the mural loomed enormous over them, Noah's ark flying away from the burning world.

"She didn't tell me anything else about it." Emma was speaking faster, rushing to get through it. "And she said I should go, because she had to finish Eddy's session. But I know it has something to do with really bright lights, or something . . . because every time he sees bright, flashing lights, he freaks out, and . . . I don't know. I'm sorry I don't know any more than that.

But whatever it is, I knew it's what . . . did that to him.

"So I ran to my room, and I packed up like, three things, and . . . and . . . and I tried to get my half of the money from Zaza—and I went to church. I saw Dr. Richardson watching me, so I volunteered to do the candles. Then, as soon as I got to the back—" She winced. "I started to flicker the lights . . . because I knew it would cause a reaction from Eddy. I'd seen him freak out before, and I knew it would get everybody's attention, especially Dr. Richardson's."

She ran her hand over Eddy's head gently and leaned it in her direction. He hadn't reacted during the entire story. He was unnaturally emotionless, so robotic, that his skin looked like it would be cold to the touch.

"Then, I just . . . faded into the chaos. Zaza didn't have the money yet when I asked, so I took the envelope from your jacket"—she nodded to Neesha—"and I disappeared into the woods. I went to bribe a maintenance worker, but by that point, they were all looking for me. I couldn't get over the fence without setting off warnings, so I came back to the one place I knew the instructors never went—the chapel." She looked up, behind her, to the mural in the nave. "The flood. And I've been here ever since."

"You managed to avoid them in here for a whole week?" Zaza asked.

Emma shook her head. "They're not actually Christians. None of them. No one ever comes in here, except for mass. Whatever this place is, it's just for show. And these stories"—she pointed to the murals on the wall—"they're all wrong. It's like they drew the murals without reading the actual Bible. This school isn't Christian. It's something else."

"They're not Christians," Peter said slowly. "It's not real therapy. There's no real research. Then what is this place?"

Emma took a deep breath and shook her head. "I don't know. But it's not a school."

They all sat breathless, the stale air of the misplaced chapel pressing down on them.

"It's like . . . a human laboratory. Or a training facility, or something. They're training us, and testing us, for something. That's why they're always evaluating us with *everything*, making us write in the journals . . . they're trying to, I don't know, make us supernatural or something."

The room sat in silence. It was impossible to tell if people believed her, or if they were too stunned to respond.

"That's why they recruited us," Aiden said. "They were searching local news articles, looking for the most . . ."

"*Evolved*," Emma said. "That's the word she always used. She'd say she liked talking to me because I was evolved. . . ."

"Everybody gets bussed in," Neesha said, staring at the back of a pew. "I bet no one even knows where we are."

Peter sat up in the rearmost pew. "Why now?" he asked. "For the school. Why are they gonna start doing this shit now?"

"She wouldn't have let me see it if she wasn't going to do it to me," Emma said quietly.

"But why you?" he asked.

"Does it matter?" Neesha asked.

"Yeah, it does. The school's been open for twenty years; if they were torturing people with the ARC, we'd have known it by now."

"We do know about it," she said, pointing to Eddy.

"If it failed with Eddy, why would they try it again?"

"Maybe it didn't fail," Evan offered.

Everyone turned to reexamine Eddy, focused on nothing at the front of the church. It was hard to view him as the positive outcome of an experiment.

"Still," Peter argued, "that's *one* person, at least four years ago. He might be thirty. Most of us are graduating in eight months; why do we think everybody's suddenly in danger?"

"He's right," Zaza jumped in. "They're not gonna start doing this to all of us. Which means we should go back, soon, and figure out what to do from there."

"We can't go back there!" Neesha protested.

"What else would we do? We can't stay here," Zaza said.

"They're right," Emma said quietly. "There's nowhere to hide."

Everyone was quiet for a minute, no one saying the worst part out loud: going back meant abandoning Emma.

Aiden took her in again, really looking at her, instead of the reflection of her he'd always seen. Her hair was matted and tangled, her eyes were creased, and her cheeks were red from crying. Her entire body looked weak.

Without thinking, he stood up and walked to the front of

the chapel. Her saw her shoulders tighten as he sat next to her.

"I'm sorry," he said before she could speak. "I was a shitty boyfriend. You were going through hell and I could only see how it was affecting me."

Emma nodded. "You had a lot on your mind," she said.

"But I didn't have to. You always said that—I didn't have to." He stopped himself. "This isn't about me. I just want you to know I'm sorry. I'm sure all you were getting out of our relationship was sex. . . ." He paused, letting her respond.

"Not really." She winced. "That was pretty bad, too."

He took a deep breath. "Right. Well, then I'm not sure what you were getting out of this. But I know I was taking too much."

They sat in silence. "How was the game?" she finally asked, quietly.

He shrugged. "I barely played. I think Dirk's gonna get drafted, and I'm . . ." He looked around. "I don't know what's gonna happen to me."

They sat in silence for another long moment. He could feel the others watching them; he felt exposed, in front of this many people, but he couldn't make it matter. "Okay." He finally exhaled and pushed himself up. "Thanks again for . . . you know. Everything."

He dropped himself back into the pew next to Peter, who leaned in immediately. "We gotta go back," he whispered. "There's nothing saying that the school is gonna do this to all of us, or any of us. But if they find out that we know, or that we know where she is . . ."

"Wait." Neesha sat up at the front of the church. "Wait. Oh my God."

She closed her eyes in concentration. Everyone else watched her in silence. "What?" Peter finally asked.

"They're testing us, all the time. And recording all the results, right?"

Emma nodded.

"What if something happened recently that caused all of the results to get . . . dramatically better? Something that made them think that what they were doing was working—that we were ready, or whatever. That it was time to start using the ARC."

She stared at Emma, who stared back, horrified.

"Holy shit," Aiden said. "You're right." He reached into his pocket, and in front of them, he dropped the baggie of the remaining silver pills.

NEESHA.

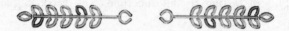

NEESHA REMEMBERED TWENTY-FOUR hours earlier, lying in her room, when she'd been paralyzed by fear that she might get kicked out. It was almost funny, thinking about all the things that seemed so serious and important then.

Scenes of her four years here played back in terrifying clarity. The free tuition, the insane curriculum, the global recruiting, the calls for exceptionalism, the emotional assessments, the meals and supplements—there was no reason for any of it unless there was some larger end the school was moving toward. It had always been there. There was always a voice, just beyond all the instructors, whispering a direction, suggesting a plan for the students.

She thought Redemption was her escape, but it was the opposite. It was a cage, in a much larger reality. And she didn't even know the worst of it. Her eyes drifted to Emma, seated with her eyes closed and her head rolled back against the altar. Emma had chased the same promise—new place, new life, the ability to be the best and the reward that came with it—and had fallen further into the trap.

Neesha walked cautiously to the front of the nave, sliding onto the ground next to Emma, taking her own piece of altar. It was a long moment before either of them said or did anything, just breathing the same air and staring forward at the same low-resolution, inky-black church, watching the spot where it disappeared into darkness. Finally, Emma let her hand fall softly onto Neesha's. Neesha slid her fingers through Emma's and squeezed.

"I'm sorry," Emma said.

"You're sorry?" Neesha almost rolled her eyes. "I can't believe I didn't know . . . all of that was happening."

"I'm really good at hiding stuff."

Neesha swallowed. "You were trying to tell me. You were trying to tell me to focus less on that stupid trophy, and I didn't . . . I should have said something."

Emma shook her head. "I set you up. I shouldn't have gotten you involved at all. I made you sell your project, then left you to take the blame. If they would have found out . . ." Her eyes fell to the floor in front of them. "When they find out. It'll be even worse for you."

Neesha tightened her hand around Emma's, her grip so delicate Neesha was afraid squeezing might shatter it like glass. In every picture of Emma in Neesha's head, the delicacy was an act, a false flag waved for attention and pity. Holding Emma's hand and sitting this close, hearing her story and reading her journal, Neesha knew it wasn't.

"It's funny." Emma's eyes were puffy from crying but soft as always, as though she was mid-joke. "A few months ago, I thought I had problems."

Neesha smiled painfully.

"I wrote in my journal, *This is the worst my life has ever been.*" Emma shook a few tears out of her eyes. "I don't know why I even thought it was a good idea to write that. It's like I was trying to make it worse on purpose." She sniveled and it echoed through the church.

"Why do you think she picked you?" Neesha asked.

"I don't know . . ." Emma's body had a small but constant rock back and forth. "Because I'm depressed, maybe. So if something happened to me, it wasn't a total loss."

Neesha let the words sit, staring down at their thumbs. "What've you even been eating? And drinking?"

"Communion bread," Emma said, again trying a small laugh. "The body of Christ. And Eddy's been bringing me water."

"That's healthy."

"It's getting pretty old." Emma turned back to the defeated faces around the room. "I wish I'd never told you guys any of this."

Neesha felt Emma shaking softly, from withdrawal, or fear, or exhaustion, or cold, or all of it. She watched her for a moment, Emma's dull white cheeks heaving with every earned breath. They couldn't go back. Emma couldn't go back. She needed help.

"We have to get out of here," Neesha whispered so only Emma heard her.

Emma didn't respond.

"All of us," she whispered again. "We have to get all of us out of here."

"I've spent five days trying to escape, just Eddy and me. Trust me, there's no way out."

Neesha nodded. Evan had sat up in the front pew and was staring at them, or rather, staring at Emma. Peter and Aiden were silent, watching them from the third pew. They were all waiting for Emma to tell them what to do.

"You know why I think the school picked you?" Neesha asked, again out of earshot of anyone around them, quiet enough to only exist in the tiny bubble they'd created.

Emma shook her head.

"Because everybody cares about you. And you know why I think that is?"

Emma stared back at her, wet eyes unblinking.

"Because you care about everybody. And that's a fucking mystery, and a miracle, and probably the most evolved thing I've ever heard."

Emma almost smiled, looking at Neesha with her eyes barely open. "You're crazy."

Neesha nodded a few times. "And that's why we're gonna get ourselves out of here. All of us. Tonight."

A few others around the room sat up, turning their faces toward hers. "Tonight?" Emma whispered in disbelief.

"No way," Zaza said, shaking his head. "No way, this can't end well."

Neesha sat up, speaking directly to him. "So either we go back in there, put our heads down, pray we don't get caught, and keep auditioning for them, day in and day out, hoping we can make it out on the other side . . . or we run like hell."

Zaza stared back for a moment before swallowing. "Okay," he said. "Okay. Tonight."

She looked up to Aiden, who was staring at the top of Emma's head. "Fuck it. Tonight." Behind him, Peter sat up and nodded. "Tonight."

Emma sat up. "What about them?" She jerked her head toward the door of the church.

"Who?" Neesha asked.

"Everyone else."

They followed Emma's gaze down the center aisle, through the walls of the church, to the school, where hundreds of students were obediently gathering in their dorms, completely unaware that their lives were controlled and engineered for torture.

"We get evidence," Neesha said, more confidently than she felt.

Emma shook her head. "How would we get evidence? There's nothing, except . . ." She stopped.

Neesha read her eyes. "Exactly."

They got wider. "I can't . . . I can't ask any of you to—"

"I'll do it." Evan had been quiet for most of their time in the church. "I—I'll g-go in there for you."

Emma swallowed, and with her last drop of remaining energy, she squeezed Neesha's hand tighter.

PART VII.

the flood.

⦾⦿⦿⦿⦿─○─○─⦿⦿⦿⦿⦾

AIDEN.

BREATHING HEAVILY, AIDEN walked down the hallway, straight for the Human Lounge. There were a few extra maintenance workers moving up and down the halls, but Aiden had been out past curfew enough to understand how to avoid them. He took a moment to collect himself. Other than the crackling of the disappearing fire, the lounge was quiet.

As Peter had pointed out, most of Aiden's life had been a low-stakes experiment. He tried to remember a time when he'd felt anywhere close to this nervous, or this helpless, and the best he could come up with were bad tournament losses and poorly attended birthday parties. When he was twelve, there was a day that his parents thought he might have pneumonia, but it turned out to just be a cold. Candy shit, as Peter called it.

But not tonight. He knocked on Dr. Richardson's door.

It took several minutes, but she answered, poking her head out slightly. "Aiden?"

"I need to talk to you—"

"Why aren't you in your dorm room, Mr. Mallet? Are you confused?"

"Something happened."

Aiden looked past her into the office—the four men crowded around her desk were the heads of the four schools, as well as Father Farke.

"It's past curfew, Mr. Mallet. If you need me to call someone to escort you to—"

"It's about Emma." The men inside the room exchanged glances.

"What about—"

"We found her."

NEESHA.

"WHAT LANGUAGES DO you speak?"

The boy in the dorm, Lai, shrugged. "English and Mandarin?"

"Peter," she whispered, and he came rushing down the hall toward them.

"We have a very important responsibility for you," Peter picked up immediately.

"Why are you speaking Mandarin?" Lai interrupted him.

"So it's private," Peter responded.

Lai's eyes widened.

Neesha tried the door across the hallway, prepping Peter for his next private conversation. If there were only English speakers in the dorm, they skipped it and moved on to the next, so as not to risk being overheard by the English-speaking staff. Almost everyone asked why Peter was speaking their native tongue. No one questioned their request.

"—but you need to start exactly at two a.m., not a second before or after. Can you handle that?" she heard Peter telling Lai, in the

last dorm on the top floor of D4.

"Two a.m.?" Lai asked, in English.

"Right," Peter slipped. "Two a.m."

"What happens at two a.m.?"

Neesha shot upward, the voice behind her pouring cold water down her back. A maintenance worker stood ten feet behind them. "What are you doing out of your dorms?"

"Oh, yes, what up? What up, what up?" Peter said, trying to shut the door.

The maintenance worker caught it with his foot. "And what happens at two a.m.?"

"A homework thing, we're trying to link up our study schedules."

"Of course," he said, pointing to Lai. "I'm sure he won't have any problems explaining it to me, then. What did these two instruct you to do at two a.m.?"

Lai was the last person she wanted to trust to lie for them. One time Lai read a poem for a girl he liked on the intercom when he was supposed to be giving a speech for class parliamentarian. Lai was completely transparent.

His eyes shot back and forth between the three of them. "In my home country," Lai started, his accent strangely strong, "we have a, uh, a—what do you call it in this country, Peter?" He switched to Mandarin; Neesha couldn't understand it, but guessed the rough translation would be, *"What the fuck am I supposed to say?"*

"Um, I guess the best translation would be . . . energy-based study session. Like a . . ." Peter switched to Mandarin, and Lai nodded.

"We believe that we must channel our collective Shōki to communicate through aura and create Kami no Ki for ourselves and our studies. So we both study . . . at two a.m."

The maintenance worker looked confused. "Well, it's past curfew."

"Our fault," Neesha said, patting him on the back. "Just wanted to make sure we got it right."

He stared back for a moment, before swimming out from under her hand and heading straight for the stairwell.

Peter turned to her immediately. "We don't have time. You have to go. I'll get as many of these people as I can."

Neesha nodded. "Good work, Lai," she said, throwing her hood up. "That Buddhist shit really does sound like nonsense."

Lai glared at them. "That wasn't Buddhism, motherfuckers, it was *Dragon Ball Z*. Now get out of my room before you get me in trouble."

AIDEN.

TEN MEN FOLLOWED Dr. Richardson as they walked, joining up along the way after they heard her radio command. At the back, a confused Yanis walked alone, speaking to no one.

"What were you doing out here?" Dr. Richardson asked as they approached the church.

"Looking for her," Aiden said, trying to hold himself together. "I thought I saw her after mass, so I followed, and . . ."

"And you spoke to her?" Dr. Richardson was a few steps ahead of the rest, walking faster and faster as they neared the building. "Or you think you spoke to her?" She was speaking loudly, Aiden could tell, to try to prove she was skeptical, but the ten men behind her proved she believed him more than she was letting on.

Fifty feet from the church, Aiden veered right, toward the forest. "I did," he said. "I guess she's been hiding out here. She said she was afraid of something in the school."

Dr. Richardson didn't react.

"I was trying to convince her to come back," he said. "But

she wouldn't. So I just told her I was going to go get her some food and come back—"

"Shh." Dr. Richardson stopped. The men behind them did as well.

"Over there," Aiden said, pointing. "There's a wide tree—she was hiding behind it."

Dr. Richardson advanced ahead of him, rounding the wide tree, and looking back quickly, disappointed. "This tree?"

"I swear she was here . . . wait." He pointed to a tree nearby. A yellow cardigan was balled up at the base. "That's hers! That's what she was wearing."

Aiden watched the recognition wash over Dr. Richardson. "Okay," she said. "Spread out, everyone. Make increasingly larger perimeters; a few of you go out deep into the forest and start working backward."

The men nodded and dispersed as she had commanded. "Emma!" the maintenance worker next to her began to shout, but Dr. Richardson threw her hand over his mouth and nearly wrestled him to the ground.

"Don't shout her name, moron." She noticed Aiden watching and loosened her grip. "We wouldn't want to create unnecessary panic over what is most likely a student's wild imagination."

EVAN.

EVAN PLUGGED IN the code to Dr. Richardson's office from memory. As soon as the lock lit green, he motioned to the hooded figure waiting in the phone booth. She came rushing over.

"Go," he whispered. "We don't have very long."

Emma stood rooted to the spot, staring at the sliver of light spilling out from the door.

"Emma, now."

"I'm sorry, I—" She looked around her for a way out. "I can't go in there. I don't even know you."

"If you don't move, what happened to you will happen to all your friends," Evan said, as a matter of fact.

Emma took a deep breath and slid sideways into the room. Evan followed, checking to be sure the lobby was empty behind them.

The office was still: four bookshelves that looked untouched; two additional tables, each covered with miscellaneous papers and folders that looked frozen there by time. On Dr. Richardson's desk sat an hourglass, a few framed photos of her with scientist types, a prototype Macintosh computer, and an electronic apparatus that looked like a baby car battery.

"Where's the back room?" he asked, wandering around the edges of the room, feeling along the walls and shelves.

"The door was over there." Emma nodded toward one of the walls with several bookshelves against it. "I—I think one of these things opens up . . . I thought there was gonna be a door . . ." Emma stammered to a stop. "I don't remember exactly."

Evan kept his eyes moving around the room, establishing patterns and searching for breaks. A number of the shelves contained multiple copies of the same book, including one row entirely reserved for a book called *Evolutionary Design*. One of the copies in the middle stuck out, so Evan pulled it. Nothing happened.

"Where was the crease to the door?" Evan asked, more urgently.

"I walked in right here." Emma retraced her steps. "And she was standing . . . God, I don't know. Over there?" She signaled vaguely toward an even wider area of the wall.

The photos on the shelves were turned in alternating directions, so every other photo faced away from the one next to it. Evan tried turning some of them, but nothing happened.

"Do you remember what angle you could see it from? Or what was in front of the door?"

"I can't," Emma said desperately. "I think I blocked it out."

Evan stopped. At the end, there was a photo with an old man, not in an office, but in a living room. Dr. Richardson wasn't wearing her usual pantsuit, or any kind of formal attire—her pants were flannel, pajamas. This photo wasn't a scientific accomplishment; it was personal. Evan tried to pull it down, but it wouldn't budge.

Behind him, Emma had started to cry softly into her hand. "I'm sorry, I swear it's—it's somewhere in here—"

"I believe you," Evan said, without turning from the bookshelf. Near the bottom, hidden between several frames, was an inconspicuous wooden cross. But it wasn't a normal cross; it was shaped to match the tall one outside, its outstretched arms drooping downward at the center. He tried to pick it up, but it wouldn't budge. It was fixed to the shelf. He placed his hand over it and felt the top collapse beneath his palm—a button. As he pulled his hand back, the top of the cross began to glow yellow, illuminating the phrase carved at the bottom: *I am the Light of the World.*

From behind the wall in front of him, he heard a loud metal click, and release.

Behind one of the bookshelves, a small break in the wall formed. Without a word, he and Emma rushed to it, placing their fingers inside the crack and yanking backward. Wheels under the shelf slid back easily, leaving a small opening in the wall.

AIDEN.

AS THE MEN fanned out through the woods in front of him, Aiden walked slow circles around the outside, maintaining his panic while looking for nothing in particular. Most of the men were far enough away that they were only visible by traces of their flashlights, but one flashlight was clearly within his line of sight—Dr. Richardson hovered close enough that Aiden could still hear her breathing. She'd given up looking and turned her attention to him.

"I spoke to her myself, you know," she volunteered, over the crunching of leaves and the snapping of twigs. "On the phone. From Kansas."

He didn't respond, letting his panicked breaths fill the holes in the conversation.

"I suppose she could have lied to us." He could hear her moving closer, angling toward him. "She could have called from inside the school or something, but we have cameras for that."

Aiden kept his eyes moving, determined not to focus for too

long on any fixed spot, as his manufactured panic began to legitimize.

"In fact, we have cameras for everything. So if I was wondering why someone might go out to the woods, in search of a person who was already found. . . ."

Even though it was cold, sweat formed across Aiden's forehead. It was getting harder to avoid Dr. Richardson's stare.

She stopped walking and the woods went quiet. "Why do you keep looking back at the church?"

Aiden froze, fixing his eyes forward at Dr. Richardson's feet, away from the church. After a few seconds, her feet began to move.

"Where are you going?" he asked as Dr. Richardson passed him, but the answer was obvious.

"I'm just curious. . . ." She moved toward the church.

"But she's not in there!" Aiden rushed after her. "She was out here, that's where I talked to her!"

"Well, maybe she went in," Dr. Richardson said, walking faster.

Aiden sprinted in front of her, heading her off at the bottom of the stairs. "I don't think it's a good idea," he said desperately. "You know, for spiritual reasons."

Dr. Richardson smiled. "We have to check everywhere. Trust me, that's what your Lord would want, too."

Brushing his shoulder as she passed, Dr. Richardson jogged up the stairs. Giving her a moment to get ahead, Aiden turned to follow, sliding through the twelve-foot double doors and clicking them shut behind his back. It was completely dark in the church, and Aiden positioned himself squarely in front of the doors, the church's only exit. Dr. Richardson's voice caught in his ears—*your Lord.*

He couldn't see it, but he could hear Dr. Richardson advancing down the center aisle. She turned on her flashlight and its beam barely found the surfaces around the room. The paintings on the wall glowed dimly in whatever white light could reach them, and the illumination pivoted with Dr. Richardson's body, slowly, back and forth. She began moving more slowly, looking up and down every pew. Aiden stayed frozen in the back, squeezing the metal bar of the door behind him with the strength of the Apex in his system, when he heard it—

"Oooh." A muffled cry rang out from the front of the sanctuary. Aiden swallowed hard.

Dr. Richardson froze. "Eddy?" she asked quietly. There was no response. She was about a hundred feet away, near the front of the center aisle, but Aiden could see Dr. Richardson's face curl slowly into a smile in the second before her flashlight went out. A second later, the flashlight came back on. Then off again. Then on again.

"No, no . . ." the voice cried, louder this time, more obviously from the front right side of the room.

Dr. Richardson began to advance, flickering her flashlight so quickly it was like a strobe, calling to him. "Eddy. Your brothers and sisters compel you. Come forward."

"Noo—"

"Come forward and join your family—" Dr. Richardson called. Aiden could feel his stomach twisting over as the gravity of the danger set in. Emma wasn't lying—there was something fucked up about what they'd done to Eddy. Dr. Richardson was doing it now.

"Nooo—" The cries were constant now, sobs and gasps in between them.

"Come forward, rise to meet your family—" Dr. Richardson's voice swelled louder.

"No!"

She stopped, only the piano between her body and the noise. "Eddy?" she asked breathlessly. Her flashlight clicked off, then on, then off—

There was a loud crashing noise at the front of the sanctuary. Someone hit the piano, someone cried out in pain, Dr. Richardson grunted in struggle.

"What the fuck is—" It was Dr. Richardson's voice, trying to shout against obvious restraint. "What are you—oh no you fucking—" Her sentence was cut off by the loud snap of tape over her mouth.

In the back of the room, Aiden sighed, loosening his grip on the door handle.

NEESHA.

"I'LL BE HONEST, I thought you guys were kidding about the sweeps when you were training me." A voice with a slightly southern accent drifted around the corner. "Going into students' rooms and shit? What's the point of that?"

Neesha slid closer, angling to see around. There was a gathering of maintenance workers in the C-School Lounge, a gathering she'd have to get past.

"Yep," another voice answered. "And we never even find anything. It's just to scare 'em, I think, keep 'em from getting ideas."

"Why, though? What's the point?"

"Kids are too damn smart. They're freaks."

"What do they think kids're gonna do, though? Run away?" the southern accent protested. "Why'd they run away from here?"

"Every kid's an asset, gotta protect the assets."

Breathlessly, she slid out into the darkness, cowering as far as possible from the fireplace, clinging to the circular outer wall. Above her, the maintenance workers were congregated on the first landing, two of them facing out over the lounge.

"I don't know. I feel like maybe these kids have something special they don't tell us about. Can't think of why else you'd need so much security. Plus, why lie about it? Telling the kids we work in maintenance—"

"If one more of these little fuckers asks me to fix a toilet—"

One of the men laughed. Neesha ran her thumb over the key in her pocket.

"That's what I'm saying! The kids never do anything, hardly break any rules, but we've got forty trained military guys out here in bumfuck wherever? For what?"

"Is it a good job?"

"Sure, pay's great, but—"

"Well, then shut up about it."

The other two men laughed, and she used the moment to slide into the doorway, unlocking the door to the C-School and clicking it open.

"Y'all hear something?" the Southern accent asked, and she froze.

"Listen to this guy! Little kids got you paranoid, bud?"

"Guess you're right," he mumbled. "I'll shut up and drink my coffee."

Neesha ducked through the door and turned to sprint away. The hallway was empty, multicolored as always, the neon reds and blues of the labs more vibrant in the darkness. Her footsteps clattered loudly on the linoleum. She could hear her heartbeat pumping in her ears as she reached the door to the Pharma Lab.

She could see through the window that the room was empty. She pushed the door open.

"Schoolwork, I presume?"

Neesha froze. Dr. Yangborne stood behind her, smiling out from a lab across the hall.

"Oh," she said. "I'm sorry, I just forgot something . . ."

He raised an eyebrow.

"I was thinking about what you said, about how I should be taking more of an initiative, and so I figured . . . today was a good day to get started."

Yangborne nodded.

"So . . ." She stepped backward, turning away from him. "I'm just going to grab a few things, and—"

"How ignorant do you think we are?"

Neesha stopped in the doorway. "I . . . what do you mean?"

Yangborne was still smiling. "We test students every day. We monitor every aspect of your lives. You think we wouldn't notice half our student population was high on amphetamines?"

Neesha's stomach dropped. She stood gaping back at him.

AIDEN.

AIDEN RUSHED TO the front of the room. Zaza held Dr. Richardson against the ground, half-triumphant and half-horrified.

"I can't believe I did that," he exhaled. "Who the fuck am I? Why did I do that?"

"You have a crush, Zaza," he said, ripping off a huge piece of tape for Dr. Richardson's hands. "And people do very stupid things for crushes." They sat her up in a chair and Aiden wrapped a strip of tape around her arms behind it, then fastened it to the piano. Dr. Richardson flailed wildly within her bindings. "Keep a close eye out, and don't let her make noise, alright?"

Zaza nodded, and Aiden rushed back up the center aisle and out onto the porch.

The back lawn was almost silent. One by one, the maintenance men who'd been in the woods had started to make their way back toward the school, each one asking about Dr. Richardson, each one receiving radio silence. They came out of the forest in groups of two or three, and each time, Aiden darted behind the top pillar of the church, praying they wouldn't make the turn.

Every fifteen seconds, he checked his watch, waiting for 2:00 a.m. It was a Rolex, one he'd bought for himself before starting the school year. When he'd bought it, he'd stood with his mother, passing it back and forth, debating loudly in front of the attractive store clerk whether it was worth it to spend three thousand dollars on such a small accessory; whether he'd be able to wear it enough times to justify its purchase; whether kids at school would even care. Ultimately, the decision was made to buy it, of course, because of what it said about him, and the value it implied. It was 1:49 a.m., and at this moment, the watch was worthless.

A pair of footsteps came slogging out of the forest, slower than the rest. Aiden froze as Yanis came out of the black, whipping a stick that the maintenance workers used to clear undergrowth back and forth. His head was still up, the long beam of his flashlight scanning back and forth. Aiden tried to shrink into the darkness, but it was too late.

"Aiden?" Yanis took a few steps in his direction. "Are you still over there?" The flashlight beam hit him squarely between the eyes. "Aiden?"

"Yeah, it's me," Aiden said. "Did you find her?"

With every step closer, he could more fully appreciate Yanis's size relative to his own—a little taller and much wider, particularly in the shoulders. His head sat perched on his neck like a boulder, threatening to drop and crush him. He was like a linebacker in a Russian version of the NFL.

"No. Where's Dr. Richardson?"

"In there," he said, nodding to the forest. "She said to send somebody in to look if she wasn't back in twenty minutes. It hasn't been twenty minutes, though."

Yanis looked a little confused. "Have we checked the church?"

"Yeah, Dr. Richardson swept through it."

"How long ago?"

"Ten minutes."

"And she didn't leave anybody here, at the initial site?"

"Just me."

"Huh." Yanis stopped next to him. "Very strange, right? Why would she do that?"

"I don't know," Aiden said, staring back at the school.

"Can I ask you something, just you and me?" Yanis reached for his vest, digging into one of the pockets. If Yanis wanted to get past, he wouldn't have to try very hard. Aiden took two protective steps back.

Yanis pulled out a pack of cigarettes and offered one in Aiden's direction.

"Oh, no—no, thank you."

"Huh. Yeah, I guess I hear they're no good if you play the running sports." He put one in his mouth and lit it with a match. "I lift weights, so . . . not really so worried about the cardio. But you, you are going to be a basketball professional! *Millions* of dollars."

Aiden was lost, but played along, nodding.

"In Russia, we don't have this. We don't think athletes are so much better than everyone else, that they deserve so much more money." He took a long drag. "You know what I did back in Russia, for work? Private investigator. A very, very good one, for a lot of money, so much money, the only people who could afford to pay me is the Kremlin. So I guess maybe, more of a bounty hunter. I tracked down big criminals, enemies of state. And then one day, I get offered my best job yet, *crazy* money, to be private security coordinator. And I get on the plane . . . and I'm here. Can you believe that? What kind of school has that kind of money?"

He took another drag, giving himself time to fully exhale and watch the smoke disappear. "And yet. The students that I talk to here, they are more secretive. More afraid. Than the dissidents of Russia." He looked at Aiden. "I don't want you to lie to me. And if you feel like you must lie to me, I want to know why. You're all afraid of something."

"I . . ." Aiden stopped himself. He couldn't place what Yanis knew or didn't, whether he was telling the truth himself or it was an elaborate strategy to get information. "I'm not lying."

Yanis nodded. "The one thing that gets me through my work," he said, "is that I know I'm working for the good guys. Stopping criminals, I'm making Russia safer. Tracking students who misbehave . . ." He took another long drag. "I'm asking for honesty, one time. Did you see your girlfriend tonight? Is Emma still here?"

Aiden froze, avoiding Yanis's eyes. He couldn't tell whether Yanis was trying to manipulate him or not, but he wasn't going to give in that easily. "Yes. She was in the woods."

Behind them, something crashed inside the church, just loud enough to carry through the wooden doors and over the wind. Yanis's head shot up, then back to Aiden. "Stay here."

Aiden's face flushed. He turned to tell Yanis not to go in but caught himself—all he'd do is strengthen Yanis's resolve. He balled his fists in his pockets, thinking as fast as he could, squeezing up his chest—

"Yanis," he said, stopping him. "I need to tell you something. I lied. I didn't actually see her."

Yanis came a few inches back toward him, his head jerking up in confusion.

"I wanted to find her so bad that I thought if, for some reason, you guys came looking for her, it might make me feel better." Aiden looked sideways at his watch: 1:53 a.m. "So you can punish me however you see fit. If you have to take me in right now and write me up, I understand."

Yanis considered it for another moment longer, then shrugged. "Well, that does explain a lot." He turned back toward the church.

"Wait, why—" Aiden scrambled toward him. "You're just gonna let me off? Without doing anything about it? I lied to the school!"

"Maybe we can figure out some kind of help system," Yanis said, moving toward the door. "So you don't feel tempted to try it again—"

"I don't want any help," Aiden tried shouting. "I'll just keep lying to you . . . stupid . . . assholes—"

"Don't be ridiculous, Aiden," Yanis said.

"*Seriously?*" Aiden shouted after him. "You're not gonna do anything about all of this? You're just gonna let me walk away?"

Yanis stopped at the door of the church. "Aiden, I'm afraid something bigger might be going on here," he said, whipping the doors open.

Aiden watched them close and said a silent prayer, then charged in after.

EVAN.

THEY STOOD FROZEN in the doorway. Evan could feel the cold, sterilized laboratory air spilling out, smelling like Lysol and metal.

Emma wasn't lying. The ARC was real.

It was cold, polished white metal. The top expanded out into the ceiling and it was impossible to tell where it went from there. The bottom was rounded into a soft edge, just an inch across at its tip, where three holes were populated with a mess of exposed copper wire.

Emma walked up to it slowly, placing her hands against it.

The computer system around it was just as incredible. There was a control station directly in front of the machine, but the screens stretched all the way up to the ceiling, covering every corner of the walls in the circular room.

"Let's get the picture," Evan whispered, "and go."

Emma nodded, her hands shaking as she raised the Polaroid camera to her eye and snapped a photo. The flash popped like a gunshot around them.

Immediately, he grabbed her by the hand, pulling her away, out of the room, through the office, and back to the lobby. The Human Lounge was still empty in front of them, and unless instructors decided to break their routine and police the common rooms this late, their path to the front gate would be unblocked.

"Wait," Emma said behind him. "Wait, no, this doesn't—this can't—"

The words caught in her throat. In her hands, the Polaroid was developing slowly, the colors fading in from white to form indistinguishable shapes.

It didn't look like anything. From the picture, the ARC looked like an ice cream machine, or a dentist's office.

"Okay," Evan said, snatching the camera from her hands and sprinting back into the room. He tried several different spots, different vantage points, and through the scope, none of them could capture the size of the ARC. He scanned the room, settling on the large stack of computer processors and monitors face-to-face with the machine. "What if we get up there?"

Emma stared at it, frozen in soft shock. "I—I can't climb that. I can barely walk."

Evan ran to the base of the machine, hoisting his leg over the first railing, ignoring the buttons he might be pressing along the way up. He threw his right leg over, but couldn't find anywhere to counterbalance without reaching his right arm—

"Ah!" He fell to the ground, his busted arm flopping outside the sling uselessly. The camera hit the ground next to him.

"We have to go," he said, regathering himself, ignoring the pain shooting up into his shoulder. "We have to go without the picture."

"What about everyone else?" Emma asked.

"They'll be fine," he said. "If we don't get out of here—"

"If we can't prove what's happening here, they're all dead. I'm not leaving without it."

Evan held his breath for a second, then searched the room for options. On the computer desk, buried in the back, was one of the school's closed-circuit radios. He grabbed it.

"What are you doing?" Emma watched him as he uncoiled it and flipped the lever up.

"Calling Neesha."

"You can't do that."

He didn't stop, so she rushed over to put a hand on the radio. "Evan, what if someone in one of the other offices is listening?"

Evan nodded. "Then I won't say anything."

NEESHA.

YANGBORNE TOOK A few steps across the hall. He walked straight toward her, then past her, into the classroom.

"Come in," he said, beckoning her to follow, and she did.

"Dr. Yangborne, I don't know what you think I have to do with that, but . . . it wasn't my idea."

He smiled. "Don't worry, Neesha. You aren't in trouble."

"What?"

"In fact, the opposite. We all think you're doing excellent work. As I'm sure you know, your trials are responsible for a dramatic uptick in student performance."

She clambered to catch up. "Why didn't you . . ."

"Say something? We didn't want to interfere. Your tests are tests we can't do ourselves. If we provided every student with amphetamines, we'd be liable for the results. However, if the students take them on their own . . ."

"I . . ."

"You've permanently changed history here, Neesha. In one week, you've done something the school has been trying to accomplish for decades. Your discovery is not just the most dynamic for this year, but perhaps of all time. I'm sure you know what that means?"

She shook her head, and Yangborne smiled. Delicately, he moved toward her, passing her in the doorway and heading straight for the trophy case in the front of the classroom. He unlocked the case and lifted the four-foot Discovery Trophy out from the bottom.

"You can take it now, if you'd like." He set it on the table between them.

Neesha couldn't move. She'd pictured this moment a thousand times, hoisting the trophy high while cameramen snapped photos of her. In her head, the room was full of classmates—so everyone else could see what she'd done. They were applauding, wildly, for her.

"It's a nice perk," he said. "But this trophy is nothing compared to what you're capable of. Do you have any idea the resources this school has? Its ability to impact the world?"

She swallowed. She did know. She pictured it every night before she fell asleep. Light from the window bathed the photos on the wall, the museum of Redemption's past discoveries, casting a minefield of reflections along the ground between them.

"What is this place?" she asked quietly. "What do you all . . ."

Yangborne wasn't surprised by the question. Instead, he kept smiling. "It's exactly what I've always told you it is: a facility for the most important research in the modern world. We're evolving the way humans think. And soon, we'll transcend even that. Don't you want to be a part of it?"

Behind Yangborne, the radio clicked, a few soft beeps. They both glanced at it, then back to the trophy.

Yangborne pushed it closer. "Come forward, Neesha. You've earned your place here."

Her heart slammed against the inside of her rib cage. Her mouth was dry. She felt herself pulled to the front of the room, magnetized by the trophy. Inside the case, it always seemed so far away, but this close she could see its reality: smooth edges; the sharp, reflective design at the top, shooting light upward; the Redemption logo carved into the base, ready for a name to be engraved. Her name. Her place in history would be solidified. Her future would be assured. Her family would be taken care of. Everything she came to school for—everything they came to America for—would be hers. She gripped the sides of the trophy.

The radio clicked again, three times, but more noticeably than before, the beeps a little longer. Neesha stood taller, listening.

"Congratulations, Neesha," Yangborne said. "You've just secured your place in history."

The radio clicked again, three short beeps.

Three short, three long, three short.

It was Evan's SOS call. They were in trouble.

Neesha exhaled as she lifted the trophy from the table. "Thank you," she said. "For everything."

She pulled the trophy back and in a fluid motion, swung it at his face, shattering the glass against the side of his head.

AIDEN.

THE CHURCH DOOR closed and both of the flashlights at the front disappeared. He couldn't hear anything ahead of him, from Yanis or Zaza, until a voice at the front gently called out. "Hello?"

"Who's in here?" It was Yanis.

From behind the tape covering her mouth, Dr. Richardson began to scream. She rattled the bottom of her chair against the wooden floor, and Yanis charged at the noise. Aiden snuck down the side aisle, getting to the front just as Yanis descended on them.

Zaza clicked his flashlight on just in time for Yanis to knock it away. "What's happening?" he shouted, scanning the room with his own flashlight, landing on Dr. Richardson.

Zaza didn't hesitate. He threw himself toward Yanis, catching him in the upper chest and knocking him off-balance, but only for a moment. Yanis recovered in time to catch Zaza's next blow and send it curling back inside itself with twice its strength. Zaza continued to fight, dropping lower to drive Yanis backward, but it was a man against a mountain, and it only took a few seconds for Yanis to stop Zaza's momentum and collapse him to the ground. Aiden stayed where he was, watching by stray beams of a flashlight. No one had noticed him, cowering in the shadows, giving himself an escape down the far aisle.

Dr. Richardson hadn't stopped shouting from behind the tape. Yanis crouched to examine the makeshift bonds affixed to her skin, but Zaza wasn't done yet. He threw himself against Yanis's back, screaming. Yanis tried to rip him off but couldn't, nearly falling onto Dr. Richardson's chair before shifting his weight back and driving Zaza into the ground. They rolled together, crashing into the holy water basin—the basin against which Aiden had thrown Eddy a week ago. Zaza tried to get back up, but Yanis took out his knees, again collapsing him to the ground.

Yanis rushed to where Dr. Richardson was lying, surgically removing her tape. "Thank the fucking Lord," she exhaled as soon as it was off her mouth.

"Easy," Yanis whispered. "We're in a church."

He moved limb by limb, slicing the tape slowly with a knife from his belt. When Dr. Richardson was free, she shoved herself away from the chair and stumbled to her feet, glaring down at Zaza.

"Take him to the chamber in the GRC," she said. "No food, no water, nothing. He's going to be punished worse than anyone in this school's history."

"Dr.—"

"He tried to tie me up! God knows what he'd have done if you didn't find me!" She was screaming into the shredded edges of her vocal cords. "Did you see the tape they put across my face?" Their flashlights were still in constant motion, but every occasional pass over Dr. Richardson's face revealed bloodred marks around the corners of her mouth and eyes.

"What happened?" Yanis asked Zaza. "Why did you do this?"

"Because he's insane!" she tried to answer for them. "A fucking savage!" Dr. Richardson crouched in front of Zaza. "Your life is about to become a literal hell," she whispered. "Get up."

Yanis didn't look so sure; he looked almost sick staring down at Zaza, a bloody mess on the chapel floor.

Dr. Richardson stumbled down the center aisle to the back of the chapel. She pulled a radio from the wall and flipped the switch on.

Yanis tried to pick Zaza up, but it was obvious Zaza barely had control of his body. Yanis tied a knot around Zaza's arms, behind his back, loosening it to the point of comfort and lifting him as gently as he could, using his shirt to wipe some of the blood from Zaza's nose. Aiden cowered in the far aisle and watched.

"Dr. Richardson for anyone else," she screamed into the radio. "Carl, Lisle, Luc, anyone! We need a sweep, immediately! I was just attacked by students!"

She released the talk button and noise began to filter in, loud and muffled from the static. Aiden crept closer, listening.

"Hello?" Dr. Richardson tried again. "What's going on?" She let off the button, this time long enough for the sounds to clarify, and Aiden recognized the voice—Billy Ray Cyrus. It was "Achy Breaky Heart."

She had done it. Neesha flooded the radio.

"Can anyone hear me?" Dr. Richardson tried to scream over it, but the song was cranked. "I need a sweep! Someone!"

She screamed and slammed the radio against the wall. *"Fucking idiot!"*

Yanis, dragging Zaza under his arm, reached the back door and pushed it open, night air rushing in.

Dr. Richardson followed them out. "Lock him up, then get out to maintenance and call for a sweep, immediately. Everybody, I don't care who they are. Nobody's sleeping until every student is locked in their dorms and accounted for."

Aiden crept out the door behind them.

Dr. Richardson was hobbling down the steps. "What time is it now?"

Yanis checked his watched. "One fifty-nine—oh. No. Two a.m."

"Then get the sweep started at exactly two—"

She froze, staring up at the long, cold walls of the dorms, slanting away from each other into the blackness of the night. On either side, a few lights clicked on, slowly and randomly, then went out. A few more, these ones closer, began to turn on, then off, then back on.

It rippled outward, a wave of flickering lights washed across the walls until every light in every dorm had joined. Hundreds of dorm rooms, in every direction, began flashing on and off, pouring yellow out into the night, then yanking it away with the precision of a programmed show, the entire complex twinkling like Christmas lights against the icy blackness of the Utah wilderness.

"What the . . ." Aiden heard Yanis breathe.

"Wait . . ." Dr. Richardson shouted. "Wait! They're all drawing power! They're trying to—"

Rippling from the center outward, every yellow light went black, followed by every guide light, and every exit sign. The light atop the cross, the yellow glow of the maintenance garage.

The whole complex was down.

Dr. Richardson spun to Yanis. "Go, now. Send ten men to my office. We're under attack." She took off sprinting for the GRC.

EVAN.

HE TRIED ONE more photo from under the machine. With a loud clicking noise, the camera flashed, taking all the light in the room with it. Every overhead machine and whirling noise. They sat together in perfect silence for a moment.

"Holy shit," Emma breathed. "It worked."

They were huddled behind the curve of the ARC, the only spot in the room invisible from the door. Their backs were up against the metal of the machine, their arms touching. She hadn't said anything; he hadn't either, instead keeping his eyes closed, focused entirely on her, their breathing falling into rhythm.

He knew exactly what he wanted to say. He'd written it in his journal, said it aloud to himself a hundred times. He'd pictured himself meeting her at the big wooden cross after church, telling her exactly what she needed to hear. It had been a perfect plan, from the way he would look to the way she'd be feeling to the words he'd say. He didn't have any of those things anymore, except the words. But he did have two minutes.

"I knew you needed someone."

He couldn't see her, and she didn't say anything. That was okay.

"I knew you needed someone, because I noticed that you were sleeping a lot, and walking around with your head down instead of up, and . . . my mom used to do those things whenever she needed me around more. And I noticed it right away when I moved in across the hall from you, and then, when I heard you read your poem—"

"My poem?" Emma asked. He could tell from the direction of her voice that she was looking at him.

"The one you read on May fourteenth at the church . . ." He took a deep breath. "*'I'll hold your place next to me, eternally, endlessly. . . . This world was never big enough, but you still tried to make a place for me. . . . We all deserve forgiveness, I know you could wipe the slate for me . . . you'll find me here again, a different form, the same memory.'*"

Evan swallowed. "It was my mom. Speaking to me, through you. I thought I failed in my mission, but you taught me I could have a new one. That's why I'm here. That's why I came to save you."

Closing his eyes and offering a silent prayer, he moved his right hand and set it gently on top of her left. She didn't flinch or protest, leaving it there to be touched, warm nerves connecting beneath their skin and tying them together, his color filling her in.

She cleared her throat. "I didn't write that."

"What?"

"The poem? That's not mine. That's a song, by the Sick Buffys."

"Wait, but . . . b-but, you . . . the Sick Buffys?"

"Yeah, they're a band. I don't really even like them anymore."

"B-but then . . . why did you read it?"

"I don't know, I just thought it sounded cool."

"B-but . . . but y-you . . ."

Evan fell silent, processing, feeling himself falling away from her. His brain was clear and reflective; everything that was inside him was now outside him; the plastic pieces of the poem were broken on the floor in front of him. It wasn't Emma's words; it wasn't even Emma's thoughts. It wasn't a message, sent to him through an angel—it wasn't even a poem. It was just words. He'd never even heard of the Sick Buffys.

"I'm sorry to hear about your mom, Evan," she said, pulling her hand back. "But that has nothing to do with me. You don't know me at all. And what you did to me was messed up. You realize that, right?"

The air had been drained from his lungs, the life drained from his chest.

"You weren't helping me," she said. "You were using me to try to fix yourself. That's not love."

Footsteps came sprinting through the door, faster than he could react, and by the time they turned around, a flashlight bobbed into view.

AIDEN.

OUTSIDE THE SCHOOL, with all the power offline, you could almost convince yourself that everything was normal.

Aiden sat alone, atop a large rock in the first cut of the forest, behind the maintenance building. He'd watched, safely fifty feet behind, as Yanis had dragged Zaza back into the school, then watched as Yanis went charging back out to the maintenance building to call a sweep. The instructors and security, much less organized than usual, were starting to stumble across the lawn and into the dorms, flashlight beams appearing in random windows around the complex.

From where he sat, their plan had gone off almost without a hitch. The sweep had started just in time to pull everyone from the front gate. The power to the electrical fence was off; Neesha had stopped the sweep from starting too early; Evan and Emma had been given plenty of time to get the picture; now all that remained was the vehicle. At this point, now that everything had played out accordingly, they'd all make it out, safely, together.

Except Zaza. He wouldn't be escaping. He'd suffer severe punishment, a "literal hell," as Dr. Richardson described it. He couldn't get the image of Zaza's eyes out of his head: stained with blood and bruise, searching in the dark, begging for backup. Aiden couldn't have done anything, just like he couldn't do anything now, or anything for the hundreds of other students at the school. But sitting there in the chapel, hopeless and in the dark, he couldn't help but feel like Zaza's fate was his fault.

He heard footsteps coming up the path, away from the church. He ducked behind his rock, until he saw it was Peter, staying low and sprinting along the path. "Peter!" he called.

Peter's head spun wildly. He flew toward Aiden. "Holy shit, buddy!"

"Oh—" Before Aiden could protest, Peter tackled him in a wild embrace. They tumbled backward into the forest. "I guess we're friends now."

"Holy shit, buddy," Peter said again. "I can't believe it. The kid's plan worked. We might all actually get outta here."

Aiden stood up and brushed himself off, not saying anything.

"Shit. What happened?"

Aiden swallowed. "Yanis got into the church and Dr. Richardson escaped. It wasn't until after two, so everyone else should be fine, but . . . Zaza's not getting out."

Peter's face fell. "Shit."

"I know," Aiden said. "But I don't think there's anything we can do—"

"It's not just that." Peter looked back over his shoulder.

"Everybody else was still in the school. Neesha, the kid . . ."

Aiden's voice broke. "Emma?"

Peter shook his head again.

After a long moment, Peter turned to the maintenance shed. "Alright, well, we're not doing anything standing here. You ready to go steal a bus or something?"

Aiden ignored him, staring past him at the nearest path back to the school. "No. You get the bus. I'm going back in."

"What? No, that's a horrible idea. How are you possibly gonna improve that situation?"

Aiden rocked back, a little confused. "I—I don't know—"

"Even if you get in there, if Dr. Richardson has them, they're not getting out. Not tonight, anyway. We're best off waiting to see who makes it out, then going. Otherwise we might not have a chance."

Aiden took a deep breath. "I just have to, okay? I can't . . . just sit out here."

Peter stared at him for a long moment, then smiled. "Damn," he said. "Look at you. Not so candy shit anymore, huh?"

Aiden nodded. They clasped hands once more and took off, sprinting in opposite directions.

NEESHA.

"OH MY GOD," she heard Emma exhale as she entered the room.

"Camera, now," she called, and caught it without breaking stride. She leapt to the machine and started to pull herself up. The only light in the room came from her flashlight, now on the ground, throwing long shadows of the ARC up the wall of screens. She couldn't turn around; if she took a second to consider the fall, they'd be a second too late.

Her vertical instinct came back from her climbing days, three-point balance between her limbs as she swung the forth, up several stacks of monitors. Within sixty seconds, she'd found a ledge, ten feet above the awesome machine. She adjusted the photo through the scope, lining up the corners to capture the awesome reach of the ARC's size.

Click. The camera flashed with a satisfied purr.

"Okay, let's get outta here," Emma whispered.

"I'm not sure I got it," Neesha said, adjusting herself. "I've got six pictures left, I'm just gonna take all of them."

"They're all gonna look the same, let's—"

There was another flash of light from the camera, a single strobe to remind them of the room they were in and the massive machine behind them, and then blackness again. One, two, three, four, five more flashes exploded across the room, dangerously visible in the pitch-black room. "Okay," she whispered. "That's it."

Outside the room, they could hear the faint shuffling of feet in the hallway growing louder. Neesha looked to the ground, wavering in her balance as she tried to judge the jump. "I don't know how I'm gonna get down from this," she whispered. "I can't see shit."

"We have to go. Don't worry, I'm right below you," Emma whispered. "If you have to fall, just fall into—"

The door to the waiting room slammed. They all froze.

It felt like it took a lifetime for the footsteps to cross the office, for the bobbing light of the flashlight to crawl in and over them. As soon as it was far enough inside to catch the rim of Emma's face, the figure holding the light let out a long, loaded sigh.

"You don't know this," Dr. Richardson said, smiling, her face floating in the light reflected from the ARC, "but you've come back on purpose."

Emma pressed her lips together so tightly they began to shake. Neesha could see tears welling up in the corners of her eyes. Dr. Richardson stepped forward, blocking Emma from the doorway, coming within arm's distance of her face and reaching out.

"What are you so afraid of? This is exactly what you wanted."

Emma shook her head. "I'm not staying," she said, her voice unsure. "I'd rather die than be in here with you."

Dr. Richardson frowned. "Don't say that. It isn't honest." She noticed Evan, hovering behind her. "Mr. Andrews. This is surprising. To go from an obsession with Emma to spying on her, to . . . whatever this is. All with so little emotional intelligence and social awareness. You're evolving, in a very . . . interesting way. All the same, thank you for bringing her back. She's very important to the work we do here. Just the two of you?"

Dr. Richardson scanned the rest of the room with her flashlight, mirrors and screens sending fragments of light bouncing around the circular room, revealing pieces of Neesha as she clung to the wall, ten feet above where the doctor stood.

"Yes," Emma said, but Dr. Richardson kept rotating, ninety, one hundred twenty, one hundred fifty degrees—

"I am the light of the world," Emma spat, and Dr. Richardson stopped, turning back to face her. Emma held up two fingers in a peace sign.

"You are," Dr. Richardson said. "Which is why you're back. Can you imagine all the hard work we did together just disappearing? It would have been devastating. It would have set this school back . . . well, I can't even tell you how long."

Emma continued to hold the peace sign up, strangely defiant, in Dr. Richardson's direction, her eyes flittering back and forth between the doctor and the computer monitors on the wall.

It wasn't the monitors Emma was looking at, though, Neesha

realized. It was her. Her heart leapt. It wasn't a peace sign. It was the number two. Neesha used the strap of the camera to fasten the photos to its base.

Dr. Richardson pushed a few buttons behind her, and the control panel buzzed awake. "Cute trick with the lights, but this room runs on a generator. I can't risk drops in here."

She turned back to Emma, now silhouetted by the electronic glow behind her. "Others were starting to panic about never finding you, but I didn't. No one else spent the time together that we spent; a connection like that doesn't just break because of a bit of fear or confusion. I mean, what did you think you was going to happen to you, running away? Were you planning on devolving to the Emmalynn of two months ago? Sad but without purpose? Hating herself, just for the sake of it?"

Emma was rocking back and forth in place, her fingers still holding a two in Dr. Richardson's face.

"Or did you think you were going to get better, somehow? Magically? People always seem to be so afraid when they get that close to themselves. And I understand; the closer the mirror, the more you can see the flaws—the pores in the skin, the hopelessness. But I knew eventually you'd figure it out, whether I had to explain it to you or not—"

Dr. Richardson flipped another switch, and the ARC behind them began to glow blue, rumbling to life with a low-frequency hum. "You can't escape the person that you are. You can only feed it. That's how you grow.

"And whether you know it or not, that's why you're back.

We were getting closer to who you really are, and I don't think you fully appreciated how important that work was." Dr. Richardson turned around to reach behind the computer monitor. "You're our savior, Emma. You just don't know it yet."

"There's only one savior," Emma proclaimed boldly—too boldly, her voice loud enough to hear its cracks—and her two fingers became one. That was it, the signal. With Dr. Richardson's head bent over a monitor, Neesha tossed the camera down, into Emma's hands. Emma caught it and hid it quickly in her jacket.

Dr. Richardson turned in time to see Emma's hand go flying back up to her face. "Who's that?"

Emma swallowed. "Jesus Christ."

Dr. Richardson almost laughed. "Right. Whatever you want to call them." She moved slowly to the ARC, running her fingers along its side. "While it warms up, what do you say we try a little therapy, huh? I suppose you can come too, Mr. Andrews."

Her hands on their backs, she led them out of the room, sliding the bookshelf shut until it closed with a thud, leaving Neesha alone in the soft blue glow of the ARC.

AIDEN.

"YOU DON'T UNDERSTAND," Aiden said, standing tall in front of the group of maintenance men outside Dr. Richardson's office. "I need to speak to her *now*."

"We're in the middle of a maintenance sweep—"

"—this is *why* there's a sweep, dumbass."

"Excuse me?"

"I guarantee you, if you lean your head in there, tell her 'Aiden Mallet wants to talk to you,' she's gonna say, 'What the fuck took you so long to let him in.' I swear to God."

There were nine maintenance workers milling in the Human Lounge and Dr. Richardson's lobby, one stationed at each of the diverging hallways. The tallest one, with shaggy black hair and a thick beard, was standing over Aiden. RICK, according to his name tag. "It's not happening."

Aiden looked from guard to guard around the room, all of them turned and focused on him. "You guys know what you're protecting in there?"

None of them said anything.

"Oh, you're all a *part* of it? You all believe in this torture shit?" He turned back to the bearded man. "Or just you?"

They all turned away to ignore him. Aiden wandered back to the middle of the room, his chest heaving noticeably. None of the guards were checking on him; if he wanted to turn and go, admit that his plan was a flawed one, he could. But Emma was behind that door.

He took one more deep breath.

He turned and ran straight for the bearded man, catching him off guard with a huge right hook to his earlobe. The man buckled to his knees and then to the ground, clutching his head. Three guards from the room rushed over, lunging toward Aiden, but he used the fallen man's body to shield himself.

Instructors came rushing down the stairs behind him. "What are you doing?" one of them screamed, but Aiden didn't hear it. He edged around two chairs toward the fireplaces, flames dancing on his face.

"No!" one of the maintenance workers who entered the room shouted to the instructors. "Continue the sweep. Reece and I will handle this." They edged around the perimeter, trapping Aiden in the corner, his back to the fire.

Without waiting, Aiden launched at the nearest worker, but the man was ready, receiving his fist with a shoulder and curling Aiden over with a punch to the gut. He swung his left leg as Aiden fell, driving him back, stumbling, toward the fire. Aiden caught himself against the bottom of the fireplace just in time.

"Stop! He's a student," an instructor shouted, loud enough

to draw their attention, and Aiden dove for an upright chair, toppling it back into Rick. Rick recovered quickly, accepting a punch while wrapping his arms around Aiden in a firm bear hug, trapping him and cutting off air. The other worker came over and took his time setting up for a military-grade right hook. Aiden heard a crunching sound from his own jaw.

"You're killing him!" an instructor screamed. "He's a boy!"

"Shut up!" the bearded man spat at her. "You'll wake the other students." He dragged Aiden's body to the middle of the lounge. "Bring him to his room."

Aiden rolled over to a hunch; the fire danced across a stream of blood pouring from the center of his face. He lifted his head slightly, woozy.

This wasn't his breaking point. Not yet.

He pulled himself up and charged at the guards. Reaching for the backs of their heads, he managed to slam one into the doorway before tumbling off, completely out of control of his own body.

"What the *fuck*!" the other screamed, and spun on him. Aiden rushed to his feet, dancing around the far edge of the room. Blood was pushing his hair back up out of his face; he felt himself smiling.

It didn't last long. The first worker grabbed him by the shoulder and threw him to the ground. The other drove a straight kick into his back so hard that Aiden's head snapped forward.

They began to circle him. "Don't make us hurt you any more, kid. Whatever this is, it's not worth it."

The workers who had been guarding the exit doors had

abandoned their posts. Three instructors huddled in a far corner together. Aiden's vision was slipping in and out of focus.
One more shot to the head, and he'd be out. He raised his hands
to protect himself.

From the hallways that converged on the Human Lounge,
he heard running, banging, a voice shouting, muffled through
the walls at first. The maintenance workers looked away from
him, their hands dropping as the voice became clearer—"Fight!
Motherfuckers, there's a fight!"

Students began to stream onto the landings of every floor,
rushing out from both directions to see what the commotion
was. They filled in, faster and faster, the instructors trying to
urge everyone back to sleep, but the students were too electrified to care. They formed an arena around him, four floors of
landings, packed with students.

To his right, Peter fought his way to the railing of the second-
story landing. He'd come to Aiden's rescue. He screamed down
at him, "Go, buddy!"

Aiden charged for the nearest guard. The students exploded
with excitement.

The guard closest was still focused on the students, and
without turning, took a jab straight to the face, backing into
the other guard, and giving Aiden an angle to slide past, continuing to fight with his back to the fire. The other guards were
slow to advance, exchanging wild glances with each other. One
shot a look to the instructors, who were panicked and hiding in
the corner. "Do someth—"

But Aiden was on him, crashing a fist down just in time to

catch his chin, again landing a punch without taking one, causing the crowd to go crazy and the workers to recoil as a unit, none of them sure whether they were even allowed to touch Aiden with this many students around.

One of the maintenance workers had turned to crowd control. "Go back to your dorms," he shouted at the wall of students, at least a hundred. "Return to your dorms immediately, or everyone will be—"

Their screaming swallowed his sentence. Aiden had run straight for another one of the guards, ducking a punch and driving him backward to the ground. Aiden continued to bulldoze over him, landing on his feet at the other end.

Rick had given up on trying to de-escalate the situation or trying to handle Aiden with care. He turned on Aiden just as he regained his balance and threw a hard left hook into the side of Aiden's gut. He ran at Aiden again, catching Aiden's fall by driving a knee into his chest. He finished by grabbing Aiden by the shoulders and throwing him back into the center of the four workers. Aiden's head snapped back, twisting and popping joints in his neck that had never bent before. Every joint and muscle that was used to holding him in place had begun to cave, shredding like thin plastic stretched over old toothpicks.

He tried a massive swing at one of the workers, and it missed without even being ducked. The worker twisted Aiden's arm back around his body, subduing him until Aiden managed to drive the worker off him with a kick to the shin and then one to the gut. Every time he lunged at them, their unwillingness to fight eased up, and they began to try harder. With every punch he got less responsible and less in control; the maintenance workers seemed to only be getting angrier, punching with less abandon; he could feel his joints giving up—

"What's happening here?"

Aiden froze first, and the guards stiffened. From the bottom up, students began to quiet, their screaming rapidly disintegrating to a heavy silence.

Dr. Richardson walked into the Human Lounge, horrified. "What is happening to this school? Mr. Mallet," she said, walking straight for them. "What has gotten into you?" She grabbed Aiden by the shoulders. He felt a small pinch where her right hand gripped his shoulder; he tried to squirm but she gripped him tighter. "You need help," she said, and the edges of her face immediately began to swim outward, into the light from the fire. His whole body began to feel warm, and his limbs got heavy. His body folded involuntarily into the outstretched arm of a security guard, and he flowed with the movement toward the door.

By the time he was passing Dr. Richardson's office, it was impossible for him to delineate one detail of the physical world from another. He was pretty sure the hallway was empty, but there might have been people everywhere. He thought he saw the light go out in Dr. Richardson's waiting room, but it might have been a light going out in his head.

"Where are we taking him?" someone asked. "Her office?"

"No, she said the chamber in the GRC."

Aiden felt his consciousness slipping.

"What the fuck?" That voice was Dr. Richardson's. "Where did they go?"

"He's right here—"

"Not him!" she was screaming. "The other two students in here, where did they go?"

Aiden's brain was completely clogged, everything shutting down; the last thing he heard was Dr. Richardson screaming, "Lock it down! Lock the whole fucking school down!"

EVAN.

HIS FEET WERE tired; his chest was aching. He'd just come inches from being tortured and spent long enough there to rationalize the fact that it was going to happen to him. He was flying through the hallways of the school, one false prediction or missed calculation away from falling right back into it. But the only thing Evan could think about was his right hand, alive with Emma's inside it, her soft skin fusing to his, her whole existence curling into his palm.

She wasn't speaking, or even really breathing loudly, but kept up every step of the way, trusting his instinct, watching his feet as he moved. "Are you okay?" he'd asked when they'd started to run, and she'd nodded.

He'd never navigated a sweep in the dark before, without at least lawn and safety lights; this one had dozens of variables. There would be more people than usual. The electronic locks of the school would be down; the mechanical locks would almost certainly be in use. They sprinted inward, away from the noise and commotion, toward the GRC, but the doors inward were locked. Instead, they followed back out, taking a hallway toward the C-School. Noticing flashlights from both directions, they fell back into an empty girls' bathroom.

"Okay," he said, checking his watch and counting backward from when he'd seen the last staff member go flying by. "We've got forty seconds for them to make it through this hallway."

"Then where are we going?" she asked, her voice perfect even when it was leaking out around the tears welled up in her throat.

"You're going home," he said.

She sat in silence, staring at the door, panting, but not releasing his hand. She was squeezing her eyes up into tiny balls. "Thank you," she whispered, and squeezed his hand tighter. His whole world stopped turning. His watch started beeping.

"Okay." He took a deep breath. "Let's go."

They ran laterally, through the second cut of academic buildings around the school, away from Human Sciences, through the theater, through the P-School, and then out to the gym. If this was a traditional sweep, there wouldn't be anyone even checking on this level of buildings, but this wasn't a sweep anymore. It was a manhunt. Still, he didn't have any choice but to trust the pattern, that the unoccupied places would stay unoccupied, even today. He left a new wave of adrenaline as they hit the gym—below, the stands were perfectly quiet.

A single maintenance worker was walking wider circles around the gym's exit door, but not wide enough to allow them to sneak in behind him without being seen or heard as he turned.

Evan surveyed the area for an advantage, remembering the small breaks in the bleachers of the student sections, and the bottles of alcohol usually stashed below them. Silently, he led Emma to the area, and instructed her to lie atop one of the bleachers.

Evan returned to the front of the stands, staring at the maintenance worker, waiting for him to make the farthest turn of his circle. "Oh, shit!" Evan whispered, purposefully loud enough, and sprinted away from the door.

"Hey! Stop!" The maintenance man dutifully charged after them, making the long run from his post to the area behind the stands, just in time to watch their tiny bodies go shuffling through the bleachers and out the other side. They sprinted to the door, a hundred feet closer, and before he realized their plan, they were exploding onto the back lawn.

Evan guided them out into the fog. All the flashlights across the lawn had successfully descended upon the door to Human Sciences, but none of them had noticed the students sneaking away from it. The fog, and the uninterrupted darkness, had given them the perfect camouflage. They cowered against the edges of the wild grass to make themselves small, supporting each other's hands, and as they rounded the maintenance shed, they noticed a yellow glimmer of light. A school bus was parked behind the shed.

In the front row, he saw Eddy, seated alone.

Emma shook her hand free and raced up the bus steps as soon as the door opened, swallowing Eddy in an embrace. "You did it," she whispered to him. Eddy had been tasked with hiding behind the maintenance shed and waiting until Peter and Aiden stole a vehicle.

From behind them, Peter came jogging up. "Pretty nice ride, right?" he said, slapping the bus. "Nobody even noticed it's missing."

He looked into the bus, then back to Evan. His face fell. "Aiden's not getting out," he said seriously. "But he just saved your asses."

He scaled the stairs, two at a time, and took a seat behind the wheel. Evan didn't move.

"Let's go, buddy," he said. "Time to get the fuck out of here."

Evan watched as Emma cradled Eddy's face, holding it against her own, crying over a smile. Emma wouldn't leave until they knew they'd be able to get a photo, to save everyone. Emma made her love for everyone else more important than herself. That was her power.

"What about Neesha?" Evan asked quietly.

Peter and Emma both looked at him.

"She's still in the office," Emma whispered. "If she's not caught already."

"Sorry, buddy," Peter said. "We're gonna have to come back for her another day."

From where they were standing, he could see the gate, unlocked and unelectrified, vulnerable. They'd done it. He'd done it. He'd saved Emma, and now he was going to escape with her. But if all love was important, then he couldn't forget about the love that he had been shown tonight, the most important love, from the person who had sacrificed the most for him and vouched for him when no one else would.

He turned back to look across the lawn. "I have to go back for her."

"No way," Peter said right away. "No fucking way. We agreed, anybody gets caught, we leave without them. . . ."

Evan didn't budge.

"Kid, get in the fucking bus. We're moving, now."

He looked to Emma. She was still holding Eddy but staring back at him. "You can get in there without getting caught?" she asked.

He nodded.

Peter fell back against the driver's seat. "You're serious about this?"

Evan nodded.

"Alright," Peter growled. "Hurry, buddy. Or we're leaving without you."

NEESHA.

THE ARC ROOM was soundproof, so whatever was transpiring outside the office, it was in a different world. Neesha clung to a lip of the wall, the only thing keeping her balanced, squeezing it between fingers on both hands with rapidly deteriorating strength. She couldn't stay up here forever. Eventually, they'd come back in here, and as soon as the full lights were on, she'd be entirely visible. She held a deep breath, then released it, letting go of the bar and dropping to the ground.

By the grace of the holy whatever, she landed on the floor clean, her legs and hands absorbing her fall with painful, unexceptional impact. She checked her limbs, her neck, her head—everything was intact. She fumbled along the top of the computer system, where supplies were stacked. She felt her way to a sharp instrument, some kind of delicate lever, and clutched it in her hands, hiding behind the ARC.

For thirty minutes, she sat. Outside, in Dr. Richardson's office, she pictured Evan and Emma starting to endure the first moments of torture: drugs, memories, machines; everything seemed on the table after Emma's description. And all of it would soon be coming for her.

Maybe she deserved it, to bear the weight of everyone else's punishment, to account not just for what she'd done but what she'd done to everyone else. None of this would have happened if it wasn't for her, after all. The school wouldn't have seen the false spike in results; they wouldn't have moved Emma into torture. Students were panicking, crashing, almost dying from Apex, and why? So she could win some fucking trophy?

The massive door behind her slid open.

It was silent. The ARC refracted the flashlight beam into a thousand shimmers around the room, but no sound entered. She looked back to the door to the office, waiting for Dr. Richardson to come through.

"Hello?" a tiny voice whispered from the doorway. "Neesha?"

Her body melted. "Holy shit, Evan?"

He came rushing in, materializing in the shimmering light. She dropped the lever and threw her arms around him. "You came back," she said. "You saved me."

He pushed his way out from under her. "Not yet," he said, and he grabbed her hand.

Her heart flattened again as she remembered their plan's failure to this point. "Did she get Zaza?" she asked as he guided her through the dark.

"We can't," Evan said, poking his head out Dr. Richardson's door.

"Evan, if we don't, she'll kill them."

"She'll kill us—"

A flashlight flipped on in front of them, pointed directly at their eyes. It was overwhelmingly bright, but by the time Neesha blinked herself back to clarity, her whole chest collapsed.

Yanis was holding the flashlight, standing in the middle of Dr. Richardson's lobby. He grabbed them by their shirts, steering them to the chairs in front of her office. "Sit down," he whispered violently.

She didn't, buckling her knees to fight back.

"Sit down, Neesha," he ordered again.

"Fuck you," she said. "Fuck you for working for them, fuck you for all of this—"

As soon as Yanis reached for her, she swung at him, screaming, "Run, Evan!" but he received the blow without flinching and yanked her into the chair. Evan didn't even have time to stand up.

He secured them both with tape and waved down another maintenance worker outside the room. "Get Dr. Richardson," he barked, then closed the door, leaving a small crack to the outside hallway.

He stared between them. "Whatever you all are up to, it's not worth it."

He perched on the table, spreading his legs to maximize the threat of his size. Every time Neesha'd spoken to him, he'd been perfectly calm; now he was visibly angry.

Evan spoke. "I thought—you weren't going to do anything to hurt the students."

"That's what I do now," Yanis growled. "Respond to threats."

"What's going to happen to us?"

Yanis shook his head. "I've heard this school is pretty good at punishment. Right, Neesha? Isn't that what you said?"

"You lied."

Yanis shook his head again.

"Yes you did," Evan began to shout. "You said you wanted to help us—"

"I *am* helping you—"

"Y-you said you wanted to help *her*! And now you're torturing her."

Yanis was quiet for a moment, absorbing Evan's tiny wrath. "*Torturing* her? If going to this school is torture to you, I suggest you widen your view of—"

"Don't be fucking stupid!" Neesha joined in. "We know what you all were doing."

"What we were doing?" Yanis's voice softened.

"Training us, just so you could torture us! We know about everything—"

Yanis stood up but she didn't stop.

"—and more than that, everyone knows. And you may have us in here, but this isn't going to last long. There are students that have already gotten out of here, and they're going to fucking *ruin* you—"

"*Wait.*" Yanis held his hands to his face, as though trying to stop an imaginary bag from going over his head. "All of this tonight—kidnapping Dr. Richardson, breaking in here—is because you think they're . . . training you?"

"They are. It's n—it's not a school," Evan spat.

Yanis processed for a moment before speaking again. "Training you for what?"

A noise from the corner of the room stopped his sentence dead. The door to the room creaked open, and Dr. Richardson stepped inside.

There was makeup obscuring the edges of her eyes, and her normally straight hair had swelled in volume, windblown and blocking parts of her face. Slowly, she pulled it back.

"Where is she?" she asked quietly.

Neither of them made a noise.

"Where is she, Mr. Andrews?"

Neesha could feel the light pulsing and Evan shaking in his chair next to her, but he kept his mouth shut.

"If you're here," Dr. Richardson said lightly, begging Evan to offer her something, "then maybe . . ." She looked to her office, to the secret door that was still open.

"Who are you talking about?" Yanis asked, bewildered.

Dr. Richardson didn't say anything to him, grasping Neesha's wrist.

"Do you want me to go get somebody else—"

"No," Dr. Richardson said.

"Are you sure?" Yanis asked.

Dr. Richardson ignored him. Neesha could feel her glare

from below, and the slow and terrifying curl of her fingers against her skin as she squeezed.

"I'll take them one by one in my office. Keep everyone else out." Neesha felt herself pulled to her feet, but her eyes stayed on Yanis, who was watching Dr. Richardson's wrist intently.

"I'd like to be there—"

"No," she cut him off without looking at him, and dragged Neesha toward the door.

"I know where she is," Evan said, standing up.

"Sit down, Mr. Andrews—"

"A-and you're never going to find her."

Neesha felt rage rise inside Dr. Richardson. Dr. Richardson's eyes jumped back and forth for a moment, then she sighed. "Fine. But you're next." She pushed Neesha back into her chair and grabbed Evan's wrist. Evan fought back, wriggling to get away from her, but she clasped him by the back of the neck, dragging him forward.

Neesha stared in horror but Evan wouldn't return her gaze. His eyes were fixed blankly on Dr. Richardson's face. Without a word, she marched him into her office, slamming the door behind her.

EVAN.

"YOU KNOW, I realized I was wasting a lot of powerful thought energy being upset about what happened here tonight. But do you know what I remembered?"

Evan didn't respond. The plastic bands tightly gripping his arms were on an electrical system that must have been operated near to where he was sitting; every time he tried to fight back, a small jolt of electricity rocked his skin. If he could figure out where it was, he might be able to figure out how to get out of it.

"I remembered that I am creator and created. I get to control how I think, and how I think will influence my reality. It's one of our most simple credos, but it's one that we firmly believe: I do not make *the* world, but I do make *my* world. I choose where I stand. I control my emotions. And in doing so, I control my world."

None of the computer systems or machines in the room were on except the one that mattered, the ARC behind him; its base glowed blue, with a low hum, consistent and melodic, pitching

up as the machine pulled more energy, pitching down as it settled. For the moment, Dr. Richardson had only taken a white,
rectangular clipboard off the desk, and was sitting cross-legged
in front of him on a stool, reading off it.

"Anyway," she said, without acknowledging him, or stopping
her eyes as they ran across the page in front of her. "Tonight
was a frustration, but ultimately, we'll persevere."

Evan squeezed his tongue between his teeth and prayed that
everyone else had gotten out already, and Dr. Richardson would
be entirely wrong.

"Just need to tie up loose ends."

"W-what are—are—"

"*God.* Your stutter. It's insufferable."

Evan could feel himself shaking; still he tried to smooth his
voice. "What? Are you going to do?"

"We're going to do an experiment. It probably will fail, but
that's the whole point. That's how we evolve. Weeding out our
undesirable traits. Our failures."

Evan could feel the power of the machine behind him.

"I-is—this wha-what happened to—to Eddy?"

Dr. Richardson nodded into her clipboard. "Edward failed,
too. We think. We won't know for sure, until—well. It's a lot."

"What happens?"

Dr. Richardson stopped reading. "Okay," she said to her
lap, then set the clipboard on a small table next to her. She
pulled her stool closer, looking into Evan's face with a passive
stare, her eyebrows raised. "In order for you to understand

the importance of what you're about to attempt, you need to know some of the important history of this place, and of our people."

"I'm no-not your people."

She smiled. "Oh, yes. Yes you are."

NEESHA.

NEESHA WATCHED YANIS stare at the door where Evan and Dr. Richardson had just disappeared.

"You just signed his death warrant," she said.

Yanis didn't react. "I . . . I don't get it."

She sat up, battling the tape. "Then let me make it crystal clear. This school is experimenting on students. They're preparing us, like fucking animals, to use us in whatever fucked-up experiments they're running. And just now, when she said 'you're next'—that means she's going to do it to me. And you're protecting them."

It was silent for an impossibly long moment.

"So this whole time," Yanis said slowly, tonguing the inside of his teeth between phrases. "That's what you were all afraid of?"

Neesha nodded.

"I've been looking for Emma . . . for her? So she could . . ."

Neesha nodded again.

"They can't—I mean, she wouldn't . . ." Yanis marched up to

the door to Dr. Richardson's office and slammed the handle, but it wouldn't budge. He felt along the face of the door, over to the edge, and slid his finger down it. He slammed his hand against it in fury. "This is reinforced steel. Why would a psychology teacher . . ."

Neesha didn't say anything.

Yanis backed away from it, weightless until his body connected with the wall. He stared at his own hands for a long moment. "The boy," he said, barely loud enough for her to hear. "The one who can't speak . . ."

"He was a sociology student," Neesha said. "He had the Bible memorized. He had friends. They did that to him. And he's been stuck here ever since."

Yanis looked mortified.

"Hey," she whispered. "You're supposed to protect the people around you, right? You said that you're one of the good guys. Did you really mean that?"

She watched him reclaim himself, inhaling through his nose and curling back up to his full posture. "I did. I do."

"Then help me get out of here."

His eyes shot around the lobby. Through windows, they could see several other maintenance workers moving through the building. He nodded.

"What about the others?" she asked.

"Aiden's in my office. In the GRC."

"What about Zaza?"

He nodded. "Same."

Neesha sat up a little farther. "You have to help me."

His eyes lingered on Dr. Richardson's door for a second longer. "Okay," he said. "Okay—" He moved quickly to unbind her. "We can go to my office, grab your friends, and—where do you need to go?"

"The back lawn, behind the maintenance shed."

He nodded. "I can get you there."

Neesha marched to the door, but Yanis didn't move. She turned around.

"What about . . ." He nodded toward the closed door.

Neesha swallowed. "He's a hero." She stared through the door, cringing at the image of him inside. She said a final prayer for Evan and turned to leave the room.

Their walk became a run as they tore down the Human Building hallways toward the GRC. Yanis stopped in the middle of the hallway and spun on her. He grabbed her aggressively by the shoulders and threw her against the wall, forcing her hands together behind her back.

"Ah," she screamed. "What the fuck are you—"

"Shut up," he barked loudly, shoving her farther into the wall. "Dr. Richardson has been looking for you—"

Neesha swallowed her response, letting her forehead fall against the wall. Past him, down the hallway, she could see another maintenance worker, his head turned in their direction, watching.

"Sorry," he whispered between his teeth. "That was a little hard, I'm sorry." He turned her away from where the man stood and began to march. "Pretend to fight back a little."

"Gladly." She swung her right foot back toward him, connecting with his shin. Yanis winced behind her.

After they were gone, Yanis started marching her toward the C-School exit, then veered right, through the P-School. Once inside the GRC, he let go of her hands, and she began to sprint toward his office door.

Aiden and Zaza were seated in the only two chairs in the room, as far from the door as possible. Both of their heads were hanging in the dark. Neither looked up when they entered.

"Guys," she said cautiously.

Zaza's face shot up when he saw Neesha with Yanis. He began to scream. "No! Let her go! She didn't do shit!"

"Guys!" She tried to calm them, but Zaza had descended into full-on panic. "No, no, no! She doesn't deserve this! She didn't have anything to do with—"

"Zaza," she said, grabbing him by the face. "I'm here to get you out."

His eyes were electrified with shock and bright red with tears, but the second they met hers, his face melted into her shoulder. "Ah, fuck . . ." He sobbed against her jacket.

"You did it, you little plebe."

He sniveled. "Who's inert now, bitch?"

She squeezed his hand.

Aiden wasn't speaking, his whole face dripping with blood and sweat. Yanis scooped him up by the arm. "Every exterior door is locked, mechanically. We're going to have to figure out another way."

"There's a window on the second floor," Neesha offered, cautiously checking Zaza's expression.

"I can catch," he offered.

They ran through the hallways with heads down, ready to jump into punishment formation at any point. Yanis kept his eyes high and around, Neesha kept hers forward, charging toward the C-School Lounge.

"Hey." A maintenance man emerged from a door to their right. "Aren't you—"

Before Yanis could say a thing, Zaza swung hard at the man with a right hook, without stopping their momentum. It wasn't powerful, but it was enough to send him stumbling backward. "Sorry," he mumbled to the man as they passed.

"Holy shit," Neesha muttered to him. "Where'd that come from?"

Zaza smiled.

They reached the lounge, where Neesha went straight to work on the second-floor window, cutting a precision circle with Yanis's blade. Zaza moved around the room, muscling the furniture in front of every door. Yanis stayed on the ground floor at the exposed door.

Aiden was standing but swaying, still unable to raise his eyes. "Hey." She grabbed his face. "Can you handle this?"

Aiden nodded.

"I think we're ready," she said, leaning over the railing.

He looked up to face her. "If anyone hears it, I can give you two minutes. As soon as you're out, run. Don't look back, don't wait for anybody."

"You're not coming?" Neesha asked.

Yanis shook his head. "You've just told me every student here is in danger." He paused, regaining his composure. "I can help them if I stay. What kind of a person would I be if I left?"

Neesha stared at the door as he closed it behind him.

EVAN.

"IN 1797, A man named Claude Richard was taken from his farm at the base of Puy Griou in France. Three weeks later he was returned to his village from the skies with a magnificent truth. He'd just been made humanity's final prophet."

Evan sat frozen.

"He'd been taken aboard a spacecraft, by a superintelligent species called the Alohim. They told him of their history: how twenty thousand years ago, they had birthed humanity in their image. How they had periodically checked in to ensure humanity was progressing. And how they planned, when humanity had reached the proper evolution point, to assimilate them into the Alohim, to rise and become one with their creator."

For a moment, Evan forgot about the restraints on his wrists and the dire seriousness of the situation. He stared at Dr. Richardson, unblinking and disbelieving.

"Claude Richard returned and shared the message with the people of Griou, and, of course, they were very skeptical. After all, their entire lives were built on a sound understanding of the physical universe, and unwavering Catholicism. It's how they survived; they couldn't challenge those pillars of belief because some farmer said he was taken by aliens. But Claude persevered, and explained, and as soon as they became willing to listen, they realized something: the message of the Alohim, and the proof of their existence, didn't challenge existing beliefs and mythologies; it united them.

"In fact, it explained every last mystery of science and religion. It explained the historical record they already shared through their faith. Think of the stories, told as fact throughout all of time, lacking practical explanation. The garden—not a divine birth, but the arrival of the Alohim to this planet, the scientific synthesis of human life. The flood—a warning from the Alohim that the Earth was poisoned; and the ark—a spacecraft, sent to preserve the most evolved in humanity. The great messengers—you know them, Mohammad, Jesus Christ, the Buddha—prophets, all trained by the Alohim, sent to keep us on the path toward redemption, but confused by the masses for idols of specific religions.

"But Claude Richard knew the people would understand when the moment was upon them. They would come awake, they would realize they were not worshipping a god, they were not worshipping Allah or the Buddha. They were worshipping the Alohim."

Evan could see each of the stories Dr. Richardson told vividly, hidden directly in front of him, on the walls he stared at once a week. The chapel wasn't Catholic. It was . . . whatever this was.

"The most important part of Claude's message, however, was that he would be the final prophet. Humanity was finally mature enough to understand its origin. Which meant the Alohim were preparing to make their return. Humanity was almost ready for ascension.

"They asked two things of humanity, and Claude relayed them: a council of the world's most evolved beings to ensure the species was ready, and an embassy to host them."

Evan looked around him, trying to keep up.

"The Griou separated from the villages around them to form their own society. Their civilization would be geared toward evolution; they would reward the most intelligent among them; they would create a meritocracy that put the most evolved in power. They would be prepared when the Alohim returned.

"But the French Revolution meant there was no land or material available to village folk in France. Most of them had farmed the base of Griou their entire lives, with no mobility. It would be impossible to prepare an embassy in time. But . . . there was land in the American West.

"In 1804, two thousand Griou sailed to America, and upon arriving, began to walk until they found somewhere that felt like home; somewhere no one would find them. When they found Utah, completely empty, they settled, and they built their embassy, and they waited.

"And to ensure the continuation of their people in this new land, they would build a school, where they could train their young, influence more, and continue to evolve, so that when the moment came, they would be ready. For nearly one hundred fifty years, the Alohim Research Center—the Redemption Preparatory Academy—has been preparing for the arrival of the Alohim."

It was silent for a moment. Evan couldn't tell if the school made more or less sense, or even if Dr. Richardson was being serious. But he could still feel his wrists, bound to the chair. "So—what happened?"

"What's *happening*, Evan, in the present. You're in the embassy; you're a subject. You're a member of the most important—and ultimately, the *only* important—experiment in human history."

Evan swallowed. "To Eddy."

It caught Dr. Richardson off guard, and she almost winced before returning to her attentive smile. "Right, the experiment. Claude Richard was my great-great-grandfather. He was a true prophet, but he didn't understand the message of the Alohim. He assumed their return would be immediate, in his lifetime, but of course the Alohim have their own understanding of time. Evolution requires hundreds of years; *I* knew it would take time.

"Moreover, he assumed the Alohim would return on their own to test humanity. What he failed to see was that the visit to Claude *was* their test. They weren't going to return in the future on a randomly chosen date, just to check in. They were waiting for us to let them know.

"That has been my contribution to the mission of the Griou. I established the recruitment department, to search for the most evolved young people. I traveled to prestigious universities and found world-class minds, showed them the light and allowed them to design experiments and curriculums, geared toward evolutionary results. And for my own part, I began research into how we communicate."

She stood up. "We've made unbelievable progress, evolving humans into more advanced states, both physically and emotionally. We've recruited humans nearly identical to the Alohim as Claude described them, physically. We've developed new technologies for sharing information across mediums of all different kinds . . . including the language of the Alohim."

Dr. Richardson opened a plastic container on the back of Evan's chair and began to pull out thick copper wiring. "The Alohim have evolved past verbal language. Instead, they're able to openly share information through shared electron environments; a collective brain they can all access. No secrets, no manipulation, just shared intellect. *That* is where they're waiting for us.

"Space itself can serve as a shared electron environment; most people don't know or understand this. If you openly share information across electrons, you can openly share information across all of space. However, it's a poor conductor, so the message sent needs extreme voltage, to cover enough ground to reach them. We know that, but we haven't perfected it yet." She paused. "But we will."

"Ah!" Evan jumped as he felt an incredibly sharp cut on the left side of his forehead. Dr. Richardson held a small knife.

"This part hurts a little." She placed the end of one of the copper wires into the wound, and quickly closed it with tape. Evan could feel the grinding of the wire against the inside of his skin; the empty nerve receptors and blood vessels around it began to ache and scream in pain.

"Ex-except th-this school is done."

"I'm sorry?"

"Ah!" Evan screamed, another cut, this time on the right side of his forehead. "Emma knows everything," he grunted through the pain. "And sh-she's already long gone."

Dr. Richardson walked back over to the desk against the wall without looking at him.

"Th-this whole fucking place is about to get sh-shut down. In fact, they're on their way back right now. With authorities."

She pressed several buttons on the keyboard in front of her, typing slowly. The pain set in further on both sides of Evan's forehead.

"S-so have your fun with me!" he screamed again. "This is the last—"

"Evan." The screens in front of Dr. Richardson began to blink green with light as she turned around, smiling. "This school has existed for almost two hundred years. Do you think one student with a wild imagination is going to have any effect on our work? Do you think there are 'authorities' over this kind of work?"

"It's not just one student." Evan fought to keep his lip from quivering. "There's five of them."

Dr. Richardson rolled her eyes.

"Y-you're lying."

Dr. Richardson shrugged. "It's your prerogative to think that."

"Y-you're lying!" Evan screamed. "You almost killed someone over Emma, earlier. You're t-t-terrified of her getting away and ex-exposing you. If n-not, why would you e-e-even care?"

Dr. Richardson paused, looking slightly pained. "Because she was almost ready."

All the screens on the walls came to life, and the entire room pulsed with green and yellow light. In the lights blinking off the sides of her figure, Evan could see Dr. Richardson loading up a syringe with milky white liquid. He felt vomit forming behind his teeth, foaming to get out. His heart was beating so fast it was beginning to hurt his ribs.

Dr. Richardson spun, the syringe in her hand. "Come forward and join us. It's time to speak with your creators." She stood perfectly upright, her hands held out on either side like a cross, bowing at the center. It wasn't a cross—it was them. *The light of the world*, he realized, was their brains.

"E-everyone saw what you did tonight—"

"No," she said. Her voice was still perfectly flat. "Everyone saw what *you* all did. Everyone saw that I handled it."

"B-but—b-but . . ." The copper wires and the restraints and the humming machine were pushing Evan's stutter to a breaking point. "When p-people see that Emma is—"

"See her when?" She walked over with the syringe. "You think she's coming back here?"

"A-are you—you putting me out?"

"No," she said. "I'm waking you up."

The tip of the needle glistened. "The movement of the electrons through the brain is at its highest when stimulated by emotional response. This is a hormone, created by Yangborne's students, to help you out a bit."

The needle hit his forearm and Evan screamed as she forced the drug into him with increasing speed. "L-let—let me—"

Dr. Richardson smiled and removed the needle as Evan sputtered himself to a stop.

"Most people think that human evolution is based around acquiring traits that make us more able—physically and mentally stronger. But evolution is led by one central, nuanced tenet: the ability to survive. So yes, physical, mental strength, these are all necessary components for an evolving species, but we didn't conquer the Earth by evolving physically past whales or developing more mental capacity than computers. We evolved emotionally. We built social bonds, responses to fear and sadness, collective pain . . . these are the processes that encourage us to sustain and improve life.

"These are the processes that will close the gap between us and the Alohim. Their social bonds are so strong, they no longer need to speak. Their internal controls are so strong, they can modulate their emotional response effortlessly to motivate a reaction, either from themselves or their fellow Alohim.

"Which is why our training here is geared toward that one end goal—the deepening, and controlling, of emotional response."

Dr. Richardson turned, and all around him, on every screen built into the wall, images of Emma appeared. She was sitting in a chair, staring up at the camera in front of her, smiling and talking comfortably. She was laughing, biting her lip. Evan could feel himself leaning forward, trying to hear her silence, trying to read her lips.

He shot back in his chair as the video was interrupted, for a single second, by a bright, overwhelming flash of light, erupting from the center of the screen. A screeching noise, higher than any he'd ever heard before, blared through his eardrums. Static shocks rocked the copper wires, and white-hot pain shot through his brain, starting at the exposed wounds and sizzling to the back of his neck. After a half second, it was gone.

The video was still playing, but felt quieter, duller, slower after the shock. Emma was talking now, but Evan couldn't pay attention to her. Another shock came, and he lost control of his body, shaking the chair violently with him. It settled back into the video, but less than ten seconds later, there was another shock, brighter and louder.

The video continued for what felt like a lifetime, the shocks getting more and then less consistent, and finally, the tape ran out, the video froze, and the screen turned off.

Dr. Richardson frowned at the computer in front of her. "Your emotional response is . . . very small, in terms of neural activity." She looked across a few more glowing green charts. Evan could still hear the machine behind him, humming at the ready. "Exactly what I expected. You're incapable of emotional response."

Another image of Emma popped up. She was wearing her yellow cardigan, sitting alone, this time in front of Dr. Richardson's desk. She was scared.

"We're going to go again, you ready?" Dr. Richardson asked, and marched across the room to another station.

"Wait!" he shouted, and to his surprise, she listened, pausing at the machine. "D-don't waste me. T-teach me."

She smiled. "Evan, you're the furthest thing from a candidate. Your intellect is fine, but physically? *Emotionally?* You're primitive."

"N-no—I'm not—"

"Being good at chess doesn't make human beings evolved, Evan. Intellect isn't the only thing the Alohim have mastered; our ability to feel is what drives us forward. You have none of that. You're completely incapable of empathy. It has to be *explained* to you, and even then, you can't internalize it. It's so impossible for you to grasp, it blocks your speech!"

Evan tried as hard as he could to swallow his stutter. "Yes, I can."

Dr. Richardson let out a small, pathetic laugh, then turned back to her desk.

She pressed the button, and the video began to play. He tried to think about her, he tried to muster an emotional response.

He focused completely on the only image that had occupied his head for the last three months. Though every nerve on his body felt charred with pain, in his hand, he tried to feel Emma's hand.

"You've been obsessing over her." Dr. Richardson flipped through notes, recordings of their sessions, he was sure. "But you don't have any emotional reaction to seeing her?"

On the screen, Emma started to cry. She was ducking for cover, shielding herself from whoever was behind the camera. It was the day she'd described in the chapel; the day Dr. Richardson took up torturing her.

"She's hurting!" Dr. Richardson screamed wickedly. "What kind of person can be so devoted to something, and then completely discard its pain! You're an ape!"

He stared at her, just as he had the photo in the center of his wall for countless nights, and realized what Zaza had tried to tell him, what Neesha had tried to tell him, what Emma had tried to tell him—he didn't know the person staring back at him.

She didn't know him, either, and she didn't need him. She wasn't waiting for him or crying out for his help. He'd spent five months thinking she was his route to salvation, and he'd failed, not because he failed to save her, but because the mission was never about her in the first place. The poem wasn't ever hers. It was just words.

I'll hold your place next to me, eternally, endlessly. It was just words.

This world was never big enough, but you still tried to make a place for me.

Dr. Richardson was watching him. "Is there something else?"

Evan tried desperately to avoid eye contact.

"Wait," she said, rushing back over to her clipboard. "Oh, I know."

She pressed several buttons, and the screens flipped. It was dark, the camera stuttering as it entered a room. It took Evan a moment to realize where they were, light from the window flaring the lens, then settling over a milk-white curtain, a single folding chair, and a bed, with a woman lying in it—a hospital room.

Evan swallowed. The camera took several steps closer, craning around her face and landing just below her chin. It was Mom, and she wasn't moving. He couldn't tell if she was breathing.

"There's some response!" Dr. Richardson clapped a few times.

The first flash of electricity hit him squarely in the temples. His body recoiled.

"Stay present, Mr. Andrews. All that matters is this moment, right now."

The camera stayed focused on her, circling her unconscious face. She looked peaceful, as though she'd moved on from whatever was behind her.

He tried to picture her awake, behind the chess table on the TV dinner stand, awake, on Rye Beach describing the movement of the ships, awake, on the hospital bed, but the images weren't there, and now they never would be. Every time he would come home, from now until forever, the chair in the living room would be empty, the chess pieces would only move on one side, the TV would be off.

This was the real mission, and he'd failed it. The empty seat next to her in the video was the place he was supposed to be holding. He was her cure, and her salvation, and when the moment came for her to face God, he wasn't there. And now he'd never be forgiven.

"Now we're getting somewhere!" The machine whirred louder.

Evan could feel himself dying, as though organs were shutting down, refusing the additional pain. But he wasn't going to face his judgment without first facing her. *I'm sorry*, he apologized to her in his head, his eyes watering as he stared into her face. *I'm sorry. I wasn't there for you.* He could feel himself moving closer to her, closing the distance he'd built. *I'm sorry.*

On the screen, it was as though his mother heard him. Her eyes fluttered open, she noticed the camera below her, and she smiled.

I'm sorry, he thought again, closing the open electron environment between them. She mumbled something, and Evan leaned forward, everything in his body rushing toward her, pouring out in front of her. The machine set off a shock wave of light and sound, but he didn't back down. When his mother came back, her lips were moving again, mouthing something that he could only hear in the deepest corner of his brain.

"It's okay," she told him. "I'm okay."

"Yes!" Dr. Richardson was screaming. "This is it!"

This world was never big enough, but you still tried to make a place for me. He could hear the words in her voice. *We all deserve forgiveness. So go now, you're forgiven.*

Her eyes closed once, and she drifted off. The mission was complete.

Evan took a deep breath, all that his chest could find, and exhaled every bit of it. He closed his eyes, cutting the images from his brain and ignoring the increasing intensity of shocks around him.

This wasn't happening right now. This was a year ago. He controlled his proximity.

The video of Emma wasn't happening now either. Now she was in an escape vehicle, rumbling away from the school. Mom was safe. Emma was safe. The mission was complete.

"What the fuck," Dr. Richardson shouted back at him. "What the fuck is that, what happened?" She began to slam the side of the computer.

Squeezing his cells together, focusing in exactly the way he'd always been able to focus, Evan's brain shot back to chess. The King's Gambit, the Bobby Fischer cop-out, to load up all your pieces on the strong side to give the impression of a strategy, and then to reverse that strategy and attack the weak side. He remembered his last game against his mom, her rook-to-D4 move that had ultimately handed him the victory, the way she apologized for being so wrong, the way he apologized for always beating her.

Dr. Richardson spun on him. "No!" She slammed her hand on the glass screen behind her, nearly breaking it. "No, what happened to it? What are you doing?"

Evan glared back at her, simple pieces of the chessboard and their specific functions in his mind. He could hear the machine behind him slowing down.

"You did that on purpose?" Dr. Richardson asked. "You created that, then you took it away?"

Evan took several gasping breaths, refocusing on the simple pain in his head, and none throughout the rest of his body. Slowing, he inched his swelling eyes open, swallowing as he found Dr. Richardson's figure in front of him.

"That was a real reading." Her voice felt like it was being shouted across the back lawn at him. "Legitimate activity. We were so close, and then . . ." She grabbed him by the face. Forcing his eyes open. "Evan, answer me. The empathy you felt, right there? Was that a performance? Was that a controlled emotional reaction?"

He didn't answer her, and she let his head fall back. She began moving around the room, out of focus in front of him. He could hear her writing, punching buttons on the computer, but the lights in the room stayed on.

"What are you doing?" he asked, still halfway suspended in a nightmare.

She didn't answer. He felt her hands against the bottom of his chin, her thumb jarring a small hole open in his mouth.

Something poked in between his lips, something hard, a straw.

"Drink," she said. "It's water."

He did as she instructed, cold water splashing against his tongue. He sat in silence as she delicately, one by one, removed the wires from the top of his head.

When he opened his eyes again, her face was two feet from his own. "Congratulations," she said. "You've just proven yourself worthy of legitimate development. You've earned yourself another six months."

She released the binding, and he fell forward, collapsing onto the ground.

Limb by limb, he pulled himself back up.

"You're going to let me go?" he said, the words slurring out.

"Oh God, no," she said. "You just became my primary subject."

He took a deep breath, and let it go. By the grace of Mom, he was alive.

NEESHA.

THE WINDOW SMASHED open, sending shards of glass flying in every direction. The sound shot across the open lawn. All seven visible flashlights on the lawn spun toward them. Without thinking, Neesha took two steps into the window frame and leapt to the ground.

She hit the ground and rolled, then sprang to her feet, taking off away from the maintenance building and back toward the chapel. She could feel the flashlights following her, scanning around and past her. She cut across the rocky areas between paths and dove down to hide herself for a second, before standing to run again.

She was a hundred yards from the window when she saw another body ease its way out. One of the flashlights noticed, tracking the body on the way down.

"Ah!" she started screaming. "Ah! Ah!" the sound kicked off the mountains, reverberating too many times to form discernible words.

The flashlight whipped in her direction, away from Zaza. As

soon as she saw Aiden drop from the window, she fell into the wild grass and froze.

Two staff members, headed for the base of the window from opposite directions, approaching the spot, slowing as they reached where Zaza's and Aiden's bodies were lying. She breathed silently, praying, as the flashlights converged. They disappeared for a moment into the ground, right on the spot where Zaza had fallen, before shooting back up toward each other. They panned inward, revealing each other in their gray maintenance suits, then across the grounds, and landed on the school bus. Silhouetted in their light, two hundred feet in front of them, Zaza and Aiden popped up off the ground, sprinting toward the bus.

"Ah!" she screamed, leaping up to run as well.

From the forest behind her, at least ten flashlights turned to expose the bus, bathing it in light, but too far away to see the detail. She led them back toward the bus, at least twenty feet ahead of them, panicked screaming now close enough to cut through its own reverberations. "Start the engine!"

The engine roared to life, the bus's headlights washing over the grounds, the staff, and the exposed front gate. Ahead of her, she saw Zaza crash into the door of the bus, and watched as Emma wrestled him in.

The bus started to move, slowly, away from her. She was close enough to the maintenance workers that she could hear their footsteps behind her, around her, gaining on her. A dozen more flashlights had emerged on the lawn, screaming at the bus to stop.

The bus picked up speed, swerving inward toward where Neesha was running, and she picked up speed with it.

"Come on!" Zaza was screaming to her from the doorway of the bus, hanging out to reach for her. "Come on—"

The sound of a gunshot reverberated across the campus. An instant later, the back window of the bus shattered.

"Don't slow down," she screamed back at him. There was the rip of another gunshot, and the aluminum siding of the bus crunched inward with a horrible shriek.

The bus jolted forward again, almost throwing Emma out of the side door. She reached for Neesha, grabbing her hands and linking them, trying to pull her forward, but the bus was moving too quickly, and the ground caught Neesha's feet and yanked her backward.

"Fuck!" she heard Peter scream inside the bus, letting off the accelerator, throwing the bus's momentum backward, shooting Neesha's forward, crashing her into the side of the door and onto the bus.

"Go!" she screamed at him from the stairs. He slammed the accelerator to the floor and the bus rocketed forward as another shot shattered the right-side rearview mirror.

There was too much noise inside the bus and inside her own head for her to focus on any one piece of it, but she yanked herself up the stairs, toppling over Aiden as they swung the door all the way shut. They all crawled, heads down, into the center aisle.

Peter was behind the wheel, heading straight for the gate, ripping toward it at least forty miles an hour across the rocky ground. One more shot rippled behind them as the bus leapt for the gate. The bus shuddered as it hit the metal fencing, bounding slightly backward, rocking hard against its back wheels and then lurching forward.

Neesha fell into a seat of the bus and Emma collapsed on top of her in a hug. Out the window, the road outside of Redemption was barely distinguishable from the forest around it, but they flew through it with the intensity of a video game, fifty, sixty miles an hour over tiny creeks and jagged rock edges.

"You made it," Emma said. "You made it—"

"Shit!" Peter shouted from the front. They'd just come around a bend, and in front of them was a massive bed of bushes and branches, directly in the middle of the road. The gravel disappeared into it, as though a tree had come to claim the road back.

"Is this a dead end?" Neesha asked.

"I don't know—" Peter eased off the accelerator.

"Did you not turn, earlier, when—"

"There were no turns."

Zaza stood behind him. "Do you wanna stop and . . ."

"Nope." Peter shook his head. "We're going through it."

He hit the gas, banking right to try to avoid the root of the tree, but impact never came. They cleared effortlessly, immediately, as though the whole forest was painted on a curtain.

Peter eased the bus to a stop. Behind them, the bushes and trees had swung back to look perfectly intact. There was no road, no vehicle marks, not even any real dirt to sink into. It was concrete, made to look like a real forest. The school was completely hidden from the outside world.

"It's like . . . it's not even there," Emma said.

"Where do we go now?" Peter asked from the driver's seat.

Neesha turned around. There was a highway in front of them, stretching endlessly in both directions, as if reality had been set on a permanent loop. The only thing separating one mile from the next was a small handmade billboard, with a drooping cross painted in the middle. It read: *YOU are the LIGHT of the WORLD*.

"Forward," Neesha said, and the bus rumbled away.

ACKNOWLEDGMENTS

thank you.

writing this book has taken sixteen months,

& all the love that anyone around me can spare—

addison never questions all the stupid things we do; like sleeping in a trailer for two weeks & hiking up remote mountains in Utah.

my family never doubts the crazy stories i tell, or my ability to tell them.

caleb never reads a draft without sending me a few texts to gas me up.

my life mates never leave an idea unexplored or an opinion untested.

savannah never lets me spend more than sixty seconds with my head in the sand.

my band brothers never let me forget who i am & what we're about.

my friends in LA never leave an evening unturned.

my friends around the country never leave my mind, not for more than a moment.

ben & harpercollins, joanna & new leaf, jason kuppermann— you're worth breaking the format for. you're wonderful & thoughtful & the reason my life has turned out as it has.

most of all, thank you to anyone & everyone who's read a book, been to a book tour, or told a friend about it. i hope you'll keep letting me do this for . . . ever.

A devastating loss shrouded in mystery.

Samuel Miller's debut is not to be missed!

JOIN THE

Epic Reads
COMMUNITY

THE ULTIMATE YA DESTINATION

◄ **DISCOVER** ►
your next favorite read

◄ **MEET** ►
new authors to love

◄ **WIN** ►
free books

◄ **SHARE** ►
infographics, playlists, quizzes, and more

◄ **WATCH** ►
the latest videos

www.epicreads.com